BENEDICT BROWN

MW01623126

A CORPSE IN A LOCKED ROOM

IZZY PALMER BOOK SIX

Copyright

First edition April 2021

Cover design by **info@amapopico.com**

To my wife Marion,
my daughter Amelie
and my accomplice Lucy.

Welcome Note

To new readers – hello there, if you're new to The Izzy Palmer Mysteries, or have only read Izzy's Christmas book, this story jumps back into the main flow of the series with boyfriends abroad, uncertain proposals and fledgling theatrical careers. With regards to the previous mysteries though, this book is spoiler free and can be read as a standalone.

To existing readers – let's get back to it!

Chapter One

"It was like kissing my brother."

"You don't have a brother." For such a creative person, Ramesh can be incredibly literal at times.

I tried again. "I know that. I mean… Imagine kissing your sister, that's what it felt like."

"Seriously, Izzy?" His voice rose in disgust. "Why would you even put such a thought in my head?"

I watched as he played out this nightmare scenario, his face contorting and his eyebrows rippling like tiny waves.

We were sitting in a café beside Camden Lock where I'd just finished up another case for the world renowned 'Private I Detective Agency'. It wasn't quite as illustrious-

Ooh, fancy word! Look at Izzy, everybody! She's so smart and clever and knows all the words.

Be quiet, brain!

It wasn't quite as impressive as some of our other cases, but as the old saying goes, 'small businesses who pay rent in central London can't be choosers.' Mrs Snuffles the cat didn't stand a chance against the great Izzy Palmer. I'd brought that moggy home to her owners (only a tiny bit more pregnant than before she disappeared) in a matter of days.

Which is why Ramesh and I were sitting out in the North London gloom on a Wednesday afternoon in March, celebrating my success over a couple of hot chocolates. I'd even paid extra for whipped cream and a chocolate flake.

How hedonistic!

Now who's using long words?

Ramesh and I had been through this conversation several times since my boyfriend's departure for a six-month stint working as a doctor in Peru. I thought I'd have one last go at explaining it.

"You're missing the point, Ra. When I went to the airport, I was full of butterflies. I could barely feel the ground beneath my feet, and everything was perfect; the way he looked at me, the words he said. He was my Danny – the boy I'd been dreaming of since I was eleven years old – and I loved him so much in that moment."

"And then he kissed you?" Ramesh, inevitably, sang.

I hesitated for a moment before confirming it. "Yeah, then he kissed me and it was like I was kissing my…" I didn't finish that sentence in case we got stuck in an endless loop. "I'm not saying it was a bad kiss, it was just wrong somehow. My lips suddenly felt as if I'd had Botox, my tongue fell asleep in my mouth and, when he pulled back, he looked at me in absolute horror."

"You're overthinking this, Izzy. The same thing happened to me with Sandy Inglis when I was fourteen." Ramesh's eyes stared off across the canal into the foggy middle-distance. "Ahhh, Sandy Inglis, the love of my young life. I'd had a crush on her since playschool and I finally got the courage to tell her how I felt, on a school trip to see 'The Sound of Music'. I suppose, like any boy experiencing Rodgers and Hammerstein's stirring tale of Nazis and nuns for the first time, I was on a high. Sitting at the back of the coach on our way home, something inexplicable came over me. I grabbed Sandy by the lapels of her burgundy blazer and our mouths locked onto one another's."

Still gazing into the ether, his tale had come to a stop. I gave him a gentle kick under the table. "And?"

"And it was a massive let-down. She didn't know what she was doing with her lips, her suction was way off and she kept tapping me on the back like she was trying to get my attention in a post office queue."

"So what did you do?"

"What could I do?" he replied, as if there was really only one answer to this question. "I disengaged and gave her a precise breakdown of everything that was wrong with her technique."

As with most of Ramesh's stories, I was left wondering what was fictional, what was real, and what was the point in the first place.

"That poor girl! You must have traumatised her."

"Hardly, Izzy. We came up with a plan to improve her kissing. I gave her a six-week crash course, complete with lunchtime study sessions and a particularly exhaustive PowerPoint presentation. By the end of it, she was kissing like a pro."

"I'm not sure that 'kissing like a pro' is most women's aim in life." Like the burnt-tongued addict that I am, I'd downed my hot chocolate and was trying to get the last traces of foam from the bottom of the upturned cup.

Suddenly tired of the conversation, he shot up from the table and looked at me disapprovingly. “Now, if you don’t mind, Izzy, some of us have work to do. I really should be heading back to Croydon.”

I was sorely tempted to get another drink for the road, but he didn’t give me a moment. He was already halfway to the high street when I threw my empty cup in the canal and followed after.

Only joking! I’m not a psychopath. I carefully removed the algae-based, biodegradable cover from the recycled cardboard cup and put them both in their respective waste recipients.

“So are you going to tell me what happened with you and Sandy?” I asked when I caught up with him.

The nostalgic joy that had previously shaped his face instantly disappeared. “Well… when the six weeks were over, she left me for my best friend Ronnie Goulding. They ended up getting married and having three children, so I like to think that all my effort was worth it.” He broke into a somewhat questionable accent, which sounded Scandinavian for some reason. “The student had become the master.”

I let his words sink in and tried to work out what message I should extract from his story. Nothing came to mind.

“That’s not the point, Izzy.” He waved one finger at me dramatically. “The point is… Well, I don’t actually remember. But Sandy Inglis messaged me on Facebook a few years back and told me I was the best kisser she’d ever met. So take that, Ronnie Goulding!”

I considered returning to our previous topic, but wasn’t sure I could handle another of his unrelated tangents.

Despite the grey skies overhead, Camden was as bright and bubbly as ever. Tourists from every nation on Earth bustled past us on their pilgrimage to the Stable Markets. The smell of freshly baked cupcakes wafted over from a stall and there was an old man standing on the corner singing a sea shanty. I don’t think he was a street performer so much as a cheerful drunk.

My old haunt had become far less grungy since I was a teenager. I used to make weekly visits to the vintage stores (5 items £20!) in search of stripy waistcoats and leather jackets that I was certain would show my schoolmates how cool I was. Sure, Camden had become gentrified and touristy, but some little facets of weirdness still held their own. There was a bloke with luminous dreadlocks selling friendship bracelets (and almost definitely weed), a young rapper was reciting his poetry in front of the Electric Ballroom and, in one of the shops we passed, I noticed a t-shirt which said "Poirot Lives!"

When we'd soaked up the atmosphere for long enough, Ramesh reignited our conversation.

"I forgot to tell you, I picked up the post from the office this morning." One of the major perks of our friendship these days was the fact that Ramesh liked pretending to be my secretary. "There's some interesting stuff that could lead to more work."

He fished in his courier bag for a clutch of letters. "There's a woman in Mill Hill who claims that her three-year-old daughter is planning to murder her – though she also spends a few paragraphs on her fears that Prince Charles wants to overthrow the Queen. So, maybe that's not the one for you. But there's a bloke in Edgware who wants you to spy on his wife."

"Does he suspect her of having an affair?"

He lowered one eyebrow. "No, nothing like that. He just wants you to spy on her."

"Yuck; pass!"

"Okay, what about finding a missing squirrel for some old dear in High Barnet?"

"A live squirrel?" I felt the need to check.

"Yes." His voice took on a mysterious quality as he laid out the startling enigma of the missing rodent. "She says Squibbles the Squirrel used to come to her garden at five o'clock every afternoon for a piece of shortbread biscuit and a chat. He hasn't been seen for over a week. She can't pay you much, though she does make a mean fruit cake, which should easily compensate you for any inconvenience."

I let out a sorrowful breath. "With the pittance I've been making recently, a fruit cake doesn't sound like too bad a reward."

He gave me one of his most sympathetic frowns – they always make me feel better.

"There was one more thing," he said, as he walked his fingers through the papers to extract a neat manila envelope. "I didn't open it as I thought it might be something personal."

Coming to a stop in front of Camden Town tube station, I took the letter from him and weighed it in my hand. He was right; there was something which set it apart from the missives from nutters, time wasters and animal lovers we normally heard from. The paper was clearly good quality and the handwriting almost anachronistically perfect, with scrolling tails on the capital letters. The fact that it was addressed to "Isobel Palmer" greatly reduced the list of possible senders too. Outside of a few people in my family, the only person I could think of who occasionally called me by my full name was Lady Penelope Gravely-Swans (yeah, I'm friends with the Queen's *first cousin once-removed*, no big deal.)

I was rather disappointed when I hungrily ripped open the envelope and it wasn't an invitation to some fancy society ball, but a letter from a distant relative. I skipped to the end and discovered the name of a woman I hadn't spoken to since I was eleven. Not the queen's cousin after all, but my mother's.

Same difference.

I moved out of the way of a noisy German tour party and leant against the wall to read the letter.

Dear Isobel,

You may not remember your visit to Castleton Square Manor when you were a child, but I certainly do. You came with your mother to see me, and I have to apologise for not receiving you in the most welcoming of manners. I have often thought about that time and wished it could have run a different course.

To that end, I would like to speak to you in person. As such, I request your company this coming weekend at a family party I'm hosting. Please let it be understood that this is not a summons. Where once I would have demanded your presence, today, older, mellower and perhaps even wiser, I merely invite you to share a few days with me, here at Castleton.

I have many fences to mend and bridges to rebuild, and I sincerely hope you'll agree to this most earnest request.

Yours with great sincerity and affection,

Elizabeth Louise Castleton

It was not a message I could have expected. I hadn't heard from the woman for almost twenty years and had to wonder whether she'd seen me on television or read about my previous cases in one of the papers. It hit me deep down inside. As I stood stunned in that throbbingly busy neighbourhood, the letter drifted from my grasp to land on the dirty pavement.

"What is it, Izzy? You look like you've seen a-" Ramesh began, his voice soft and sensitive, before he got distracted by one of the market stalls across the road. "Actually, hold that thought. I've got a hankering for churros!"

Chapter Two

The word which, I can only imagine, Ramesh failed to utter was *ghost*. And, though it's a cliché, it certainly felt that way.

My mother's uber-rich cousin Elizabeth lived on a vast estate in the Peak District. I had only been to her luxurious manor house once, when I was eleven. During the visit, our host was proud and snobbish and her two diabolical children harassed, tormented and framed me for assault so that I was sent off to be punished by their maid. Luckily, the staff at Castleton Square Manor didn't fulfil their miserable boss's demand. I had a fine time, stuffing my face in the kitchen and binging on detective fiction from the impressive library. This was still not enough to make me want to return.

We travelled south of the river in silence. Well, Ramesh licked his sugary fingers in a rather too gleeful manner, which made me wish I wasn't in such a bad mood and had snagged some churros for myself. When we got to Croydon, he went back to his real job at Porter & Porter and I stayed on the train to head home.

"Mum, I've had a letter," I said as soon as I stepped through the door. I had no fear of my mother not hearing as she is in all places at all times.

"I know, darling. Me too. Isn't it wonderful!"

I found her standing on a coffee table in the living room with two of her husbands (well, one current, one ex) sticking pins into her. They were not indulging in a spot of amateur acupuncture, or carrying out some dark voodoo ritual. In fact, they were helping her prepare costumes for her upcoming one-woman residency at the London Palladium. My mother rebranded herself as Bu-Bu La Mer – a sort of British Liza Minnelli – and, for some reason, her public were lapping it up. On the back of a viral video and an appearance on Graham Norton's chat show, ticket sales were rocketing.

She was dressed head to toe in pink and blue zebra print, and my fathers – biological and otherwise – were commenting on their creation like expert tailors.

"The hemline is perfect, but I think it needs more *oomph* somehow," my normally sane stepfather, Greg explained. "Don't you think, Ted?"

"Yes, she needs to be a touch more…" Dad searched for the perfect word. "A touch more predator and a little less prey!"

They both stood back to consider this dilemma.

"Izzy, my love." My mother pointed to the sofa, which was covered in fabric swatches and fashion magazines. "If you look in that pile over there, you should find the perfect mask."

I did as commanded and handed her the diamante encrusted tiger's head, which she swiftly put on and admired in the full-length mirror that they'd borrowed from my bedroom.

My father clapped and let out a cheerful, "That's just wonderful. It says, 'You'd better watch out, I'm fierce.'"

"That's right," Greg took up the thread. "It says, 'I'm a wild animal, but with a soft underside you might just enjoy.'"

Personally, I thought she looked like a crazed extra from the stage version of 'The Lion King'. The two men let out a happy sigh before a look of sudden self-awareness crossed their faces and they both peered at the floor.

Greg cleared his throat. "Would you like to drink a beer, Ted?"

"That sounds like a very good idea. Or two beers even."

"Why not several? And we could cook some meat on a barbecue, perhaps."

My mother was less keen on the plan. "But it's five degrees outside and we haven't finished here."

Greg jumped onto the table to give his wife a very smoochy kiss before replying. "Don't worry, Rosemarie, my love! I'm sure that Izzy will be able to help you." Plumping his chest up and grunting in a manner which I assume he considered masculine, he made his way over to the door. "We hate to leave you, but there's a football match starting that Ted wants to watch."

"That's right, the footie! We've no time for... ladies' things," Dad said in an unusually gruff voice as he and Greg went to the back lounge to carry out some stereotypically macho activities that they never normally had the slightest interest in.

Once they'd gone, I could finally get to the topic I needed to discuss. "Mum, you're not seriously thinking of going to see Elizabeth this weekend?"

She held out one hand and stepped down from her pedestal like Marilyn Monroe singing 'Diamonds are a Girl's Best Friend'. All that was missing were her two male assistants.

"Yes, I am, Izzy." She'd clearly made up her mind. "And you're coming with me."

"Not a chance." As I said these words, I had a premonition that I would live to eat them. "Elizabeth Castleton ordered her maid to beat me after her evil brood made up terrible lies. I don't want to be in the same region as her, let alone the same house."

Mum made her lonely puppy face and, if I'd had any resolve before this point, it instantly crumbled. "But the whole family will be there. I was on the phone to your uncle Bradley this morning and he says Elizabeth has quite the party planned."

"Well, if Uncle Bradley's going, then sign me up." I should point out that my voice was marinaded in thick, runny sarcasm. My mother's brother Bradley is about as much fun to pass the weekend with as a dose of cholera.

I crashed down in our reclining armchair and yanked the footrest up like the belligerent child I am.

My mother softened her voice before speaking. "Listen, Izzy. Bradley said that Elizabeth was very keen to have you there. He said that she'd been reflecting on her life and realised the mistakes she's made. She wants to make up for what happened."

I crossed my arms huffily and looked out of the window.

"And besides, the family have been talking for months about your detective agency. You're a bit of a celebrity these days, you know!"

I pretended that such self-indulgent arguments held no sway over me and she leapt forward to push home her advantage.

"Think how it will feel to show them what a success you've made of yourself." She opened her hands wide, like miniature explosions, and peered around at an invisible audience. "Imagine standing before your great-aunt Dolores – who was surprised when you told her that tall people are allowed to vote – and Uncle Bradley – who still calls you Ian – and telling them about your big television debut!"

Okay. So it's not a big deal or anything, but I might have solved a murder on national television on the day of the last royal wedding and Mum's family might have heard about it, which might have made me feel the tiniest bit ecstatic. Actually, there was no *might* about it. I'd spent my whole life being the freak of the family and now I was a highly respected private detective. I'd solved at least six-

Eight!

Thanks! I'd solved eight murders and found any number of pets. It was about time I enjoyed my moment in the sun. Not that I was willing to admit such thinking in front of my mother.

"I suppose that, if I do go, I'll be able to tell everyone about your burgeoning stage career so that you don't have to sound too smug." I delivered this line with just the right amount of nonchalance. Even Ramesh would have been proud of my acting.

"That's the spirit, Izzy. And you can protect your poor cousin Axel from his father. You know how they fight."

"Okay, mother, you've convinced me. It would be rude to skip out on a family function."

It was the first time in my life I'd had a conversation with a Swarovski-studded zebra/tiger hybrid – though, knowing Mother, I doubted it would be the last. Despite the fact I couldn't see her face, it was impossible to miss how pleased she was at her victory.

"Run along now, daughter dear," she said with a suspicious cackle. "You have a call with Danny this afternoon, and I'm off to convince your fathers that there's nothing quite so manly as sewing sequins onto a leotard." I had no doubt that she would succeed.

Just the mention of my boyfriend's name was like a shot of adrenaline to the heart and, without another word, I thundered upstairs to my bedroom. This led to a shout of "Softly, Izzy!" from all three parents, despite the fact that one of them hadn't lived in the house since I started secondary school. Sorry, am I the only one whose mother collects husbands? Right. Thought so.

I plonked down on my bed and opened my laptop, just in time to accept the incoming call from the man of my dreams, light of my life, Dr Danny Fields.

"Hi Danny!" I practically screamed at him as all the pent-up energy I felt from the five whole days we'd gone without speaking rushed through my body. "How are you-"

"Izzy, listen. This isn't working." His words hit me like a basketball to the face.

Ahhhh! He's breaking up with us! Do something, Izzy. Do something now!

I admit I was panicked, but, given the situation, I think I came up with a really quite sensible solution.

"Danny, will you marry me?" I asked, and he looked even more nervous than before, so I just kept babbling. "It's the perfect answer to any relationship problems. That's what my parents did, and they stayed together for a surprisingly long time."

Danny narrowed his eyes, as though he'd finally worked out what an idiot I was. There must have been a delay on the line as it took a few heart-breaking moments for him to say, "Izzy, I can't hear you. I don't think your microphone is on."

As my heartbeat returned to the levels of a comparatively healthy human, I made a silent wish that Mum would finally work out how to use a computer properly and stop pressing the mute button when she wants to hang up a call.

I clicked the mic on. "Is that better?"

He smiled and a feeling of pure harmony flooded between us.

"Hi, Iz."

"Hi, Danny." I had a severe bout of stomach ache just then, but, somehow, in a good way.

"It's nice to see you."

"It's nice to see you too."

Sadly, this was as far as we normally got into our calls before things got awkward. Danny was there in my room with me, transmitted across six thousand miles of internet from the jungles of Darkest Peru. I could talk about any topic I wanted to; share my innermost thoughts with my childhood sweetheart, who I had finally revealed my feelings towards after books worth…

Odd expression, but continue.

…of near kisses and near misses. I could tell the man I loved anything, but the words wouldn't come.

"Did you find that cat?" he tried, and I could already see the strain he was under to maintain this pseudo conversation.

"Yes, thanks. Are you still surrounded by potentially lethal cases of dengue fever?"

He laughed at me. Luckily, Danny is one of the very few people on Earth whose laughter makes me feel *more* confident rather than less.

"Oh, yeah. Lots of dengue fever. All the dengue fever, in fact. I've got dengue fever up to here." He was rambling, which was preferable to the silence that often marked our exchanges.

I couldn't explain it. Whenever I wasn't talking to Danny online, I was thinking about him. But when we did talk, we had nothing to say. It was my fault for waiting until the very last moment before he went away to smush lips with him. I couldn't be sure if the terribleness of that kiss was due to nerves, pressure or – surely the most obvious option – he actually was my brother, my parents had given him away at birth to our future neighbours Kevin and Celia, before having me almost exactly nine months later.

Perhaps energised by the fact I'd finally worked out what must have happened, a thought popped into my head.

"I'm going to a posh family function this weekend at Mum's cousin's house near Derby. The invitation said I could bring a partner." That feeling of love, hope and elation surged through me once more. "It's a shame you're not here."

We had a gushy moment then – a different kind of awkward silence – before he had a go at the old 'speaking'.

"Hey, you should take Ra instead. Think of the hilarity that would ensue as he made a total hash of pretending to be your big macho boyfriend. Classic Ramesh!"

"Yeah, that would be funny."

"Have you asked him whether Patricia agreed to marry him?"

I let out a little sigh, as this was another issue that was playing on my mind. Ramesh had called his girlfriend before Christmas and left a message on her answerphone proposing, but he hadn't mentioned it since. "No, and I feel terrible. If things are bad between them, I don't want to ask about it and make him feel worse."

"Maybe they're engaged now and it slipped his mind."

I showed my disbelief on the matter with a gentle, "HA! Have you met Ramesh? He doesn't really go in for keeping things to himself. He once took out a full-page ad in the Croydon Advertiser to celebrate the fact he'd won the role of *seventh brother* in a local production of 'Joseph and the Amazing Technicolor Dreamcoat.' If he was engaged, we'd know about it."

"Yeah… You're probably right." A brief laugh died away and we both knew what was about to happen.

A hush gripped us that was near impossible to escape from. We looked like those funny looping videos people make on their phones, as we struggled to come up with a topic that could fire us back towards normal conversation. There was a list in my head of potential ice breakers – the British government's current agricultural policy, the perfect length of time to cook pasta, Morris dancing – but they were all absolutely rubbish. I could tell from the finger that Danny kept raising and putting back down again, that he was going through the exact same phenomenon. Our brains were on strike!

……

……

……

See! Normally, my silly old brain would have made some hilarious, sarcastic comment then, but no! Nothing!

"Star Wars!" Danny shouted in desperation, which led to a brief discussion of the fact that we'd both seen a few of the films and didn't have a strong opinion on them.

"People who stand on the left on escalators!" I went with, as, after his attempt it was clear that scraping the barrel was very much permitted.

"I don't like them," he replied. "Skinny Jeans?"

"Invented by the devil!" I shouted back. "Battenburg cake?"

"Never eaten any." His head twitched about and I could tell that he was searching for inspiration from whatever was in front of him. "Goats?"

This was the nail that broke the camel's skull. It was no good, there was no coming back from "Goats?" and we both knew it. We sat in the kind of excruciating noiselessness that precedes a poorly attended funeral. We were more than just quiet, we were a vacuum, sucking noise in from all over the universe and turning the volume down to zero.

"Sorry, Danny. Mum's calling. Bye!"

I'd hung up before I knew what I was doing and instantly felt like

I'd just punched a seal pup. Danny's adorable face hung on my screen for a few seconds to make me suffer just that little bit more.

Izzy, what were you thinking?

Don't even start, Brain... If you'd just...Why didn't you...? Ahhhhhh!

Chapter Three

I took a couple of days to recover from this episode by barricading myself in my room and transferring all work calls to Ramesh's phone. It seemed like the grown-up thing to do.

Life was simple in my childhood bedroom with my complete Agatha Christie library and the posters from all the coolest movies that came out in 2004 (I'm looking at you, 'Shrek 2' 'Spider-Man 2' and 'Harry Potter' 2). In fact, very little had changed since then. I still had my collection of Care Bears on my dresser, which was itself covered in glow-in-the-dark stars (though I had scrubbed off the felt-tipped declarations of my love for James Blunt at some point in my twenties). I'm sorry, but I don't like change. I like things to stay exactly as they are forever so that I never have to feel bad about missing anyone or making any stupid decisions.

Obviously, I was aware of the fact that, over the last year, my whole life had been upended. I'd left a job I hated, started an intermittently successful business, made a bunch of new friends – from a tech millionaire to a sort-of princess (still no big deal) and admitted to Danny that I'd been in love with him since we were kids.

I knew, deep down, that there was nothing to be scared of…

Except for the possibility that Danny would leave me, we'd never speak again, my business would fold and that I'd exaggerated this whole *being friends with a princess* thing, as, despite hanging out a couple of times over the last few months, she probably only saw me as a useful contact in case anyone in her circle of friends got murdered (again).

So, as I was saying, change: bad! Staying in my bedroom eating the toasted cheese sandwiches, which my stepdad slotted under the door to nourish me, and ploughing through golden-age murder mysteries: good!

I was enjoying Christie's 'After the Funeral', in which an old lady is cruelly murdered by… actually, I hate spoilers, read it for yourself. I was enjoying my third Christie of the week, when Mum decided she'd had enough and called on some big strong men (well, Ramesh and Dean) to help barge the door open.

"I could have been naked!" I put my hands up to cover my chest, even though I was sitting beneath my duvet, wearing a sweatsuit and an extra cuddly jumper.

The invasion force parted for my mother to march into my sanctuary like Darth Vader – who, now that I thought of it, did make the original Star Wars trilogy kind of iconic. I stashed this thought away, in case I ever spoke to Danny again.

Mum started in on her lecture. "Enough of this, Izzy. I've no idea which mini-drama you're going through this week, but we've a trip to pack for and you're being a massive baby. I thought we'd got past all this last year!"

Dean, my aforementioned tech-millionaire friend, was wandering wide-eyed around my room like a seven-year-old at a dinosaur exhibition. He took in the artefacts of my adolescence and chuckled to himself. "You play the accordion?"

No one was paying him any attention as my mother, in another of her extravagant costumes, was still shouting. "Get out of bed and downstairs this instant, or I'm cutting off your sandwich supply."

"You wouldn't dare!" My voice matched the décor. "Also, why are you dressed as Mother Teresa?"

She wasn't going to be distracted by such an obvious ploy. "Either you start packing for our weekend away, and come downstairs to help the boys finish off my costumes, or I'll throw some clothes in a bag and have you manhandled into the car."

Ever my mother's willing apprentice, Ramesh took a few steps forward with his muscles flexed in an attempt to look tough. It didn't work.

I threw the duvet off me and swung my legs out of bed. "I've changed my mind, I'm not going with you. It doesn't matter how many murders I solve, our family will still laugh and call me names like always."

"Not an option." As you may have realised, when Rosemarie Palmer sets her mind to something, she is not easily dissuaded. "You're coming and that's that."

I tried to recall past arguments where I'd triumphed over her, but I'm not sure there'd actually been any. Luckily, Danny's idea came back to me. "Fine, but I'm not going alone. What I need is moral support. What I need is a fake boyfriend." I turned to my fake secretary, who had given up on looking dangerous and was hugging a Care Bear. "Ramesh, you don't mind taking on the role, do you?"

He tossed Funshine Bear back down and put his hands to the side of his face.

"Seriously, Izzy?" In case his outraged tone wasn't clear enough, he allowed his jaw to hang open for a few moments. "I'm a pre-engaged man! How do you think my pre-fiancée would feel about me swanning off with the first woman who needs a fake boyfriend?"

This did nothing to help me understand whether Patricia had agreed to marry him or not, but there were more important issues to deal with.

"Dean, are you busy?"

Ramesh let out another offended shriek. "Oh, I see how it is, Izzy Palmer. I say no and you're straight on to the next man. You didn't stay heartbroken for long!" He immediately stomped from the room with a melodramatic huff, before turning back with a question. "Also, what are you making for dinner tonight? I'm allergic to carrots this week and I don't want to get all bloaty."

My good hard stare was enough of a reply and he flounced off downstairs.

"So, how about it, Dean? Will you be my boyfriend?"

He paused to think before answering in his usual gruff, loveable manner. "Sure, I'll do it. Fiona's away at a conference, so I was going to stay home and play computer games day and night until I fell asleep on the remains of my dinner. Whatever you've got planned is guaranteed to be healthier."

Dean and his girlfriend had only been going out for a few months but were already living together. Danny and I had known each other most of our lives and had finally managed a first kiss.

"She won't be jealous?" I felt I should check as there was some history there.

Dean let out a short, moody chuckle. "No, not at all. As soon as she got to know you, she realised that you're no threat to her whatsoever. It's quite funny actually, we were laughing about it only-"

"Yes, thank you, Dean."

"So, it's sorted then," Saint Teresa of Calcutta announced. "Pack your bag and then make us all dinner. I've promised the boys a carrot-free feast for all the hard work they're doing."

She sounded like a slave driver, which, when I made it downstairs, wasn't far from the truth. Dean, Ramesh and two of my dads (there's a third who retired to the seaside) were spaced out around the dinner table, sewing, pleating and hot-gluing a particularly exotic outfit that looked like a cross between a flamenco dress and an aviary. It was covered with stuffed robins, bluebirds and ducks.

I'm not going to lie. I was quite excited to see her show.

I made a truly delicious spaghetti Bolognese (sans carotte) before being roped into the production line after dinner. And though I didn't get to bed until two in the morning and my hands felt like pin cushions when I finally did, I was glad that (not for the first time) my wise mother had pulled me screaming into the world. We chatted and joked as we worked, and it was nice to be with the ones I love.

When the morning came, Dean arrived with his chauffeur to take us north. His sleek, black Jaguar saloon could only fit four passengers though, and so my mother was forced to leave one of her husbands behind. Not that her ex had been invited in the first place.

"I think the very concept of a 'plus one' is ridiculous," she said several times that morning. "What if you have more than one to plus?"

"It's the practical solution," my father insisted. He had popped by to stand in the hall as we rushed about getting ready. "It's not like I'm really part of the family these days anyway, and I don't fancy driving up on my own."

"Don't you say that, Ted," my mother took her ex-husband's hand and looked at him with a sincere expression. "You will always be a part of this family."

I'd almost got past finding anything that my parents did strange, but their continuing friendship still bemused me a little. Mum dashed back upstairs and Dad went to talk to the chauffeur about the swanky car.

Ramesh surprised me by stepping from the lounge as I lugged Mum's luggage outside. "Izzy, do you mind if I stay in your room for a few days?"

"Did you sleep here last night?" I was suddenly worried that, despite his talk of *pre-engagement*, he and Patricia were, in reality, *post-break-up*. "I mean, of course you can, buddy. Or you can take Danny's room in the loft; that way you can stay for as long as you like."

His grin was replaced with a slightly beleaguered expression. "No, that's alright. I should be finished with my project by the time you get back. Your mum's sewing machine is much better than mine, and Patricia will be busy with work this weekend. I'll keep your dad company."

I would have asked him what project he was talking about, but my mother reappeared in one of her travelling outfits – big yellow hat, matching floaty dress – and ushered me through the door. Since becoming the all-singing, all-dancing viral sensation known as Bu-Bu La Mer, she had tried to dress the part at all times in case her multitude of fans should spot her at the motorway service station at Newport Pagnell.

My stepfather was busy packing the car, but found the time to shout his catchphrase at us. "*Come along, Rosemarie*. Bradley says that there'll be a cocktail reception at two o'clock. He says that, the last time he went to Castleton, the sausage rolls were to die for."

We stuffed the Jag with our bags and jumped inside for Dean's chauffeur, the ever-silent Giles, to get us on the road. Ramesh and my father were waiting on the doorstep to say goodbye. The thought of spending a whole weekend without me was clearly too much for my dear friend and, like a small child after a family visit, he ran down the road to wave us off.

As I have the longest legs by approximately three metres, I got to sit in the passenger seat. We shot through Surrey, with Giles's nippy manoeuvring making up for his serious lack of conversational skills, only to join the motorway and spend the next hour and a half managing an average speed of *slower than an old man with a Zimmer frame.*

Greg had a nap, Mum decided it was the perfect moment to practise her routine for the new show – her song selection, did help me understand some of her more outlandish sartorial choices, though I still couldn't figure out where Mother Teresa fitted in – and Dean unexpectedly did his part as a backing singer. He had a rather nice baritone, which I certainly wouldn't have imagined from talking to him, looking at him, or having known him for the best part of a year.

None of that mattered though, as I had a book with me. A book! A passport to thrills and relaxation; a portal to infinite universes, and the only item I need to make the world seem like a far more sensible place. Poirot poked about in the lives of the Abernethie family and, just as he got to the truth about the murder of poor Cora Lansquenet, we pulled up at the gates of Castleton Square Manor.

Chapter Four

Even though there were a stream of cars waiting, the smartly dressed guard on duty would close the gates between each one and spend a couple of minutes checking the credentials of every passenger. When our time came, Mum was so excited that she sang her name and Dean harmonised with his own. I despaired at the impact she could have on people. When I first met Dean, he could barely make eye contact and spent most of the time actively trying to avoid social interaction. Now here he was singing at strangers.

I miss the old Dean, that guy knew how to be surly.

The equally surly guard – who looked like he'd just come from an audition for (non-speaking) servant #2 on Downton Abbey – mumbled his acceptance and waved the car through the gates. Driving on to the property filled me with a sense of adolescent dread. Images came back of my tubby little cousins running away from me through the house, their cruel laughter the only trail for me to follow, and I had to bite the inside of my mouth to push the thoughts away.

The gravel drive which led up to the main house was longer than my street back in West Wickham. There wasn't a stone out of place, as though someone had groomed it like a monk in a Zen garden. On either side of the car, there were neatly laid flower beds and, further out across the estate, I could see tennis courts and a swimming pool. The place had clearly changed with the times. I didn't remember such features on my first visit there two decades earlier.

This wasn't the only change I noticed. As we approached the grand entrance in front of the house, I spotted a young man and woman with long-barrelled shotguns. They had an assistant with them to load the trap, and the girl, who had the recognisably green eyes of the Castleton family, watched our car pass as her brother stood forward to shoot.

My cousins Tedwin and Noémi had slimmed down and prettied up over the years. Tedwin, who had been as round as a one-pound coin the last time I'd seen him, was now broad and chiselled. He'd clearly inherited his father's looks, as he was nothing like his mother. His hair was dark, his eyes brown, and his jawline looked like it had been surgically transplanted from some 1930s matinee idol.

Noémi had red hair and freckles, like all the women of her family going back generations, and her features were fine and attractive. Those intense green eyes locked onto mine as we drove past, but there wasn't a hint of a smile on her lips, even as she absentmindedly poked her brother in the ribs and made him miss the target. His temper flared in response, and I had to assume they hadn't changed so much after all.

Our arrival in front of the large, boxy manor house caused a bit of a stir. I was suddenly glad that we weren't pulling up in Ramesh's neon pink Datsun or Mum's antique yellow Corsa. In fact, as I got out of the millionaire's car we'd arrived in, every last guest and servant turned to peer. I spotted distant cousins and a crumbling great-uncle, and even they looked impressed to see me arrive in such style. If it hadn't been for Mum and Dean loudly finishing up their rendition of 'I Got you, Babe', I would have felt pretty cool indeed.

There was valet parking for most people, but we didn't require anything so workaday. We had Giles, who would park the car off site for the weekend and come back to pick us up whenever we needed him. I felt dreadfully guilty at the idea that he'd be stuck in that car as we let our hair down, but, when I collected my handbag, I spotted a pile of P. D. James novels under my seat and I knew he had the right idea after all.

Making sure that no one was looking, I unzipped the top of my bag to show the selection of Dorothy L. Sayers books I'd brought with me and nodded as if to say, *you and me, we're not so different after all.* He clearly didn't understand what I meant and crumpled his brow as if to say, *please get out of the car and leave me alone.*

"Rosemarie, you old battleaxe!" I heard my uncle Bradley shouting down from the entrance. He had a glass of something fizzy in his hand and had no doubt arrived early to enjoy the maximum amount of freeloading possible.

"Brad, darling!" Mum beamed up at her older brother and, for the thousandth time in my life, I wondered how she could put up with the odious brute.

My uncle was a big deal (in his own words) in central heating in the East Midlands. He was a stout, rectangular man with no chin and a voice like sandpaper. I have honestly detested him since I was two years old. He ran down the stairs, Mum ran up and they met in the middle to give each other a hug.

"I've been looking forward to this for weeks!" he said, and I wondered why Mum and I had only just got our invitations. He stuck his hand out for my dear, sensible stepfather to accept without a smile. "Alright, Gregory? Nice motor you came in. Is it yours?"

"It's mine actually," Dean interrupted, already having the measure of the man. I'd given him a full rundown on my family and exactly what flattering lies he should tell them about me.

My uncle was a little taken aback by the suavely coiffed young gentleman in the Hugo Boss suit, and stumbled over his words. "Uh. Oh yeah. And you are?"

"Dean Shipman. I'm the CEO of X-Tec Spyware. Perhaps you've heard of us? We're the biggest manufacturer of micro surveillance equipment in Europe."

Uncle Brad was the kind of person who's only happy when he's the richest human in sight and fought for a comeback. "Only in Europe?"

Not for the first time, Dean impressed me with his ability to overpower people with a torrent of businessy jargon. "Second in the world, but we hope to address that when we expand into North America next year. A market flotation should follow soon after."

Clearly stumped by that one, Bradley peered around for an easier target and, you guessed it, landed on me. "This your boyfriend is it, Ian?" He let out his staccato laugh. "Done well for yourself, you have. Always assumed you were a raging lesbian!" His awful voice echoed across the grounds and I wondered if there was anything in my purse that I could use to stab him to death.

Try the nail file! No, wait, use a pen, it's more poetic!

"I call her Ian," he explained, grabbing Dean's wrist tightly as he did so, "because until she was about twenty she looked the spitting image of a boy I knew from school. Ian Darling his name was, and she was the spitting image of him. I swear."

Even Mum wasn't enjoying her brother's performance, but she threaded her arm through his, to ascend the stone staircase to the main entrance. "Is your new girlfriend with you?"

"Deidre? Nah, she had a big night out last night in Derby and is sleeping it off. I've got to be honest with you, Rosie, it's not working out. I think she's too old for me. You know how I like 'em young, and Deidre is past thirty." My uncle had been married three times and was engaged to his fourth. He was like a reverse Benjamin Button in that, as he got older, his partners miraculously got younger.

"What about Axel?" I asked, half wishing that my poor cousin had stayed at home to have a holiday from his odious father.

"Yeah, the little prat's here somewhere. Probably picking his spots and crying that his dolly's broken. Ak ak ak!" Each note of his laugh cut through me like a chainsaw.

"Izzy!" a voice called and I would have been happy if it was Genghis Khan or Justin Bieber, so long as they got me away from my uncle Bradley.

I turned to see Tedwin and Noémi scampering across the lawn towards me, their faces bright and sunny. I stopped to wait for them and their perky looks remained even when they were close enough to see the grim expression I had perfected just for them.

"It's so good to see you," the older of the two, a cold, calculating girl asserted.

Her brother continued the spiel. "Mother told us you were coming and we've been so excited. We broke off the shoot just for you."

You know that old saying, *forgive and forget*? Well, I've never heard of it.

I'd already worked out my opening line back in the car. "It's funny, I would have expected you two to go in for blood sports more than clay pigeon shooting."

Clearly missing the note of disdain that I'd worked so hard to cultivate, Noémi laughed and said, "Oh, no, not at all."

"In fact, we're both vegetarians." Tedwin was even more handsome up close, which didn't compensate for the fact he was a smug, demonic creature from the pits of hell.

"We're so impressed by your detective agency." The girl cleared her long undulating hair from one eye with a snap of her neck. "Tedwin even took clippings from magazines."

"I did not." The boy jabbed his sister in the arm for misspeaking. "And besides, you've been obsessed with our 'big cousin Izzy' since we were kids."

Noémi blushed at that and couldn't find her words.

"That's great," I said, unable to put up with their act for a moment longer.

I turned to head inside as Tedwin spoke again, his voice rising in desperation. "We're sorry!"

I looked back and imagined that I could see these two words hanging in the air between them in a comic book speech bubble. Noémi stared down at the ground and, when she finally spoke, her tone was softer, kinder and less confident.

"We're sorry for the way we treated you back when we were kids. We really are. It's just…"

Her brother took over again. "We were so excited about you coming to stay and probably didn't behave how we should have. We really wanted to be friends with you because you were so much cooler and more streetwise than us."

Ha! Enjoy the moment, Izzy. That is the first and last time that anyone will call you streetwise.

"If you're still angry and don't want to talk to us, that's fine." Noémi's hands hung limply at her side, and there was something very childish about her. This glimpse I received was not of the shrewd and scheming girl who had practically disfigured her own brother to get me in trouble. There was something sweet and open about her. "We just need you to know that we aren't the little monsters we were back then."

"Don't worry about it," I replied, giving nothing away of what I was feeling inside. "It's water under the bridge."

My voice cold, I turned to head into the house. They clearly didn't get the message as they both bounded after me.

"Oh, what a relief!" Tedwin let out a posh giggle.

"We were so worried you'd never forgive us."

Linking arms with me on either side, they chatted away, full of enthusiasm for all the things we could do together now that we'd put the past behind us.

Chapter Five

I felt another wave of emotion crash over me as I crossed the threshold into the house. The place was just as I'd remembered it. I'd hoped that, with the passage of time, I'd come to exaggerate the opulence and grandeur of Castleton Square Manor, but if anything, it was more glamorous than I'd described.

The entrance parlour could have fitted an exhibit of antique buses inside, and everywhere I looked there was gold leaf. There were three crystal chandeliers hanging from the intricately decorated ceiling, two great marble staircases swept from the first floor – like an upturned fleur-de-lis – and, in every alcove and cornice, classical sculptures looked down placidly at their guests. It was exquisite, and I had to take deep breaths as I took it all in.

"Hey, Ian!" Uncle Bradley called. "This boyfriend of yours is a bit special!"

"Fiancé," my mother corrected him. "Izzy and Dean are engaged."

I was about to pull my mother aside and tell her to calm down with all the play-acting, but had second thoughts.

If we're having a fake boyfriend, he might as well be our fake fiancé too.

Over by an immense buffet table, Dean had drawn a crowd. My grandparents were there, hanging on his every word and a number of relatives whose names I couldn't recall had gathered around to listen.

"That's right, Izzy got me to spy on her own best friend!"

Everyone burst out laughing at the story. As he addressed his new fans, Dean had a smoothness about him that I found quite disturbing. My nerdy, paranoid acquaintance had been replaced by a young George Clooney.

My two second cousins were magnetically drawn to the spectacle, so I was tugged along with them.

"She always was a bit of an oddbod," Uncle B kindly explained. "I remember when she was a kid she used to… Here, Ian, what was that weird thing you always used to do?"

I sighed and tried to wish myself back home like Dorothy Gale. Sadly, my shoes weren't red or ruby encrusted, and, now that I looked, appeared to have some chewing gum stuck to them.

"Reading?" I replied with great effort.

Bradley laughed and so did my grandparents. "That was it! Reading! Head in a book all the time, what an absolute weirdo."

Dean did his best to make things better, but I could see it would do no good. "That's just one of the things I love about Izzy. She's incredibly well read. In fact, if it wasn't for her, I-"

"Never mind that," my grandfather put in, sounding like an outdated prototype of his boorish son. "Tell us more about all the money you've made with your company. Ak ak ak!" His laugh was like a pneumatic drill.

I was saddened to see both Mum and my selfless grandmother fawning over the moronic men in my family. Dean attempted to get us back on track by talking about another of my cases, and Noémi gave my mother a big hug to welcome her. The conversation soon came to a halt though when a woman in a purple velvet dress with a plunging neckline appeared at the top of the stairs.

"Good afternoon, everybody." I wouldn't have recognised her if it weren't for that deep, dramatic voice. She waited for silence before continuing. "Thank you so much for coming. A family reunion like this is long overdue."

There was some sycophantic laughter then from Bradley and a few like-minded cousins. Just as loud was the murmur of surprise as we took in the new, improved Elizabeth Castleton. The woman I'd met all those years ago was a big ruddy-cheeked woman; a farmer caught in a storm, who dressed the part of the country squire. The specimen before me could not have been more different.

Her cheeks were gaunt, her lips swollen and her breasts… well, they were a hell of a lot more prominent than I remembered. In fact, her whole figure had changed. It was clear that she'd gone on more than a crash diet. She'd been under the surgeon's knife. From the chunky ball of clay she'd once been, cosmetic surgeons had sculpted something lithe yet curvy. She was ugly and beautiful in equal measure; an unfinished masterpiece which a child had decided to complete.

I didn't want to pity her or condemn her for her personal choices, but it was hard to fathom why anyone would spend so much money to look so strange.

"Looking good, Lizzie!" Bradley instantly shouted, to give me a clue.

Stepping carefully down the stairs with her long trailing skirt hitched up in one hand, Elizabeth put the other to her chest in overacted appreciation. She eyed her guests as though checking that everyone had arrived and, as the bustle of conversation returned to the party, she cut a line straight for my group.

"Hello, everyone." She still spoke with a pompous tone and those green eyes hadn't changed in the slightest. There was a coldness to them which had terrified me when we'd first met.

"Mummy, we were just talking to Izzy," Tedwin began, but his mother didn't look at him.

Noémi was quick to take her turn. "Isn't it wonderful that-"

"Not now, children!" she managed to snap without losing her polite tone. "I'm talking to my guests."

Bradley had already muscled his way to the front of the group and kissed her on both cheeks, which he always did when trying to impress people. "Ravishing. That's the only word for you, my lovely." I was standing on the other side of Elizabeth and his eyes flicked between us. "'Ere, Ian, you should take a page out of my lovely cousin's book and stop dressing like a middle-aged man. Might not look too bad if you scrubbed up a bit."

I involuntarily peered down at my comfortable brown trousers and thick Aran sweater and completely failed to come up with a response. Luckily for me, I had my supporters in the crowd. Even though my mother looked on, mute and apologetic for her inability to tell her big brother where to shove his nasty comments, Dean came to put his arm around me, before an unexpected defender spoke up.

"Don't be such a swine, Bradley." Elizabeth stared the musk-scented spiv down. "If you keep peddling such nasty views, I'll have one of the servants escort you out."

For the second time since we'd arrived, Bradley had to fumble for his words. "Yes… I mean, what I was trying to say to Izzy was… well, it was only a joke."

Elizabeth straightened her back and her inflated bosom heaved itself up accordingly. "I'm going to take my *lovely cousin* Isobel on a little walk, so I hope you all enjoy the apéritif."

She turned without another word, and I followed along obediently.

Before I could thank her, she looked at me tenderly and said, "I'm sorry about your uncle. For some reason, in our family it's always the rudest voices that we have the most trouble answering back to."

We began our turn about the room and, like the Queen from her coronation carriage, Elizabeth waved politely to her guests.

"You didn't seem to have too much trouble back there," I told her. "Bradley looked like he'd been slapped in the face with an electric eel."

She nodded appreciatively. "Yes, as I tried to show you in my letter, I've learnt a lot about myself over the last few years." Her words faded out and she came to a stop in front of an alabaster statue of a tragic heroine with a spear through her heart and her arm outstretched. For a moment, the two women's expressions were perfectly matched. "I will never be able to tell you how sorry I am for what happened the last time you came to stay. I knew what my children were capable of, but I was too proud to admit they could be lying. I was too eager to show your mother how perfect my life was, but that was far from the truth. My dear Matthew had died very shortly before your visit and I was a shell of a person. I don't think I've entirely recovered even now."

I didn't want to think that I'd held onto my anger for so long, but on seeing her there, so repentant, the corked-up emotion fizzed from me.

"Thank you, Elizabeth." My voice came out cracked and weak. "Thank you for saying that and writing the letter when you did. I would have held onto the sad memory of my time here forever otherwise."

She put her hand on my shoulder and I could tell it was not a natural gesture. She was not a warm woman and never had been, but I appreciated this small kindness. We both looked around the room then, as if Castleton Square Manor itself deserved to be included in our discussion. Elizabeth smiled and nodded to a few more guests and I noticed that her two children had angled themselves around to keep an eye on their mother as they chatted to my grandparents. An old man in military uniform came down the stairs at a canter, and I recognised him as the General – or that's what everyone in the family called him at least. He was my great-uncle and, though I'd met him at several events, I didn't know Elizabeth's father's first name.

"There's Daddy." Her whole attitude changed as she caught sight of him. "I'd better go and see him, he was in a foul mood when I left him earlier and I don't want him ruining the party."

Despite her words, she stayed looking at me and delivered one last comment before parting. "I have to say, Isobel, that I have read every last article I could find about you in the papers. I watched and re-watched what happened at Lady Penelope's wedding and I was so very impressed. You're a marvel, Isobel Palmer, and I'm so glad you could brighten up our little do."

She smiled her fragile smile as she left, and I worried that her stitched-together face might fall to pieces from the effort.

I stayed where I was to take in the scene. Everyone appeared to be enjoying themselves. Maids and butlers were serving drinks on silver trays and, tucked in one corner behind a forest of palms, a string quartet were playing Pachelbel's Canon.

Elizabeth was right. Her father did not look amused and waved his hand through the air irritably. Though he never raised his voice, his disapproval had attracted his grandchildren's attention, and Tedwin and Noémi zoomed across to protect their mother from his anger. I would love to have heard the discussion, but it was carried out in whispers that didn't travel across the room. I could only try to lipread what was said and, unless they were talking about peanut butter sandwiches, I don't think I was much good at it.

A neat young man who I didn't recognise came to see Elizabeth then. She answered him distractedly, which caused her father to erupt again. Once he'd said what he had to, the General's loose jowls went in for one last outraged shake and he stormed from the room.

Chapter Six

"I did try to make you sound impressive," Dean told me when we were next alone. "I've always thought my family were impossible, but you've got some real beauties in yours."

As he sipped his champagne, he looked rather chic. It was amazing how much he'd changed from the rude, oikish person who had reluctantly confirmed my alibi when my boss was murdered a year earlier.

"I appreciate the effort, mate." I took a glug of champagne. "And thanks for coming. This can't be much fun for you."

His not completely hideous face became smiley. "Are you kidding? Getting to witness the monsters in someone else's family is the best. Have you got any really racist relatives? Or how about an incredibly boring one? Like, so boring that I want to rip my ears off? I get a curious thrill out of terrible people."

I would have taken this opportunity to tell him how weird he was, but the head butler appeared with a gong. Somewhat inevitably, it went bonnnnnnnnng! And everyone quietened down to listen to his announcement.

"Ladies and gentlemen, lunch will now be served in the dining room."

I was feeling pretty full already…

I told you we shouldn't have scoffed so many of those tiny sausages!

… but I had faith in myself that I would be able to wolf down a three-course meal and probably quite a bit of cheese and crackers after. The dining room was spectacular. Laid out like a wedding banquet, with the flowers and decorations to match, no expense had been spared. There was even a head table where Mum, Bradley, Elizabeth and their other first cousins were watching over everybody like the wardens of the feast. I noticed that there was an unoccupied seat beside Elizabeth and that her father hadn't appeared for the meal.

"Looks like we're on the kids' table," Tedwin joked, as we found our place on the seating chart.

"Much better," Greg replied, with his typically well-spoken composure. "That means we can make a mess and no one can complain."

Noémi smiled and sat down next to me. Dean took advantage of the fact I was much lower than normal to give my neck a fake, but affectionate nuzzle. I reacted as though this was just what I wanted (though I thought he was taking the act a bit far, to be honest) and a few of his fans at the neighbouring table nodded approvingly.

The heirs to Castleton Square Manor had another opportunity to show just how friendly they now were. Tedwin blushed away whenever his sister mentioned my name and they both bombarded me with questions about my cases, what it was like to discover a body and whether I still got freaked out by blood and gore – to which I lied and said, "Nope, doesn't bother me in the slightest."

I tried not to pay them too much attention. There was a constant conveyer belt of delicious food and it ran right up to our table. The first course was a cold soup of cucumber and Spanish ham (muy rico!) the main was a chateaubriand steak (délicieux!) and the dessert was the tastiest tiramisu I'd eaten in recent memory (sorry, I don't know any Italian!). I washed each delicious mouthful down with some sort of eye-wateringly expensive wine. I'm no expert on such things, but it was strong, red and had a definite aroma of fermented grapes.

There must have been at least fifty people there and, though there were a few faces I'd never seen before, I recognised the majority of them from various functions over the years. Looking around at the Gibbs-Castleton family made me feel like an anthropologist. It was easy to spot trends in the ranks. The male line clearly held to the Bradley/Grandfather model of human specimen, whereas the majority of the women, I'm sorry to say, were downtrodden mice who couldn't have got a word in if they'd had the will to try.

Though I still didn't trust my second cousins, at least they broke the mould. Tedwin was attentive and polite and Noémi an utter chatterbox. They may have been growing on me just a tad, but I wasn't letting my guard down. Another rebel in the family was Bradley's twenty-year-old son, Axel, who came over from his table towards the end of the meal. It can't be easy living with Bradley Gibbs, and I always have a lot of time for him.

"Hi Iz!" he said in a voice that managed to be both sad and optimistic in equal measure.

"Axel!" I already sounded sympathetic. "Who've you been sitting with?"

He let out a low groan in the direction of a pernickety bunch in the far corner. “Old people. I didn’t catch their names but they told me all about the problems with my generation, so that was fun. I’m pretty sure Dad came in here earlier and swapped me off this table just to annoy me.”

You know those people who go through life feeling hard done by over nothing? Well, Axel is nothing like them because he has every reason to be miserable.

“Yeah, that sounds like something Uncle Bradley would do.” I searched for a silver lining. “Still, the food was good.”

He evacuated every particle of breath from his body in a slow steady stream before replying. “I wouldn’t know. Dad made me go out to the car to get his photo album with all his pictures of the fish he’s caught this year. I couldn’t find the car and then, when I did, it was locked so I had to come back here, get the key and bring him the album. When I finally got it, he didn’t want it anymore.”

“Would you like my tiramisu?” Dean offered, getting in on the pity party. “It’s a bit fancy for my tastes.”

“Some things don’t change at least,” I told my friend, rather relieved there were still traces of the hopeless case I’d first known still inside him.

“Yeah, give me a nice scoop of vanilla ice cream over this pretentious stuff any day.”

Axel’s eyes lit up then, and it wasn’t just because of the dessert he was about to inhale. “You’re Dean Shipman, aren’t you?”

Dean nodded and, in his naturally nasal voice, replied, “Guilty as charged, my good man.”

“I can’t believe it! I’m such a fan of your products. I read a profile of you in Techworld magazine. You’re basically my hero.” He was jumping up and down on the spot, so I relinquished my seat for him to geek out with my fake fiancé and pulled a spare chair over.

Most people had now finished their meal and the room was getting noisier. Calls of “Speech, speech!” went up from every corner and Elizabeth looked embarrassed, but rose to address the crowd.

“I wouldn’t wish to keep you from the rest of today’s entertainment, but I’m happy to have this opportunity to thank you all for coming.” She sounded shyer than when we had spoken before, and rushed through the words. “I hope you’ll enjoy the day as much as I already have.”

As she was speaking, Elizabeth's offspring jumped up from the table and raced one another across the room. They made their way there in that funny running walk that people do when they don't want anyone to know how eager they are to get to where they're going. They eyed one another hungrily. Even if they weren't the savage children they'd once been, I could see that there was something not quite right with the pair of them.

Tedwin was in the lead to begin with, but selected a poor route through the tables and almost flattened a young maid carrying a tray of coffees. So, in the end, Noémi was the first to arrive. As she got there, the neatly dressed man I'd seen earlier, who I now assumed must be some kind of paid assistant, handed her a cordless microphone.

"Before we get on with the celebration, I'd like to say a few words, if you don't mind." Noémi took her time and peered about the crowd, before shooting her brother a triumphant wink. "First, I'd like to say how wonderful it is to see so many of you here. Old faces," she looked at me just then. "… and new. Young and not so young. From north and south. It is so thrilling to have you all here together, and none of this would have been possible if it weren't for our beloved *Mummy*."

Standing just behind her mother, she put her hand out. Elizabeth flinched a little, then took Noémi's fingers loosely in her own. Tedwin tried to grab the microphone, but his sister merely turned away to shut him out.

"My mother has been such an inspiration to me. Her philanthropy is well known of course, but, as they say, charity begins at home and she has always been a warm and generous woman. Which is why I wanted to come up here to raise a glass to the founder of the feast and my own personal hero…" she seized a fresh glass of champagne from in front of Bradley – who looked like he'd already had too much to drink. "To Elizabeth."

The toast rang out around the room, as we all got to our feet. Tedwin looked furious not to have made more of an impact on the proceedings. He didn't even have a glass to raise and swayed impotently from side to side.

Something weird is going on here, don't you think?

Totally. But perhaps it's just rich people being rich people. They're all completely mad, remember?

Except for our good friend Lady Penelope.

Well, obviously! She's the best!

Bradley put a neat full stop on the toast by passing out on the table in front of him and Mum somehow ended up with the microphone.

"Give us a song, Bu-Bu!" my leering grandfather bellowed, before several more Bradleys in the audience echoed the demand.

Mother did a humble, *oh no, I couldn't possibly* gesture and five seconds later was signalling to a sound guy in the corner to cue her music. I have to admit, her production values had rocketed since her first performance at the Cova Negra hotel, which marked the beginning of her fake-celebrity fame. Not only did she have an actual backing track this time, and no longer needed to hum the saxophone solo, there was even a costume change.

"Where would I be without the people around me?
What would I do on my own?
Where would I be without my family beside me?
I might have a house, but it would not be a home."

With each line of the song, she danced up to a different member of her audience and gave them a wink or a smile.

"Where would I go when I needed a favour?
Who would lend me a buck or three?
Where would I go when I needed a saviour?
Nobody else would put up with me."

The music picked up tempo and she launched into the jazzy chorus.

"I love my faaaaaaaaaaaaaaaaaamily!
They never complain when my life's in a mess.
I love my faaaaaaaaaaaaaaaaaamily!
And they love me too, which is why they're the best."

Much like my mother, the song managed to be both affectionate and mocking, vain yet self-deprecating. She whipped the yellow dress from her shoulder to reveal a sequined Union Jack minidress, and the aging lotharios in the audience went wild.

"They may not be so handsome, or even that pleasant,
They aren't the most clever, it's plain to see,
But there is one thing which we can agree on.
We're all just crazy about me!"

As she returned to the chorus, strobing searchlights swept the room from above the sound desk. All eyes were fixed on Mum as she mounted the grand piano in the corner and fans plucked flowers from their table centrepieces to launch them at her.

All eyes but mine.

Chapter Seven

After lunch, there was time to freshen up before the family photograph. Those guests who were staying overnight were escorted from the dining room to the apartments on the eastern side of the vast, cuboid house. A squat, wiry, rather tough maid, who couldn't have been less than fifty, came to escort us upstairs. She wore a mischievous grin as she collected Dean and me from our table.

"If you'd like to come this way, please." She spoke in a clipped, polite tone which didn't hide the fact that she'd recognised me.

"It's Martha, isn't it?" I asked on our route towards the ballroom.

"Yes, Miss," was her only reply. She kept her eyes ahead and showed no further sign of having remembered me.

Martha had been my saviour on my first visit to Castleton. If it hadn't been for her, my cousins' sadistic plan would have come to fruition and I would have been punished for their fictitious crime. Once we'd left the crowds behind in the dining room, she stopped and threw her arms around me.

"Oh, Miss Izzy." Her voice had changed with her attitude and a string of tones in a thick Derbyshire accent rushed out at me. "I knew it were you the moment I saw ya." She seemed genuinely happy to have me there and bustled along the corridor for us to follow. "Wait till I tell all the old gang about this. They'll be made up!"

Dean looked bemused but said nothing as I replied. "It's lovely to see you too. You were the best part of my last visit here. Well, there was one other thing I liked."

"I remember, Miss, the detective library, weren't it?" She stopped and a cheeky grin spread across her face. "Do ya fancy a peek now?"

She didn't wait for my answer but cut off the corridor we were on to rush through the ballroom, which was already set up for the dance that afternoon. A gigantic stone staircase occupied one wall of the room and showed us that we'd arrived at the oldest part of the house. A balcony at the top linked the east and west wings, where the guest and family apartments were located.

Martha chatted away to us en route, filling me in on what the other members of staff I'd met had ended up doing. "Course, I'm the last one here from back in them days. Grew up local and never found a reason to leave but we still stay in touch."

We turned left at the top of the stairs, then followed the corridor around to come to a small, hexagonal room with bookcases covering every wall. It filled me with the same sense of wonder as when I'd first found it as a child.

"I remember it being massive," I said, scanning every last title and automatically searching out the ones I hadn't read. Dean let out an affectionate laugh at my expense, but I didn't mind. This was my happy place.

Half of one shelf was dedicated to Christie, but there were plenty of other writers represented. Sayers was there, of course, but so was Georgette Heyer, Gladys Mitchell and Georges Simenon. And it wasn't just the Golden Age of Detective Fiction, all the hard-boiled big guns were there like Chandler, Cain and Hammett and there were newer names too. Ruth Rendell, Colin Dexter and Ian Rankin occupied one of the shelves and the only thing missing was space for the collection to grow. I could have spent a lifetime there and never got bored.

I turned back to our smiley guide. "Thank you, Martha."

"You're very welcome, I'm just so happy to see ya." She beamed a little more, then escorted us out.

She led us to our suite in a dark, wood-panelled corridor, still shaking her head, like she couldn't believe it was really me. "You should come down to the kitchens before you leave, for old time's sake." With one last smile, she walked back towards the party.

"She seemed nice," Dean said, and we both stared after her until she'd disappeared around the corner.

"Yeah, lovely." I put my hand out to open the door, but was still too in awe of Martha's warm, noisy personality to go through. "It's rare that I meet someone after such a long time and they don't mention how tall I've become."

We finally went into our room, where a large double bed with barley-twist posts at its four corners occupied half the space.

Dean let out a grunt of mild surprise. "Ah... One bed. We didn't think this plan through."

I would have offered to sleep on the floor, but he spoke again to save us from such an awkward negotiation.

"So, who do you reckon the killer would be if there was a murder here?" His blunt question took me by surprise as I landed down on the puffy duvet.

"What makes you ask that?"

"We're in an old country house and you're a known murder magnet, obviously."

"A what?" My voice wavered in surprise.

"A murder magnet. Have you never heard the term?" I shook my head, so he continued. "Yeah, strange phenomenon, but I've read about them. People who attract murders wherever they go."

"Total nonsense." I lay back on the bed and considered having a nice little nap. "As if I'm a murder magnet."

He let out a classic Dean snort. "You can't deny that people die wherever you go."

"Ahem, I'm a private detective. I go where the crime is."

He was quick with his comeback. "Nope, that doesn't cover it. At least three times over the last year, a murder has occurred in your immediate vicinity without you being on a case – because you're a murder magnet. First in your office at work, then on holiday in Spain, then walking through London on a sunny winter's day."

Don't forget our trip to the caravan park on the south coast. People always forget the caravan!

I searched for a response. "I never saw a single dead body until the day I met you."

He was having none of it. "Nice try, but do you know how many murders I've been a witness to in the last year?"

I sat up to look at him. "Let me guess… four?"

"None, Izzy, not one. The main reason I agreed to come away with you this weekend was in the hope of stumbling across a corpse."

"Weirdo!"

He continued, unperturbed. "So, to return to my original question. Who do you reckon the killer would be if one of us was chopped down?"

I thought for a moment. "It depends who the victim is. If someone kills my cousin Tedwin for example, I know exactly who'll be behind it. Tedwin will be murdered by-"

"Izzy?" I heard Elizabeth's voice calling from the hall and then a hesitant knock on the open door. "Would you mind if we have a quick chat before the chaos starts back up again?"

I shot Dean an awkward look and ran to speak to her. "Of course. Can you give me five minutes to get changed?"

She nodded and motioned that she would wait outside in that strangely uncertain way of hers, so I grabbed my swankiest outfit – a sparkling black, floor-length cocktail dress with a rather cheeky slit in the front – which I had no doubt that Uncle Bradley would still find too masculine. I pinned my long, flyaway hair to my head, put a token amount of makeup on my face and left Dean to his own devices.

Elizabeth was waiting for me in the hall. It was the perfect moment to address the sleeping arrangements.

"I'm glad I got to catch you on your own, actually, as I was rather hoping that Dean and I could have separate bedrooms." She looked at me like I wasn't making any sense so I searched for an explanation. "It's just… It's just that we don't believe in sex before marriage."

She swallowed down whatever she'd been thinking and said, "Oh, are you very religious then?"

I did a trademark Izzy Palmer squirm and finally went with, "Yep, very."

She did not look convinced. "But your mother just told me the story of how, when you were at university, you got locked out of your house stark naked after you had an argument with your boyfriend."

Brilliant, thanks, Mum! How am I supposed to get out of this now?

"Yes, that's right… But I didn't marry him, so it was okay." I was aware that this made no sense whatsoever. "I reckon Dean and I have a real shot, though, which is why I'm holding off from… you know… kissy-time."

You sound like you're about four, Izzy. It's called sex. Is that really so difficult to say?

She gave a disinterested shrug. "I'm sure that, if you talk to a member of staff, they'll be able to help you." She came to a stop at the end of the hall and looked out of the window at the guests who had already arrived for the photograph.

"It's curious to see them all here," she said, in a dreamy, almost lazy voice as I approached. "When I was young, my parents used to have big parties like this all the time. After Mummy died and Daddy gave the house over to me, I was simply too busy being a mother or helping Matthew with his business. At some point I came to forget that there was anyone else outside of this place."

She started, as though coming back to her senses, then pointed to the door we were standing next to. "Shall we?"

I was surprised to discover that this dark, oaken portal led to a set of spiralling stone stairs, with an incredibly heavy old door at the top. She produced a key from her clutch bag and led me into a spacious reading room, with a cluttered desk on one side and a Chesterfield three-piece suite on the other.

"How cosy." I didn't look at her then, as I was too busy admiring this pleasantly normal space in the otherwise grand house.

"It's rather odd, isn't it? There's one on each corner of the manor. We call this one the east tower, though it's really just an old storage room I had decorated to my taste."

The wallpaper bore stripes of burgundy and green. There was a large armchair in each corner and no TVs, computers or phones for the outside world to intrude through. But the outstanding feature of the room was a selection of colourful, taxidermic birds in formation on a large branch behind the desk. Rather like my host, they were sad, beautiful and strangely unnatural – trapped in position as though about to take flight.

When neither of us had spoken for a whole minute, I found myself blurting out my thoughts.

"Is everything okay, Elizabeth?" I asked, then rushed to explain why I would pose such a loaded question. "I mean, you didn't seem to enjoy the meal very much, especially the speeches."

As everyone else was watching my mother's entirely unspontaneous performance, I'd kept my eyes on Elizabeth. The look of horror that had consumed her face had shocked me, even from the other side of the room. I traced her gaze to understand what could have elicited such fear, but it seemed she was only staring into space. Her father had arrived a few moments earlier to take in my mother's routine, but I couldn't say for sure that Elizabeth had seen him.

"What could possibly be the matter on such a joyous occasion?" A hollow smile reshaped her gaunt cheeks as she sat down behind the desk. Her hand automatically fell upon an old pulp-fiction paperback there, and something clicked in my head.

"The detective library; it's yours, isn't it?"

As a child, I'd never questioned who the gigantic collection of crime fiction novels had belonged to, but I was overjoyed to discover this connection to my mum's cousin, who smiled at the question.

"It was my grandmother who started it, but it has certainly grown under my curation. I recently acquired a signed first edition of 'The Mysterious Affair at Styles' and an early print of Edgar Allan Poe's 'Tales'. I'll have to show you them. I read in the paper what a fan of Christie you are."

All my concerns at what Elizabeth was going through were swept aside for a moment as I processed the revelation. "It was my idea of heaven, when I camped out there, on my last visit. You're so lucky to have it."

My choice of words seemed to alarm her, and the smile once more disappeared from her face. "Yes, I'm very lucky. People are always telling me I should be more grateful for my lot."

She looked out of the window in the direction of our gathering relatives. On one side of the room was a beautiful view across the elaborate gardens of the Castleton estate and, on the other, nothing but the flat, stone roof of the property.

"There is one thing I'm very grateful for though." Her expression perked up a little as she spoke. "And that's why I called you up here, Isobel. I've tried so hard to be a better person these last few years – to make up for the mistakes I've made – and you being here really is the culmination of that. What I did all those years ago, sending you off to be punished, out of sight and out of mind, was a wicked thing and I will never forgive myself."

"Well, I have." I walked up to the desk, which displayed a handwritten letter in bold black ink. "I didn't think I would be able to when I read your letter, but I see that I was just as much at fault for hanging onto something so petty for so long. Though, I'm afraid it might take me a while to do the same for your children."

She rolled her eyes. "I don't blame you, they're…" Her voice trailed off.

"They seem nicer now." This was my rather transparent attempt to fish for more information. "They've really grown up."

"Yes… Yes, they have." Her tone was frosty = and it was clear that she was holding something back. "Isobel, my dear child, I need you to know..." The silence was overwhelming as I waited for her to continue. "I... Well, I just wanted to tell you that I'm proud of all you have achieved."

"You can trust me, Elizabeth. You can tell me what's upset you." I paused, hoping she might do just that, but when she didn't reply, I spoke again. "Is that really why you wanted to talk to me?"

Her eyes flicked between me and the far window, then she smiled and the tension melted away. "Yes, my dear. Now, if we're not quick, they'll take the photo without us."

She held her bony hand out to me. It was not the answer I was looking for, but I pulled her up from her chair and we were about to set off downstairs when Uncle Bradley rolled in.

"There you are, Elizabeth." His voice was gruff and insistent from the beginning, and he barely looked at me. "Sorry to interrupt the chinwag you ladies were having, but there was that matter I was hoping to discuss."

Our host hesitated, and I could see that this was this last thing she wanted. Looking between the two of us, she finally gave in to her cousin's request. "Perhaps you should wait downstairs, Isobel, I'll be with you right away."

Chapter Eight

I tried to listen to their conversation from the bottom of the stairs, but there were no raised voices or shouted threats to give me a clue to what they were talking about. Bradley didn't look happy about it when he shot back downstairs though. He gave me one grumpy look and motored off ahead to bark at his son.

Elizabeth retained her cautious air when she emerged, but put on a smile for my sake. Our arms linked, she led me in that slow, stately way of hers, and I was happy that we weren't stuck with my uncle flapping his mouth the whole time. When we got outside, I was relieved that I was not the only one wearing my Sunday best. Though I admit I'd been far too casual at lunch, I fitted right in with the sparkling throng of relatives who were waiting for the photograph.

There were benches laid out and Mum and the rest of the Gibbs family had already chosen a prime spot next to the core group of Castletons. This placed her right next to the General, but there was none of his usual anger left in him and he seemed very engaged as they chatted. Dean looked rather jolly to be included too. As I reached my fake fiancé, he was laughing with Greg, Tedwin and Noémi. They had all become firm friends over lunch, and I suspected that my cousins were rather good at winning people over.

"Who's the man taking the photograph?" I asked Elizabeth, when I spotted the same figure who had been busy at lunch but never consumed so much as a drop of champagne or a crumb of vol-au-vent.

"That's my assistant, Fabian. He's a real wonder. I don't know where I'd be without him." She sounded rather shy as she said this, and her eyes lingered on the handsome, thirtysomething who was dressed in almost as expensive a black suit as my millionaire companion.

We took our places and Fabian started organising the rabble.

"If we could have a little hush." I noted a French accent, but he spoke in near perfect English. "That's it, pay attention. You're going to have to bunch together to fit into the camera." One thing he certainly hadn't lost was his gallic charm. "That's right. Now, the old lady with the big hat, no the plump one… yes, you. If you could move to your left three steps so that the colour of your dress doesn't blind everyone."

There was some unimpressed muttering at his rude comments, but we're British so nobody told him off. I noticed that Noémi were seething, though. She directed several sarcastic murmurs in Fabian's direction for her mother to tut at.

"I'm telling you now, madam." He stressed this last word aggressively as he pointed to my jovial mother. "I'm going to take three photos, so don't go moving about after the first. If we have to do this again because you weren't paying attention, we can stay here all afternoon." He sounded like my school chemistry teacher. "You're the one in the sleeveless dress, not me. And the forecast, as ever, is rain!"

How dare he mock the British weather! It was the British weather that propelled us forth from these beauteous shores to establish the widest empire in human history. It was the British weather which made the Brontës stay indoors and craft their poetry, and which keeps Wimbledon's courts so green!

Calm down, would you? We constantly make fun of the rain.

We're allowed to; we're British!

My brain can be a real zealot when it's worked up about something.

"Okay and, three… two… one," Fabian said, with his eye up to the viewfinder of the large black camera which was mounted on a tripod. "Weren't you listening? I told everyone not to move. Two more to go!"

My head was flooded with images of the annual class photos we'd taken when I was at school. My mum had bought them each year, so that I could remember the happy memories forever. In every last one, I ended up looking like someone in the row behind me had pinched my bum.

I got a call from Ramesh, just as the Frenchman was finishing his task.

"Yes, fine, answer your phone." He directed a scowl in my direction. "Even though I didn't actually tell anyone we had finished. What do I matter anyway? I'm only the photographer."

Fabian did scare me a little, but Ramesh is generally a texter. He normally only rings if it's really important, so I had to take it.

"Izzy, ask your stepdad whether he has a welding torch! It's an emergency!"

"What an earth do you need a welding torch for?"

"What don't you understand about the word emergency?"

I passed my phone to Greg, who provided the necessary information.

The only other thing that Ramesh had to say to me was, "Has anyone been murdered yet?"

"No. Why do people keep-"

He interrupted me before I could get the question out. "Let me know when someone dies. Byeeeee!"

I heard my father murmuring, "That's a turn up for the books; no one dead," and then Ramesh hung up.

Sticking with the weddingy timetable, after the group photo, it was time for drinks and dancing. The butler who had announced our late lunch reappeared to escort everyone to the ballroom. We were a happy bunch as we made our way there. Dean was in a particularly good mood, chatting to my mother about the possibility for crime that such old houses promised. For her part, Mum sang every answer, presumably to remind everyone of her much-heralded performance from an hour earlier.

"It's not just because there are so many novels set in old houses like this one," he told her. "I think the place lends itself to mystery."

"I absolutely agreeeeeeeeeeeeee!"

Sadly, I'd fallen into step with Uncle Bradley who was at a more subdued stage of his drunkenness. This meant that he could go into great detail on the finer points of the central heating business. "It isn't what it was. There was a time when central heating was a big deal and everyone was forking out for it. These days it's taken for granted. It's mainly new builds we work on, so when the floor fell out of the housing market, we never got back to the level we used to be at. You know the Derby Telegraph once called me the 'local king of central heating'."

I considered mentioning the fact that the Croydon Advertiser had christened me 'South London's queen of crime', but Bradley is a troll, so I ignored him and walked along in silence.

The ballroom was the jewel in Castleton Square Manor's crown. It was bigger, grander and better stocked for drinks than the entrance parlour had been. A full dance band was playing Glenn Miller-style swing tunes, and I was rather impressed to see some of my older relatives take to the floor and go spinning around one another. In a rare moment of assertiveness, my Granny Flo yanked her husband forward, and he twirled her about like they were ballroom champions.

I found a prime spot to be a wallflower, and Dean went to get us drinks. My mother wouldn't be outdone by her parents and did her best to get Greg dancing. Her third husband is more of a slow, thoughtful type, and even Mum's encouragement couldn't make up for his complete lack of rhythm, grace and spatial awareness. They ended up shuffling quietly together, cheek to cheek. It was sweet to see. It had taken her a few attempts, but Mum had finally married the right man.

When Dean arrived with the champagne, it was the perfect excuse for us not to dance. We sipped them slowly for half an hour as we chatted to my cousin Axel. When our glasses were empty, I could tell that Dean was about to ask me whether I felt it necessary to accompany him onto the floor, just as Bradley stopped by.

"Come on, Ian." He was steaming drunk again. "I don't normally dance with other blokes, but in that dress, I'll have to make an exception."

He grabbed me by the wrist, but I wasn't interested. "I'm fine here thanks, Uncle Bradley."

"Don't be such a wet blanket." Another tug. "Don't be such a party-pooper." Yank… yank. "Don't be such a… urmmm…" The thesaurus in his head had come up short.

Putting both hands on mine, he pulled with all his strength. Only, I hadn't expected quite so much commitment on his part and didn't resist strongly enough. I went flying forward, but instead of ending up in his arms as he expected, I shot past him and landed face down on the floor.

My chin made contact with the shiny wooden surface and I lay there stunned for a moment, unable to think what a normal person would do in such a situation. Behind me, Dean stepped forward to put himself between the lanky, spread-eagled woman in a ridiculous cocktail dress and her uncle tormenter.

"You've had too much to drink!" For a short, skinny chap, Dean could sound surprisingly tough and I turned to see him fronting up to Bradley. "Go outside and do whatever it is you have to do to sober up. I'm not going to let you hang around here making people miserable."

Everyone was looking. I don't mean a few people had gathered around me, I mean everyone in the whole place had trained their eyes on the scene like heat-seeking missiles. The bloody band had stopped playing and the musicians were standing up on the stage to see what the commotion was. Fabian was floating about with his camera too, and I swear he took a few cheeky snaps.

Mum had spotted me from afar and ran across to help. "Bradley, darling, I think you've had enough fun."

As I sat up, I was surprised to see a look of sheer fury in my mother's eyes. Despite her soft words, Bradley knew that he'd made a mess of things and stuttered out a reply.

"I… Yeah, I didn't mean to… You're right, I'll go for a lie down."

His head bowed, he sought the composure to make his exit, but something wasn't connecting in his brain. Instead, he staggered round in a circle for a bit until Fabian lowered his camera to take him by the arm and lead him upstairs. Elizabeth had just arrived and watched in horror as her cousin was escorted away. She mouthed a *sorry* in my direction, then followed her assistant upstairs.

I was surprised to see the General mount the stage to cover over the disruption. "Nothing to worry about everybody. Just old Bradley drinking too much. No surprise there, eh?" There was some tittering from the crowd, and he motioned to the band to start playing. "If the sumptuous Bu-Bu La Mer is here, and we give her a nice round of applause, perhaps she'd be good enough to sing us another number?"

Chapter Nine

Bradley wasn't the only one who wanted a quick getaway. As soon as everyone was distracted, I hightailed it up the marble staircase and sat on a bench on the balcony. It was the perfect spot to watch Mum's performance and feel sorry for myself.

The little drama I had been a part of hadn't quite subsided and I noticed Tedwin, Noémi and their grandfather running after their mother to lend assistance. They barely noticed me as they sped past, bickering at one another over whose fault it was that everything that day was going wrong. The Castleton kids did not appear to be the monstrous individuals they had been as children, but they clearly had a very different public face from their private one.

Dean brought me some ice for my poor bruised chin and when I pressed it against the wound, I discovered that it had started bleeding.

"Better get a plaster too then," he said with a cheerful grunt and disappeared off once more.

As the band foolishly hadn't prepared any of the music which she and Ramesh had composed for her big show, Mum sang 'Moonlight Serenade'. The subtle, simple song drew an even bigger cheer than her earlier, more choreographed effort and she dedicated it to her beloved husband in the crowd. When the song was over, she stepped off the stage, walked through the ecstatic crowd and came straight up the stairs to sit next to me.

She put her hand in mine and, for a minute or so, we said nothing, happy to take in the swelling music and the beauty of that incredible hall.

"I seem to be saying this a lot recently, darling, but I'm so sorry. I don't know why I didn't put Bradley in his place the moment we got here." She breathed in deeply before continuing. "I know what he's like, I do. But every time I'm with him, I turn into a child again, mooning at my big, brave brother."

I couldn't blame her. I knew why it had happened and how my mother felt whenever we were with her family, but it still hurt.

"He's less than you, do you know that, Mum?" I paused to see if she'd acknowledge this small but important truth. "And Grampa's not much better. You're worth ten of either one of them."

She let out a disbelieving laugh. "What are we like, eh? You with your boys and me with mine. But you know how it is, darling. Family can get to you like no one else." I felt that this statement was part explanation, part apology for some of the more trying moments in our relationship.

When she spoke again, her voice had softened. "After all that we've been through over the last year, we end up here with a bruised chin and a battered ego. 'The Sumptuous Bu-Bu La Mer' and the great detective Izzy Palmer, brought down by a bunch of old moaners."

It was a rare moment when my mother was the one who needed comforting, but I shuffled along the bench and put my arm around her. "There's a Philip Larkin poem which begins, 'Home is so sad. It stays as it was left'. I read it at university and that line has stayed with me. It's like, no matter what we do or who we become, when we go back to our families, nothing has changed. Your brother will always be rude and overbearing and you will always be in awe of him, though all he does these days is get drunk and say nasty things."

The General thundered past us for the third time, on his way back towards the east wing. He'd already been back and forth to the party once and looked as put out as ever. On seeing the teary mess we were both in, he clearly decided it would be best to ignore us. Mum and I looked at one another once he'd gone and burst out laughing.

"It could be worse, darling," she said. "We could be stuffy old bores like my uncle. Did you know that, until I appeared as a pundit at the royal wedding, he'd never spoken a word to me? But he fired off endless questions during the photograph. Have I met Lady Penelope personally? Do I know where Rupert Gravely-Swans buys his suits on Saville Row? The old snob couldn't get enough of me all of a sudden."

I grinned and held her tighter. Maybe I haven't made it clear before, but I love my mum. Now that I come to think of it, I probably don't tell her enough either.

"I love you, Mum." Her sobs grew deeper and louder before I'd finished the sentence. "You're stubborn and infuriating and I generally wonder if you've lost your mind at least once a day, but if it weren't for you, I'd be an unemployed hermit with no friends. You're the best mother I could imagine having and I truly appreciate everything you do."

Izzy! Stop it, you'll make me cry next!

Unlike my brain, Mum couldn't find any response except to pull me into her and make my shoulder all soggy. When she finally let go, she dabbed at her eyes in a shy, rueful manner.

"My makeup is running. I must look like a panda." She patted me on the knee stoically and, without another word, made the international hand gesture for, *I'm going to the bathroom to see how dreadful I look and attempt to do something about it.*

As she walked off, still wailing, Dean appeared at the top of the stairs. "What's wrong with her?"

"I said something nice and it all got too much for her. It's for that very reason that I ration out my compliments."

Dean turned his head to one side and, like an uncomprehending alien, newly arrived on Earth, watched my tearful mother hurry away to the east wing.

"I could only get these," he said, once the scene had been processed in his mechanical mind. He held out a strip of sticking plasters with pictures of princesses on. He sat on the bench to peel off the paper and place a grinning Cinderella on my chin. "This place is so big and none of the serving staff knew where to get help, so I asked the mother of a little boy and she came up trumps."

He sat back to admire his handiwork just as a shout bounced along the corridor towards us. "Elizabeth?"

It repeated over and over, getting slowly louder. I could hear doors being opened and banged shut and new voices joining in.

"You haven't seen Mummy?" Noémi asked a moment later as she peeped around the corner to check.

"She didn't come this way." I rose to my feet, but Noémi had already vanished.

"More family weirdness." Dean shook his head as though it were another funny twist in the day, but something felt wrong to me.

"Stay here. I'll be right back." I forgot about my very hurty chin and left the napkin with ice in on the bench. By the time I got to the corridor where my room was, a small search party had already assembled.

"Has no one seen her since we brought Bradley upstairs?" Noémi asked.

The General's voice was hoarse and distant. "We left the drunken fool in his room and Elizabeth said she had a headache. I went downstairs, but people were asking after her, so I came back up to see whether she would be returning to the party. She's simply disappeared."

"What about the east tower?" Tedwin asked.

The General had moved beyond his usual state of irritation and looked genuinely distraught at his daughter's absence. "I was just there. The door's locked from the outside. If she didn't leave this wing, she must be in one of the bedrooms."

"There's the detective library," I said, trying to be helpful. "Couldn't she be in there?"

The General nodded and motioned me to follow, just as Fabian arrived. Sizing up the situation in his quick, methodical way, he went with my cousins to search the bedrooms.

The old man walked with great purpose, like he was marching off to battle. We took a turn off the corridor and were soon in front of the little library.

"Alright." He placed his hand on the antique glass doorknob but hesitated before turning it, as though he feared what might be inside.

Finding the courage to open the door, he pushed it with great force to reveal nothing but books. The same old, wooden bookshelves lined the walls, but it didn't look as though anyone had been in there since we'd popped by earlier in the day.

This was enough for the General, who immediately continued on along the corridor, throwing open each door we came to. I did the same on the other side, but the only thing of interest was that the bathroom door in my mother's room was closed. I didn't like to knock and interrupt her.

We made it halfway around the four sides of the square and met Fabian and the others in the middle.

"I don't know where Mum's got to, but Bradley's still passed out on his bed. What about you?" Noémi asked, and the General shook his head.

"No sign of her."

We hung in space, like a stuttering video call that had lost its signal. A surge of authority coursed through me and I walked past them to the unembellished door of the east tower. There was something that didn't make sense to me, so I decided to put it to the test. My team trailed behind me and we mounted the short, spiralling staircase to find that the door at the top truly was locked and the key was still in place.

"I told you," the General blurted. "She must have gone back downstairs without you noticing."

"It's not possible," I replied. "I was sitting right on the balcony, I would have seen her just like I saw you."

"Mummy always locks the door when she's not inside." Tedwin was at the back of the procession, but stood on tiptoes to peer around everyone ahead of him. "She says she likes this to be a room of her own."

"And I bet she normally takes the key with her when she leaves, right?" No one had an answer for me, so I turned back to the door.

As I didn't have any pockets on my ridiculous sparkly dress to keep disposable gloves in, or even any sleeves to grip the door with, I pulled the white handkerchief from Fabian's dinner jacket and carefully unlocked the door. I took a deep breath before opening it, and, when I finally did, there was Elizabeth.

Chapter Ten

She was lying face down on the floor, not far from where we stood gazing in. If the bloodstain covering half her back didn't tell me what had happened, the large knife sticking out of her certainly did.

"Call an ambulance." There was panic in the General's voice and he turned away, unable to process what was in front of us.

Tedwin sprinted downstairs, looking for a better signal than the ancient staircase could offer. Careful not to dislodge any evidence, I slipped my torturesome black heels off and stepped inside the room. I crouched beside Elizabeth and put two fingers to her neck to search for a pulse. As I did so, her shoulder jerked backwards and her eyes locked onto mine. There was barely any life in her, but she did her best to grip my arm and cough out a few words.

"I'm glad you're here." I'll never forget this tragic moment. It was hushed and childlike, as though she were letting me into a secret. But with her brief sentiment delivered, she allowed her eyes to close and prepared herself for death.

"Elizabeth?" her father said in his typically formal voice, like he was a middle manager in a medium-sized accounting firm, asking a customer whether they were happy with the service they'd received. "Who did this to you?"

There was no response.

"Do something," Fabian shouted, running into the room in a panic.

I attempted to stem the flow of blood with his handkerchief, but it was too small. She'd already lost a lot of blood; removing the knife would have only made it worse. Tedwin had returned with a towel for me to fashion a tourniquet around her body, but it was a vain gesture.

I sat there with my hand on her back for several minutes before I was sure she was dead. No one spoke, but they crowded around to say their farewells and I felt both stupid and kind for not making them wait outside. I feared I would drip blood across the carpet and contaminate the room further, so stayed right where I was until the police arrived. It felt wrong to leave her anyway.

Of course, that's not the only reason I stayed behind. As soon as the General had taken the others back downstairs, their faces grey and grim, I studied every detail in that room from top to bottom. I took in the fancy, uncapped fountain pen that was resting on her desk, the black ink spilt across it, but no letter in sight. I saw three mystery novels lying at Elizabeth's feet, which must have fallen from the shelf by the door when she'd struggled with her attacker.

The wound in her back was not the only one. Her hands were deeply scarred, as though she'd fought with the killer to seize the knife. There was a small tear and a spot of blood on the shoulder of her purple dress too, which suggested the killer had swung with the knife and missed. But, perhaps most tellingly, as I lifted the arm which had come to a rest on my lap, I saw a trace of thick white powder beneath her perfectly glossed nails.

When the first uniformed officers arrived on the scene, I expected shouting and accusations, but there was no such drama. I explained why I'd touched the body and they guided me out of the room, with as little impact as possible.

I was escorted down to the corridor where the others were waiting, incapable of anything more than shocked silence. I found the stillness infuriating. Time was passing and all we could do was wait for the police to get on with the investigation. What I needed was the truth. What I needed was to pull my treacherous suspects into separate rooms and shoot them full of questions, one by one.

I watched and waited, in the hope that whoever was responsible for the poor woman's death would let their act slip – that their long faces and creased brows might give way to a sly, shifting look or irrepressible smile. The General's head hung despondently – he looked like he would never speak again. Tedwin and Noémi were sitting on the floor side by side, the boy with his eyes to the ceiling, his sister focusing on the floor. If anyone, it was Fabian who most surprised me. Sitting perched upon a radiator, the dead woman's assistant was clearly shaken by what he'd seen. His eyes kept flicking to the spiral staircase as if, were we to try a second time, we could still save his employer.

In an attempt to free myself from such excessive emotion, I considered the facts of the case. It was a closed-circuit murder; the four gloomy corridors of the east wing offering any number of places for the killer to hide after the deed had been done. Dean and I had been stationed at the only exit. There were no staircases up from the ground floor to that part of the house except for the one I'd been sitting next to for the fifteen minutes after our host went upstairs. Bradley, Tedwin, Noémi, the General and Fabian were the only ones who could have done it. Well, almost.

"Hello, everyone," my mother cooed in an inappropriately chirpy voice. "What's the matter? You look like you've seen a-"

I felt it wise to interrupt. "Elizabeth's dead, Mum. She's been murdered."

Her smile did not immediately abandon her. "But that's not possible, she was-"

"Where have you been?" the Frenchman asked, his voice high and strangely desperate. "Where have you just come from? We checked every room and didn't see you."

"I…" Reality had set in and Mum struggled to find her answer. "I was in our bathroom."

Fabian wasn't happy with her answer. "Then why didn't you hear us calling her name?"

Mum thought before replying. Her usual instinct to project a sunny disposition at all times was at odds with the moment, and I could see she was unsure how to proceed. In the end, she slowed everything down and, in a calm, careful voice, said, "Well, I might have heard something, but I thought it was the maid. I could never have imagined there'd been a murder."

"Leave her alone," her uncle spoke up. "There's no sense throwing accusations around." The General's sombre tone and haunted look restored calm to the draughty hallway – for about ten seconds before the place erupted again.

"And what about you, Fabian?" Noémi was the instigator and she stretched the name out aggressively.

"Don't you start!" The Frenchman's voice achieved new levels of bile and disdain.

Not to be left out, Tedwin had a theory of his own to put forward. "Nice try, Sis. Make a big fuss and no one will consider that you're the one behind this."

A great scoffing noise cut the space between them. "I'm sorry? Are you really suggesting that I would kill my own mother?"

"Quiet!"

Despite the thick carpet, endless wooden panels and heavy furnishings as far as the eye could see, the word seemed to echo about us. We turned to see a guy in a cheap grey suit with slicked back hair, a heavy gold chain and three chins.

"The name's Detective Sergeant Osborne." He spoke as though we should have known this already. "I'm in charge of the case (until my boss turns up). So quit your chatting and do as I say."

We all flinched at his unexpected arrival, but it was interesting to see the General suddenly stand up straighter. I couldn't decide whether he was bristling at the thought of being subordinate to a character like D.S. Osborne or glad that someone had taken charge.

Osborne's gaze came to rest on me. "Palmer, I heard you were here. We're going to need your help on this one."

The uniformed constable who had been standing guard at the door took exception to this. "Sarge, she's a civilian. She can't be involved with an investigation."

Osborne's slightly greasy face went two tones pinker. "Did you not hear what I said, P.C. Chandra? I'm in charge."

I could tell the woman was not easily intimidated and that she even considered answering back. Instead, in her strong Midlands accent, she replied with, "Yes, Sarge," and returned her gaze to the hall in front of her.

"Very good." The middle-aged detective ran his hand slowly and gently through his hair. "Palmer, with me."

He marched past his constable and up the stone staircase to the scene of the crime. At the top of the stairs, he offered me a set of shoe protectors and gloves.

"I'm not going to lie to you. I haven't got a clue where to get started with this one; thank God you're here." For a man with a noticeably massive ego, he had no trouble admitting that he wasn't very good at his job.

He glanced casually at the body and then went for a wander around the room. "People management, that's where my skills lie. I haven't got the first clue about red herrings and smoking guns or any of that stuff. Modern policing is all about putting the right people in the right place. Once in a while though, a special kind of case crops up, and I reckon this might be my banana skin." Without pausing for breath, he spun round and said, "Talk me through it. Tell me what you know."

He was a cold wind blowing through the manor. A brash, boastful caricature of a detective.

I couldn't find my words, so he prompted me. "I believe the door was locked from the outside?"

"That's right." I was still in the doorway, afraid of contaminating anything before the scene of crime team got there to run forensic tests. "I was the one who opened it. When we came inside, she was still breathing, but that doesn't tell us much as she'd been spotted alive and well a quarter of an hour before anyway."

"Who do you think…" he paused to pick the right word, "… done it?"

Ha, this guy's hilarious. He's like a character from a bad, seventies cop film.

I was trying to remain diplomatic, but it was hard. "I was sitting on the balcony of the ballroom until her family realised she was missing. My mate Dean stayed there after, so, assuming there's no one hidden in one of the rooms, the only possible suspects are the ones you just passed downstairs and my uncle Bradley who's had a few hundred too many."

"That's six people, including your mum?" Perhaps he wasn't so stupid after all. He could count to six and had recognised Bu-Bu Lar Mer among the suspects.

"Yes. We were here for the party. It's still going on downstairs."

"Not for long." He didn't seem interested in my observations and, picking up a porcelain figure from the desk, frowned a little before replying. "It couldn't have been a trap that was set for her? Mechanical arms, hairline triggers? That's the sort of thing that happens in the books you read, right? A knife to the back, with the real killer fifty miles away."

I looked at poor Elizabeth. "We'd find the arm, or the trigger, there's no sign of anything but the knife."

He came to a stop in front of the morbid aviary. "What do you know about the dead woman?"

"Not as much as the others. It's only the second time I've seen her in twenty years."

"But she's your cousin, isn't she? Was there a family falling out? Something like that?"

He piled his questions up like a child with bricks, and I could tell that he couldn't be trusted. He was looking for the swiftest resolution to the case, not the right one.

"I wouldn't say that, but-"

He didn't let me finish. "So, there's a feud. Your mother on one side, Elizabeth Castleton on the other, and Elizabeth ends up dead. Thank you, Miss Palmer. You've been very helpful."

"No," I tried again. "You're not listening. My mum had nothing to do with this. She'd only been downstairs for a few minutes when we found the body. She couldn't have-"

Another interruption. "A few minutes is long enough to murder someone. And you said yourself that Elizabeth Castleton was still alive when you got here. If the killer didn't wait around, then she only needed seconds to do the deed."

I pored over the corpse, desperately trying to find some evidence to show Osborne he'd got it wrong.

"The knife!" I yelled with as much pride as Archimedes jumping from his bath. "Elizabeth was tall, the wound is high up on her back. My mother would never have attacked someone from such an angle. She's tiny compared to Elizabeth." *And me*, I thought, but didn't want to make myself a suspect in his preposterous mind.

He raised one arm and attempted to stab an imaginary victim from an impractical height. "Fair enough. So, it must have been one of the men." He let out a self-assured *hmm*. "We make a great team, Palmer. We've already ruled out half the suspects and I only got here five minutes ago. Do you reckon we could get this sewn up by dinnertime? Derby County are playing tonight and I never miss a Rams game."

I really didn't know what to say to that. He kept veering between professionalism and profound stupidity.

He took a few steps forward so that he was standing over the body. "It was a joke, Palmer. You should lighten up."

I let out a laugh for some reason, even though it wasn't a joke and it certainly wasn't funny. I suddenly knew how Mum felt when humouring her big brother.

"I suppose we should talk to our suspects then." He sounded as though this was far too much trouble for him and he'd rather be doing something else. He stepped over the body and I timidly followed him downstairs.

Chapter Eleven

I took a moment to check in with Mum on my way past, but she was putting on a brave face.

Or hiding her guilt!

Come to think of it, Mum would make a good killer. She's a superb actress, when she's not trying to do a silly accent, and could charm her way around the most experienced investigators using just her smile and a few well-chosen words. I don't think it's likely though. She doesn't have that killer instinct. She only managed to watch the movie 'Babe' "once and never again" after the scene where the duck becomes dinner. It's hard to imagine her hacking another human to death.

Osborne cleared his throat to address everybody. "If your rooms are in this wing, you may retire to them, but I've stationed two officers at the exit, so you won't get out that way. If any of you are thinking that you can escape by jumping from one of the windows, please try. It would save me a lot of bother by, first, helping to identify the guilty party and, second, breaking your legs so that you can't get away."

The guy was really fond of hearing himself talk and laughed more than was warranted. "We'll be interviewing each of you in turn, and it would be great if we could wrap things up quickly. Derby County are playing tonight and I never miss a Rams game."

Oh no! He's a joke-recycler! We have another Bob on our hands.

He didn't even pretend that this was funny, but signalled to Tedwin that he would be the first interviewee.

"Sarge," the young constable interrupted as two more uniformed colleagues appeared, having searched the wing for lurking murderers. "Should we stay here or head downstairs to interview the other guests?"

Osborne pulled one sleeve of his jacket halfway up his arm and then tugged it back down again. He clearly wasn't happy with this suggestion, but only because he hadn't thought of it himself.

"No... Well, actually..." He stumbled over his answer before coming to an idiotic conclusion. "Chandra, you stay here. You other two, swap with Powell and Lowe at the door and then tell them to interview the guests downstairs."

Clearly pleased with his pace of thought, he turned with a smile and we entered the nearest bedroom where Tedwin was waiting for us. Despite only being a few years younger than me, there was something very childish about him. Sitting on the edge of the high bed, his feet didn't touch the carpet and he swung them gently above the floor.

"Why did you kill your mother?" Osborne began in a bark. He didn't take the time to sit down, but launched the accusation at Tedwin.

"I didn't kill her." He was clearly panicked. "I swear. The first I knew about it was when we went upstairs and discovered her bleeding to death on the floor." He looked like he wanted to cry, but nothing came.

"Who would want to kill her then?" The officer had already dropped his far too obvious bad-cop routine.

"I have no idea. As far as I know, no one except, my sister and grandfather would benefit from her death so-"

Osborne clapped his hands together. "Brilliant, you've been very helpful." He spun around on the ball of his feet like an overeager disco dancer, before whispering to me in a loud voice that Tedwin and anyone outside in the hall would surely have heard. "Four down, two to go."

The investigation was a joke. The man had the attention span of a three-year-old and the cognitive abilities of a poorly trained Labrador. I needed to do something before he ruined our chances of solving the murder entirely, so I waited for Tedwin to leave and pulled the sergeant aside for a quiet word.

"Do you seriously think you can rule him out, just because he said he didn't do it?"

Osborne didn't like to be challenged. He sucked his stomach in and moved up close so that his face was only a few centimetres from my own. "Call it gut instinct, Palmer. It's probably not something you're used to, but, for a career officer like myself, it can come in very handy."

He was infuriating, and I struggled not to scream. "You didn't even ask him where he was right before the murder. He and his sister came up here at least ten minutes before we found their mother. What were they doing then?"

He looked stumped again. "That's not my concern. All I need to worry about is identifying the killer, and we've only got two suspects left. The Frenchie's not much taller than your mum, the daughter neither, so that only leaves the old fella and your drunken uncle."

"Your reasoning is way off." I refused to be cowed by him, so pretended that he was my horrible, dead boss and delivered the stinging response that he deserved. "Tedwin benefits from his mother's death just as much as the rest of the family. You have to grill him and get to the truth."

He rolled his eyes exaggeratedly and then did it once more for effect. "I was willing to have you on board this investigation, but if you're going to cause problems, I might just change my mind."

I tried to come up with a reply; I promise I did. I even started in on several, but that just made me sound like I was hiccupping. "If you… Is there… My only… Ahhhhhhhhhh!"

Ignoring me entirely, Osborne stormed from the room in search of his next suspect who, I could only assume, would deny all knowledge of what had happened to Elizabeth, leaving the sergeant free to arrest the last remaining suspect.

I could hear him start in on the same routine as he entered the room where Bradley had been deposited. "Why did you kill your cousin!?" he growled once more.

I collapsed in the hall and sat hugging my knees. I'd had a similar reaction when I was fourteen years old and couldn't climb the rope in gym class, but my psycho teacher Mr Bath insisted. With my long skirt wrapped around me, I was shaking with anger until I heard a few soft words and looked up to see that I wasn't alone.

"Are you alright?" It was P.C. Chandra. She was rooted to the spot by the east tower door, but looked sympathetic.

"No, I'm not alright. A woman has been murdered, the man investigating is a grade-A moron and I'm wearing far too revealing a cocktail dress which I should never have bought in the first place!"

As my words died away, she checked both sides of the corridor before coming over to me. "I've seen this before," she said in the matter-of-fact tone that reminded me of pretty much everyone I had met in the servant's hall on my first visit to Castleton. "It's finding someone dead like that; it messes with your head. Most of the bodies I've seen have been traffic accidents. They're still hard to deal with, but this is murder."

I got a bit smug then. "Thanks, but this is not the first body I've come across."

I'm not sure that's something to be proud of, Iz.

"Yeah, I know who you are." She didn't sound impressed. "But how often have you been holding the person as they died? That's going to leave a mark."

I wanted to tell her that it was nothing to do with the blood pouring from Elizabeth's back, the rusty red stain of which was still visible on my right hand. I was going to say that the only problem I had was with her boss, who was more like a cartoon of a man than an actual man, but then I realised something.

"Wow." I sat back against the wall and opened my eyes wide to process the revelation. "You're right."

"Yeah, love, I know." She knelt down and gave me a smile, which made me feel a lot better. "After doing this job for a few years now, I'm quite good with people. Better than D.S. Osborne, anyway. People only put up with him because his dad and his grandad were top brass. No one knows what the hell he's talking about most of the time. But don't worry. D.I. Fincher will be along soon and he knows what he's doing."

"Chandra, you're off your post!" the detective sergeant hollered, as he marched out of one room and into the next. "We've got a lead. Call despatch and tell them I'll be bringing in a live one."

Chandra returned to her watch so that, a minute later when Osborne reappeared with the General, he didn't have to shout at her again.

"If I've got anything to do with it, this one will be going away for a long time."

My great-uncle looked terrified. All his arrogance and pomposity had drained away. He was not the authority figure he'd appeared when he'd strode in to berate his daughter that afternoon. He was suddenly shyer, smaller and frailer.

I stood up to meet his gaze as Osborne pushed him past.

"You've got to help me, Isobel. I would never hurt my Elizabeth. This is all wrong."

Chapter Twelve

Farce.

I was living through a real live comedy of the absurd and, for once, my mother and Ramesh had nothing to do with it.

"Tell you what, love." P.C. Chandra told me. "You go back to your room and get changed. You'll feel a lot better when you've got a nice comfy jumper and some tracky bottoms on."

I like the way this woman thinks.

I nodded and did as she'd suggested. I had to hand it to her, she spoke a lot of sense. Not just on the fundamental human need for baggy clothing over tight, strappy scraps of scratchy cloth, but what she'd said about finding Elizabeth bleeding to death. I'd become hardened to the violence of my job. I'd viewed each case as a newly discovered Christie novel that I got to be a part of, but I'd never watched the life drain out of someone before and it gave a whole different hue to the experience.

I went back to my room, which was a lot messier than my first visit, as apparently Dean had felt the need to pull the sheets off the bed. I changed into the exact uniform that the constable had recommended. Pulling on my fleece hoodie was like jumping into a hot bath and I immediately filled my tracksuit bottom pockets with random useful stuff. I was about to shove my mobile in when it started to buzz.

"Izzy, this is urgent!" Ramesh was practically screaming down the line.

I was used to him blowing everything out of proportion and decided it could wait. "Ra, there's been a murder."

"That's only to be expected, Izzy, now listen-"

I was slightly offended. "I'm not a murder magnet, if that's what you're implying. Have you been speaking to Dean?"

When he spoke again, he sounded a little guilty. "I'm really sorry, Iz. I know you rely on me to help you with your cases, but you're on your own this time."

"Thanks, Ra. I'll try to cope."

Ha! Sarcasm; the highest form of wit!

"Now listen to my problem! I need you to ask your mother whether she has any sheets of thick leather we could use. She's not answering her phone."

"We?"

I could hear my father in the background. "That's right, Izzy. I'm helping Ramesh with his *project*. It's very exciting. You're going to be so surprised when you find out what it is." He sounded very pleased with himself. "Normally, I'm the last person to know about any surprises that you and the gang get up to, so I'm rather proud to be the first this time."

Ramesh seized control of the conversation. "So, will you ask your mum for me, Iz?"

"Her cousin was just slaughtered by a knife-wielding maniac and she's a suspect. I'm not sure it's the right moment."

His voice was suddenly distant. "That poor woman! I can't imagine what she must be going through."

"Seriously? Now you find your sympathy?"

"I'm not a monster, Izzy. If Rosemarie is having a difficult time, I feel dreadful about it." There was a pause before he came up with a suggestion. "You should probably leave it twenty minutes before asking her about the leather."

"And the wagon wheel!" Dad added.

"Oh, of course. Ask her whether we can use the ornamental wagon wheel in her garden, please. I'll give it back on Monday. In fact, you know what? Just get her to ring me, that's probably easiest."

"Whatever you say. I'm going now. Bye!" I pulled the phone back from my ear and he listed a few more items he'd forgotten as I hung up.

Back in normal, human clothes once more, I really did feel better. I looked into the mirror on the ancient dresser and gave myself a pep talk.

Hey, that's my job!

"Izzy Palmer; the famed detective who has already solved the murder of a millionaire, a journalist, a Hollywood star and countless others."

Countless? I can count to eight quite easily!

So much for pepping me up.

I started again. "Izzy Palmer, internationally renowned detective."

They love you in France!

"Izzy Palmer, who has a one hundred per cent success rate for solving murders."

And finding missing cats!

"Izzy Palmer is about to solve the case of the murdered cousin."

You go, girl! Shoot for the moon!

I smiled at the strong, confident woman in the mirror. There would be no fear or uncertainty this time. I was ready for whatever Castleton Square Manor had to throw at me. I pulled the door to my room open and went to search for Dean.

"I didn't like to move from here until you'd told me otherwise," he explained, when I found him just where I'd left him at the top of the stairs.

I felt a bit guilty, but I was pretty sure he'd have been playing games on his phone the whole time anyway. "I appreciate it. You've heard what happened?"

He nodded and puckered his lips together in a morose grimace. "Yeah, I'm really sorry, Iz. An officer told me."

"Did anyone leave the east wing while you were out here?"

As we spoke, a forensic team tramped past us on their way to the crime scene. They were already dressed in clean overalls and one had a hood up that made him look a bit like an alien.

Dean waited for them to pass before answering my question. "Only that loud-mouthed detective with the General. He kept shouting 'make a hole, make a hole' even when there was no one in his way."

"Yep. D.S. Osborne isn't amazing at his job." I sat on the stone bench beside him.

The ballroom beneath us was nearly empty now. The only people remaining were the band, who were packing up their equipment, and a few members of staff, collecting abandoned drinks and moving furniture. It was another example of Osborne's ineptitude. Though the murder itself happened half a house away, this was the last place Elizabeth had been before she was killed and who knows what evidence a competent officer might have unearthed there. I had to at least hope that the other guests had been spoken to before they were allowed to leave.

"Are you okay?" Dean asked, when I hadn't said anything for a minute. "You're very quiet. I'm not used to you not talking."

Under normal circumstances, I might have been offended by his comment, but there were more important things to worry about. "I'm just trying to remember as much as possible about the crime scene before it fades from my mind. There are so many things which don't add up."

"Maybe I could help?" He sounded almost self-conscious. "I mean, I'm no Ramesh, but maybe if we go through what you know, it will make things clearer."

It was yet another chance for me to look at my friend and think, *wow, this guy has changed.*

"Well… the big question I keep coming back to is, why was the door locked when we found Elizabeth?"

Dean's techy brain whizzed, and he instantly came up with a good explanation. "To make sure she died, I suppose. Maybe they didn't have the guts to finish her off. Maybe the killer saw all that blood from the first wound and panicked. They left her bleeding to death and locked the door so that she couldn't call for help."

"You're right, you're not Ramesh. He would have suggested that the killer locked the door because Elizabeth was in love with another woman and they didn't want the truth escaping." I thought about Dean's far more sensible solution. "The only problem with your idea is that it doesn't explain why the killer didn't take the key. That would have made it all the more difficult for her to get help. There must be something that I'm not seeing."

Dean seemed irritated not to have solved our enigma and gave it another go. "Alright then, I've got it. The killer locked the door to prove that it was murder. They didn't want anyone thinking Elizabeth had killed herself." He sounded pretty cocky, and I gently set him straight.

"Ha! Nice try, but Elizabeth's hands and arms are covered in defensive wounds and the blow that finished her off was right between the shoulder blades. There were signs of a struggle too – books fallen to the floor, her chair upturned. I don't think there was much risk of anyone mistaking it for a suicide."

He let out a trademark grunt and stood up. "I wasn't there with you, so I don't have the whole picture. Fill me in on the details. This is just like debugging an app. If we work through everything methodically, we'll get to the right solution."

I was about to do as he requested, when we heard voices coming from the east wing.

Mum was first. "Hello? Is anyone here? It's just that, I've been waiting around for some time now and nobody has come to see me."

Uncle Bradley must have heard her call and emerged from his room. "Yep, I'm here. Splitting headache though. Don't know what they put in the rum and colas here, but I was knocked right out until that bloody policeman came in firing questions at me."

Tedwin was next. "Has he gone?" he shouted and, before this sentence was out, I heard footsteps pounding in our direction. He called again. "Oh, no you don't, Sis. Don't even think about it."

A moment later, Noémi appeared on the landing, pelting towards us with a face filled with rage. Her eyes were focused on the entrance to the family's apartments, but Tedwin was only metres behind her and catching up all the time.

Clearly getting into the spirit of things, Dean sprung forward to join the race. As much as I hate running (or any kind of exercise that makes my heart beat at the wrong speed) I was swept along in the chase for… for something.

"I'll kill you, Noémi," Tedwin lovingly informed his sister. "You're a psycho hellseed devil monster and I will rip your head off before I let you get hold of this place."

As we turned the corner into that maze of rooms, Noémi looked back over her shoulder to toss an insult in her brother's direction. "I'd like to see you try, you little runt!"

The way they spoke was filled with the same malice and fury they had displayed when we were children. The sugar and spice act they'd employed that day had been tossed aside and their true nature was now on show.

I was severely out of breath by the time we reached the small office they were leading us to. I had flashbacks to my first moments in Castleton Square Manor when I was a child and the sound of their wicked laughter rang in my ears.

"Where's the key?" I heard Noémi say as I arrived. She had already pulled aside a rug to reveal a safe built into the floor. Turning the dial with all the precision of a locksmith, she pulled the door open and extracted a padlocked metal box. "Where is it, Teddy?" She had gone back to using her sickly-sweet voice now that she needed something.

Tedwin huffed out a reply. "She never told me. I assumed you knew."

Dean had taken a seat and was enjoying the spectacle. The only thing missing was popcorn.

"Not a problem," Noémi pronounced as she stood up and seized an old silver candlestick from the windowsill, then placed the box on the desk. "You may want to stand back, Mr Shipman."

Dean jumped aside just as she raised the blunt object over her head.

Go on. Say it; just like a murderer!

Okay, yes, there was something homicidal about the glee she took in smashing the padlock again and again until the box buckled and the metal housing that the lock was attached to gave way.

"Easy as pie." She'd reserved her widest grin for her brother as she dropped the candlestick to the floor and flung open the box.

The four of us clustered together to peer inside.

"Empty," I said, as the others were clearly too shocked to speak. I could guess what they were looking for, but still had to ask. "What were you expecting to find?"

"Her will, of course." Tedwin was just as vicious as Noémi and pushed me out of the way to peer into the safe in case his sister had missed something. "The solicitor!" He rushed back to the desk to seize the phone.

"Ahem." Noémi cleared her throat, and we turned to see her on her mobile. "Hello, is that Mr Jaggard? This is Noémi Castleton. Yes, of course I'll wait." There was a pause, during which time she put her hand over the mouthpiece and directed a quick dig at Tedwin. "Silly boy, I've had his number saved in my phone for just such an- Oh, hello, Mr Jaggard. Yes, this is Noémi. We met at the garden party mum threw last year. Yes, it was a lovely day, wasn't it?"

She made a *bla bla bla* hand gesture towards us, then continued in the same sunny tone. "I'm afraid I've got some terrible news. Mother has been murdered and we were wondering what happened to her will." Another pause and I watched as Noémi's jolly expression crumpled before my eyes. "What do you mean, she changed it? When? Why?"

"Don't mess this up, Noé!" Dishevelled from our run and clearly panicked by the events which were unfolding, Tedwin spoke as if his sister was responsible for the news.

"No, Monday isn't good enough." Noémi's voice became higher and more indignant. "I want you round here with the will right this moment… I don't care if it's your mother's eightieth birthday. My mother has just been murdered and the only thing that can possibly make me feel better is knowing what's going to happen to her fortune."

Chapter Thirteen

Noémi failed in her attempt to convince the solicitor to pay a visit at the weekend. She and her brother retreated downstairs, bickering as they went.

"I get why you're so into murder mysteries now," Dean told me on our way back to the east wing. "All fun and games."

This cheered me up. "I'm so glad you agree. They're the best. Well, except for the poor person who has to die. It really isn't nice for the victim at all. But leaving them aside, mysteries are great."

When we got to the landing, my uncle was leaning on the balcony, watching the drummer pack away the last bits of her kit. With the disruptive arrival of D.S. Osborne, I hadn't stopped to weigh up our suspects, but if any of them was a born killer, it was Bradley.

"Izzy, my darling. I was hoping to talk to you." His voice was almost mournful. "I feel terrible about what happened earlier. I never meant anything by it. You know what I'm like, always saying the wrong thing, but I'd never do you no harm."

I could tell that it was the effect of the booze wearing off that had got to him, more than genuine remorse. This was the man who, at my fifth birthday party, had chatted up the entertainer and taken her to our garden shed, when she should have been performing magic tricks for little Izzy's amusement. The man who, at the dinner to celebrate my graduation, got up and made a speech about how studying literature was a complete waste of time and I should have gone into central heating installation.

"That's alright, Uncle Bradley."

He let out a guffawing laugh. "I knew you weren't the type to hold a grudge, eh, Ian?"

"Yep. No hard feelings." I pushed my emotions down inside me, locked them away in a metal box, put it in a safe and then threw away the key and forgot the combination. This was how the women in my family dealt with people like Bradley. It's a proven technique.

No, Izzy! Don't be like your mother and grandmother and a thousand others before them. Call him out for the pig that he is.

Mum was standing at the other end of the balcony and had seen the whole thing. The fact that she'd had to witness my meek capitulation fired something in me and I spoke again.

"Hey, Uncle Brad," I began, my resolve strengthening. "You were right next to the east tower when Elizabeth was murdered. I don't suppose you heard her calling out?"

His arrogance seemed to fade. "Me? No, I couldn't hear a thing. I pretty much passed out as soon as I hit the bed. Like I said, I'd had a few too many Cuba Libres on top of the champagne and wine. Oh, and we stopped for a couple of beers on the way for refreshment. It's a long drive."

"You only live thirty minutes away!"

He frowned like I was being terribly unfair on him. "Yes, but Axel hasn't been driving long, and I thought he could use the Dutch courage."

It did not surprise me that Bradley had encouraged his twenty-year-old son to drink and drive. I sized him up again and noticed that, despite his smart suit, there was something very grubby about him. His hair was unkempt and his face didn't look as though it had been washed recently, with spots of brown grease visible on his forehead. And that wasn't all.

"You've got white stuff all over your hands."

He immediately pulled back from me but stopped short of hiding them altogether. "That'll be putty. Use it all the time at work, but it's a bugger to get off. We were on a job this morning."

"Izzy," my mum called, presumably in the hope of saving me from her brother. "I haven't seen Greg for a while, perhaps you and Dean could help me look for him."

"It would be my pleasure, Rosie." My friend had been lurking awkwardly but came running when she called. Just like every man who's ever met my mother, he was-

Putty in her hands?

Hmmm… no, that's too on the nose.

I hadn't quite finished with Uncle Brad. "I'll need to talk to you again later. You're not going anywhere, are you?"

"Me?" He looked as though I'd accused him of cheating on his wife or fiddling his taxes – both of which, now that I come to think of it, I'd heard him bragging about doing with great pride. "We came for the weekend and I'm not going to pass up a free holiday. This place is a home from home for me. Old Lizzie would have wanted me to stay as long as I can."

I thought about asking him exactly what had passed between them in Elizabeth's reading room before she died, but decided to wait until I had more facts.

I was already walking away when he grabbed me roughly by the shoulder and said, "I know you'll find the killer."

"Yeah, course." I formed an innocent smile. "I'll get him."

I accompanied my mother and her fan back downstairs to look for Greg. I walked in silence as they chatted. Everything was a mess in my head. I'd been right there at the scene of the crime but couldn't get a clear picture of what any of it meant. I totted up every remarkable moment from the day and tried to get a grip on the facts, starting with the room where we'd found Elizabeth.

The books which had fallen from the shelves. The ink on the table. The white substance on the dead woman's hands, which I suppose could have come from my drunken uncle when she escorted him upstairs, so didn't guarantee his guilt, no matter how much I might want it to.

But this was just the superficial evidence. There was much more to delve into and any one of the suspects (except Mum of course) could have been involved. The General had been taken away for questioning and, though I didn't agree for one second with Osborne's method, Elizabeth's father was the person I would have started with too. He'd been angry with his daughter for most of the day and there'd clearly been a disagreement between them.

What a family! If her father wasn't involved, her two-faced kids could well be. I wondered how long they'd been playing the roles of devoted offspring and what they'd hoped to gain from it in the first place. I thought back to Noémi's fawning speech after lunch and the way her mother had looked askance, clearly unable to listen to the tribute.

Was that it? Had Elizabeth caught wind of Noémi's plan to do away with her? When we'd last spoken, it was as though poor Elizabeth had something to tell me that she couldn't get out. The fact she'd been so desperate to have me at the party and even her very last words suggested that she knew her life was in danger.

"I'm glad you're here," that's what she'd said as she lay dying.

Glad that I might bring the killer to justice? But then why not give us a name? The main attack came from behind, so perhaps they were waiting for her when she entered the room, but the wounds on her hands suggested she had defended herself and would have seen something of her assailant.

A mask, then?

It would make sense and I'd have to mention the possibility to the police, though a scarf or t-shirt would have done just as good a job as a tell-tale balaclava. A towel, even.

There was a bigger mystery that needed solving first. I knew nothing of Elizabeth herself. What had transformed her from a snobbish and frumpy widow, who could see no wrong in her children's behaviour, to the person she'd become?

I thought about the slightly macabre thrill that Dean had enjoyed as he embarked on his first murder investigation, and it calmed me down. Instead of letting the weight of uncertainty pull me under, I relished all those questions and anticipated the hunt that was ahead of us.

Chapter Fourteen

By the time I came back round to the present, we'd walked right through the house and onto the front steps of the manor.

"Why on earth did you walk off like that, Gregory?" Mum moaned when we found my stepfather looking grouchy in the light evening rain.

"I didn't *walk off*, the police asked whether I had any evidence to share, I said no and they told me I should leave through the front of the property. I didn't like to argue with them and did as instructed."

There were still a few valets waiting patiently on the drive for stragglers. Several police cars occupied the space in front of them and there was a constable I hadn't seen before, guarding the entrance. Greg wasn't the only displaced person there either. Poor Axel was having a cigarette under the shelter of the stone stairs.

Wait a second! Axel's a smoker? If Hollywood has taught me anything, it's that smokers are all heartless villains. Can we really dismiss him as a suspect, even though he was in a room full of people when the victim was murdered and stands to gain nothing from her death?

I ignored my own stupid thoughts and looked beyond the drive to see Tedwin preparing his gun for another shoot. He was alone this time, with no lackey to assist him, and had to launch the trap with a pedal. Despite the fact he was a potential murderer who was holding a double-barrelled shotgun, I decided that it was the perfect moment to talk to him on his own.

I left my family to trek across the grounds, then waited as Tedwin took five deafening shots and hit three targets before the magazine was exhausted and he had to reload the machine.

"You probably think that I don't care that my mother's dead, but you'd be wrong." He broke the shotgun and finally looked at me. "I loved her very much."

This was good, I could definitely work with a suspect who started a conversation by acknowledging that he seemed guilty. "Why do you say that?"

He studied me as he spoke, his eyes running zig zags across me. "Because my sister and I just sprinted through the house in search of our mother's will, as though it were the only thing we care about. But that's just our game. We've been at it since we were kids and we're still battling. Noémi used to read the old will at bedtime like it was Hansel and Gretel."

Even after all this time, I couldn't keep the hurt out of my voice. "I remember what you were like when you were kids. I remember you conspiring to get rid of me. It didn't seem as though you were at war with one another. In fact, you were more than happy to go along with whatever your sister suggested." I paused to steady myself before asking my next question. "Do you remember what she did to you?"

"Yes, of course I do." The words shot back at me like I was a clay disk spinning through the air and he was the gun. "She burnt the skin on my arm and told Mother that you'd done it. I can still remember how it felt. It was raw for weeks and she liked to scratch the wound with her nails. As soon as you'd gone, she immediately returned to tormenting me."

I had calmed down by now and was ready with my next question. "I don't know what it's like to have siblings, but that's what big sisters do, isn't it?"

He perched on the metal cage which held the automatic feeder and looked off towards the house. "No, I don't think it is actually. I think that's what psychopaths do. Big sisters are supposed to look out for their little brothers. To be honest, I don't care anymore. She can have the house and the lion's share of the money. The sooner we disband this failed family, the better off we'll all be."

There was a humility to the way he spoke that I hadn't been expecting. It was easy to believe that his sister was the leader of their tiny gang, and I felt a little cruel to keep questioning him.

"I'm sorry, but to discover who killed your mother, I have to find out what was going on in her life. She seemed so fragile when I spoke to her today, do you know why that is?"

He looked down at the floor. "I don't know what to tell you. She'd been different for the last year. Something changed in her when Fabian came to work here. I'm not saying he had anything to do with it, no matter what Noémi might think of him. For whatever reason, Mummy had already started to reconfigure everything in her life. First it was her appearance, then her social circle and the charitable activities she was involved in."

He bit his lip and shook his head at the same time. "For years after Daddy died, she'd been practically a hermit, but that was all over. She switched to doing everything at once. She ran galas and held fetes here at the house. She even volunteered in a food bank for a while, but then it got too much for her and that's when she hired Fabian. The cosmetic surgery really got out of hand after that."

I had rushed over there expecting to strong-arm the answers I needed out of him, but his response was so light and sympathetic that it was hard to think badly of him. Perhaps I was being taken in by the skills of a talented actor, but I was coming to think that Noémi was the evil genius behind their schemes and he really was an innocent victim.

I phrased my question more carefully. "Did you talk to your mother about what she was going through? I know it's none of my business, but it sounds like she was really suffering."

"I would have." He looked away, his eyes shooting up to the clouds overhead. "My sister made a joke out of it. She said that Mummy was just jealous of her looks and was trying to recapture her youth. The surgery, all the expensive purchases around the house, the diets and a complete change of wardrobe – none of that was my mother. Our whole lives, she'd been the rock I built my existence on, but suddenly she lost her confidence and it all flaked away."

"Okay, but how do you think any of that led to what happened today?"

"It's obvious isn't it?" People are always saying this and it practically never is. What they really mean is, *it's obvious to me, and you must be a real thicko for not working out what I'm thinking*. "Some needy chap that she'd helped at one of her charities must have come in and killed her. There are all sorts of wackos about these days." He hesitated then, as he knew how bad that sounded. "Don't get me wrong, I have every sympathy for poor people, but that doesn't mean one of them wouldn't touch a bleeding heart like Mummy for all they could get."

This felt like one of those bad moments that we have a lot of in my family. It was like the Christmas day when Uncle Bradley said that "foreigners don't deserve to come to Britain cos only the British speak proper English." It was such an extreme and unlikely thing to hear that no one in the room corrected him and we carried on our game of Pictionary as if he hadn't spoken.

I certainly had a response for Tedwin though. "No, sorry. That's not right. You can't just blame some random poor person. For a start, there was no way anyone could have got into the east wing during the time when Elizabeth was attacked and there's no one left hiding there because the police have searched every room. There are six people who could have killed your mother. It lets you all off too easily if we say that someone came in off the street and did it, especially when you live on an estate with high fences and security guards."

He looked at me dead on at last. "Six? Bradley, Fabian, your mum, Noémi-"

"You and your grandfather." I let this reality settle in his mind for a moment, but he couldn't listen any longer and popped two more shells into the shotgun. "So, if you know anything that would help me rule you out, you should tell me before D.S. Osborne realises he has no evidence on your grandfather and comes back to question you."

His words came out faster then. "I didn't do it, I'm telling you right now."

"Fine, then what happened after you followed your mother and Bradley upstairs?"

"I…" He couldn't finish the sentence, so replaced the clay shot and walked back to his position. "I don't remember for sure. I think I sat out in the hall and called my girlfriend."

He raised the gun to his shoulder and pressed the trigger to punctuate our conversation and steady his nerves.

"Will she be able to confirm this?" I asked between bangs, wishing I'd asked for ear protectors.

His eyes flicked from the gunsight over to me. "No, because she didn't answer."

"Well, the police will be able to confirm it by looking at your phone," I said, to see if I could provoke a response. He was either telling the truth or too good a liar to give the game away.

He'd taken three shots now and missed each one. I wondered whether this was all I needed to know. Whether, despite the calm he displayed answering my questions, the impromptu lie detector proved his nerves weren't as steely as he'd have me believe.

"Thank you for your time, Tedwin," I said, before he slammed his foot on the pedal to launch the clay pigeon and missed the shot by miles. "It's been enlightening."

Chapter Fifteen

"So, what next?" Dean asked when I returned to the house. "Do you need me to play good cop to your bad cop?"

"In my experience, that never works. I tried it with Ramesh once and he kept telling me off for being too mean. To be fair, we were only looking into a lost dog. I probably went at it a bit hard."

What next? is always a good question in a murder investigation. Thinking three steps ahead is even better, not that I had such foresight right then. What I needed was to see my suspects all together. That's often how new evidence arises and scandals are revealed. The interaction between different personalities is always telling, but with the General at the police station and the others scattered around the house, I'd have to wait until dinner.

"I was hoping to speak to Axel, but he's not here. And where's Mum gone now?"

Dean attempted to smooth his wavy hair with the flat of his hand, but it instantly jumped back to normal. "A detective inspector has arrived who seems to know what he's doing. Fincher, I think his name is. He's gone to round up the suspects to get a fuller picture of what happened."

"That's a shame. Competent police officers are far less likely to let me poke about the place." A thought occurred to me and I decided to run with it. "Speaking of which, do you fancy a walk? There's something I need to check out."

He looked up at the darkening clouds with his usual moody grace. "Well, not really."

"Don't be such a wimp, it's only drizzling." I set off down the steps, and he sighed and jogged after me.

Dean's not exactly the chattiest person I know, but he seemed engaged with our investigation. "Would you like to hear my theory on who the killer is?"

"Absolutely. I don't have a prime suspect yet, so I'm all ears."

"Your uncle Bradley." He clucked his tongue then, like he'd come up with something pretty mind-blowing. "Think about it; he created that scene in the ballroom as an excuse to go upstairs in the middle of the party, knowing that everyone would make a fuss and follow him up and that Elizabeth would have to go with them. He'd been drinking, which never exactly reduces violent tendencies, though perhaps he wasn't as drunk as he wanted everyone to think."

He allowed himself a smile as he spoke. "The others dumped him in the bedroom and went their separate ways, only he jumped straight back up and convinced his cousin to accompany him to the east tower. He had the knife with him and stabbed her in the back, then locked the door so that she died up there alone."

"That is…" To be honest, I was a little taken aback. I wasn't used to my friends and family offering sensible, rational perspectives on my cases. "…entirely plausible."

"You're welcome." He was at his smug best. "All we need now is evidence and motive and we've got our man."

We were halfway around the property already, following a paved path through bare flowerbeds that looked eager for the spring to arrive.

"Actually, Bradley does have a motive. He called this place his 'home from home' and, just before the photograph, he came to see Elizabeth in her reading room to discuss something. Whatever it was, neither of them wanted me to know. That's why I need to talk to Axel, to find out what his dad has been up to."

We walked around the corner of the building and fell into quiet thought until Dean asked, "So is this a locked room mystery?"

I hadn't given it much thought. "Yes and no. The room was locked, but from the outside so I don't think it fulfils the tropes of the genre as there's nothing impossible about it. In a locked room mystery, the door is normally locked on the inside and you have to work out how the killer escaped. We don't have that problem here. We just have to figure out why they bothered turning the key."

"Got ya," he said and I could see his technical mind whizzing for answers.

We'd arrived at the spot I was looking for and I pointed to the mezzanine top floor. "There it is, Elizabeth's reading room." We stood peering up at the quirk in the building's architecture. Though there were only three levels for the most part, on each corner, an extra room had been added as Elizabeth had explained. Perhaps she wasn't the first member of her family who had sought solitude away from everyone.

"Yes, very interesting." Dean didn't sound convinced. "Now what did we come over here for?"

"I need to see whether the killer threw anything out of the window." I approached the imposing stone wall of Castleton Square Manor and began poking about in the bushes. "With murder, it's always tempting to assume that it's the result of some longstanding feud, a love affair or the inheritance. Sometimes though, it's just a really good way of distracting from a theft. I wondered whether the killer had gone to the east tower to steal something, been surprised by Elizabeth and thrown whatever they were after out of the window."

Dean was content to stand on the path watching me scrabble about. "What was the knife like?"

I paused my search. "Standard kitchen knife. You know, a big pointy thing for cutting meat. Why?"

"A big pointy thing? Thanks, Izzy, I know what a knife is. I meant, was it a personal knife the killer could conceal? Or was it one they might have found in the room and killed her with when they were surprised? Apparently not, which makes your theory less likely."

This is no fun. He's cleverer than us. Quick! Bring back Ramesh so that we don't have to feel stupid anymore.

I had to give it to him, he'd made a good point.

Ha! Knife point! Puns are hilarious.

No, they're not! Be quiet!

I shook my head free of superfluous thoughts and accepted Dean's argument. "Fine. So they went there specifically to kill Elizabeth, having taken a knife from the kitchen beforehand. It doesn't rule out the possibility that they were planning to steal something."

"Then what was it? What could be so valuable that they'd go to all that trouble?"

"A signed first edition of Agatha Christie's first published novel, for one. Elizabeth told me she'd bought a copy but there's no sign of it in the detective library or her reading room."

"*A book*?" He screamed the words in horror.

"Yes, a book worth ten thousand pounds if it was the really rare American edition."

He folded his arms and tilted his head. "If that was the case, then you must be the killer as you're the only one who would murder someone for *a book*."

I rolled my eyes and dived back into the roses. They were spikey and I hurt my finger. "Well, fine. Not the book then. But there are bound to be treasures up there."

"Have you found any in that bush?"

I was about to give up my search and head back inside when something caught my eye. Another of the plants further along the wall was spattered with goo. It turned out to be birds' droppings but, on the ground alongside it, there was a small clump of a powdery white substance. I knew just what it was. Well, I assumed I did. Okay, it was an educated guess.

"May I ask what you're doing?" A petite, carefully dressed man propelled himself towards us from the east side of the house. "A murder has been committed just above where you're standing. You could be contaminating evidence."

He'd made me all flustered and I, somewhat athletically, leaped from the bushes to return to the path. "D.S. Osborne told me I could…"

"Yes, well. D.S. Osborne says a lot of things, but he's not in charge anymore." He stopped himself short of criticising his colleague outright. "I'm D.I. Fincher. I apologise for not getting here earlier, I was at an eightieth birthday celebration for a good friend's mother."

Fincher was the opposite of his colleague, he was precise and serious. There was no swagger or braggadocio about him, he was simply a man with a job to do. A pair of uniformed officers had arrived and set to work poking about in the undergrowth. I was happy to see that the inspector had the same idea as me.

"So you're the amateur, are you?" He looked at me with his quick, penetrating eyes and did not sound impressed.

That put me on the defensive. "No, actually. I'm a professional detective, but unlike you, I get to choose which cases I take."

Tell him about the missing cat in Camden, Iz. He'll be so impressed.

I ignored my brain and came up with something more helpful to win over the inspector. "If you look amongst the rose bushes closest to the building, you'll find some sort of putty or plaster which I'm pretty sure will match the powder under the victim's fingernails."

Or might have been left here the last time builders were working on the house.

He creased his brow and signalled to one of the officers to look. A stocky, blonde-haired chap walked along the perimeter of the house and came to a stop just where I had.

"I'm pretty sure that's birds' muck!" he said in a deep northern accent.

"No. Down on the ground; there's a white blob about the size of a battery."

He nodded, then took a plastic bag from a zipped pocket on the front of his dayglo vest.

"Very impressive, Miss Palmer," the inspector responded. I was happy that he knew my name after all. "You're still not allowed to have anything to do with this investigation though."

"The victim was my cousin!" I said, as though this were anything more than technically true and I'd known the woman well.

His voice rose one tone and he took a step a closer. "Then you have my condolences. But if you interfere in any way, I will have you removed from the house until we've finished."

Dean thought this was very funny and let out his nasal laugh – he sounded like a nerdy kookaburra.

"I…" I began, not knowing what else I could say then changed it to, "You…" and then gave up. It made me wish that D.S. Osborne was back in charge.

"Thank you, Miss Palmer." Fincher turned away before he'd finished speaking. "I'll be in touch if I need to ask you anything."

Chapter Sixteen

"The arrogance of the man!" I waited until we were out of earshot to say anything, but Dean was still laughing.

"He's just doing his job. I'm surprised you're not happy about it. Now that a serious investigator has arrived, you can put your feet up. Or would you be jealous if he found the killer before you?"

"Oh, don't you start." It seems like everyone is against me some days. "It's not a question of me versus them. I respect the police. One of my friends is a police officer. But there are things that I can do which they can't, and that's why they should let me help."

Dean wasn't convinced. "And what if you end up contaminating a crime scene or breaking a rule that would prevent a conviction? Then you'd wish you'd left it to the police, I bet."

I tried to calm myself down by looking at the positives. "It's fine, it is." I didn't do a very good job and still sounded like I was sulking. "There are all sorts of things that I can do. He didn't say I'm not allowed to talk to people in the house, for example. Speaking of which…"

We were coming up to the kitchen door, which was hidden behind a false wall, like the entrance to a public toilet. I'd planned to stop by, and now was the perfect moment.

Not much had changed since my last visit to the gigantic yet homely space. The wooden beams on the ceiling looked just as smoky and old, the same brass pots glittered on the shelves, and the whole place still smelt delicious. One thing had changed though. The jolly, red-cheeked woman who'd been there twenty years earlier had been replaced by a newer model of cook.

"What you doing in my kitchen?" a man with a hipster beard and tattoo sleeves demanded as I stood reminiscing.

"I'm Elizabeth Castleton's cousin and-"

"And I've got an uncle who played for Derby County, but you don't hear me banging on about it. What are you doing in my kitchen?"

"We were looking for Martha," Dean intervened in that oddly confident manner he could turn on whenever it was needed. I imagine it had come in useful when looking for investors for his multi-million-pound tech startup. I wished that I possessed such a superpower.

"Ahhh, you're friends of Martha. You should have said; I love Martha!" the chef was suddenly all smiles. "Have a sit down at the table and I'll make you some tea. Unless you'd prefer something-"

"Hot chocolate!" I shouted far too loudly, though, in my defence, it had been at least a day since I'd had any and I had no idea where my next cup was coming from.

He gave me a funny look. "Okay, I'll see what we've got. Martha should be along any minute."

Dean opted for a mineral water and the opportunity to judge me. "What is it with you and hot chocolate?"

"It's unspeakably delicious. What is it with you and sour water with bubbles in?"

He ignored my damning retort and started a lecture. "You're thirty years old, Izzy. You can't live your whole life like a child. Hot chocolate is unsophisticated, bad for your health, and it will rot your teeth."

I might have let out a stab of laughter then (and pointed). "Says the man who, until this year, thought the food groups consisted of pizza, burgers and fried chicken."

He wasn't flustered by my argument. "That's exactly right, Izzy. I used to think that, but I've grown up. I started eating right, built a gym in my pool house." *Show off!* "And realised the importance of looking after myself. I think it's about time you did the same."

My hot chocolate had arrived and in response to his patronising – though obviously sensible – claims, I licked the froth off the top without taking my eyes off him.

"How's your mineral water?"

I'm pretty sure I'd got to him. "It's delicious, thank you, Izzy. Most appetising."

"Great. Shall we get a KFC for dinner tonight or would you prefer McDonalds?"

"There'll be none of that trash in my kitchen, thank you very much," Chef commented from over at the sink.

Suitably chastised, Dean and I brooded over our drinks until Martha appeared.

"Oh, Izzy, you came. How lovely to see you again. And you brought your fiancé with you too."

The bossy chef insisted that she sat down with us and Martha did as instructed.

I felt I should confess. “Sorry, Dean’s not really my fiancé. We made it up to impress my relatives.”

“I knew it!” She smiled at me then, and it was hard not to take offence.

“Sorry, how do you mean exactly?”

“Oh, don’t get me the wrong but… he is a millionaire.” She eyed Dean up like he was the Eiffel Tower or a really nice sandwich.

Sadly, I have a very thin skin and immediately launched into my defence. “No, you don’t understand. I do have a boyfriend but he’s away in Peru at the moment. He’s a doctor actually.”

“Of course he is, my lovely. Of course he is.” I could tell from the pitying look on her face that she didn’t believe me.

Sadly, I have very thin skin and refused to give up. “And very handsome. Tell her, Dean. Tell her how handsome Danny is.” I poked him in the ribs until he did my bidding.

“Ummm… That’s right, Doctor Danny is very handsome. A real Adonis in fact. He has a selection of incredibly tight black t-shirts that show off his impressive pectoral muscles.”

Martha cleared her throat politely. “He sounds… lovely.” She looked at me like I was drinking more than just hot chocolate – perhaps a mug of rum mixed with a tasty shot of crystal meth.

It was my job to get things back on track. “Anyway, I’m sorry to ask you, Martha, but have the staff been told about what happened this afternoon?”

“Yes, we have. Miss Noémi came by to talk to us. It was very good of her to come down.” Her tone spoke libraries.

I smiled and, in my nicest voice, said, “But she was a little off maybe?”

Martha rocked in her seat and blew on her cup of tea. “Well, she wasn’t exactly-”

“What Martha’s not saying is that Miss Noémi is an absolute vampire.” Chef had obviously been listening and took this opportunity to contribute. “She came down here half an hour after her mother had been hacked to pieces, and acted like she were the new queen of Castleton. Bloody cheek, if you ask me.”

Martha squirmed a little more before she delicately added her thoughts on the matter. “I wouldn’t go that far, but it’s true that she didn't show much pity for her poor mother. Which maybe isn't surprising considering-"

"Considering that she's treated that woman like nothing but a piggybank the whole time I've been here." Chef marched over to us, his hands flicking soap bubbles about as he pointed his finger up to the ceiling.

It was hard to know who to address my questions to, but I knew Martha a little and trusted her a lot. "Is that right? Was there a strain on their relationship?"

The maid looked at the chef in case he wanted to have the first word, but he backed away saying, "You say what you think, Martha. I've got nothing to do with this anyway."

"Well…" she began. "Well, you know better than anyone what Noémi can be like. She's a bit subtler than she was as a child, though she still has her moments. She was a terrible teenager, that's for sure, but over the last few years… Well, over the last few years she's calmed down. In fact, she made a real effort to be kinder to her mother."

"You're too nice, Martha. That's your problem." Chef was back and this time he pulled up a chair. "What she's not saying is that Miss Noémi changed her plan of attack, that's all. She went from screaming and insulting everyone around her, to sucking up to get what she wanted. But a tiger doesn't change its stripes and that girl is still the same selfish, greedy, money-grabbing-"

It was Martha's turn to interrupt, "Ed, go easy, would ya? You'll give yourself indigestion."

The red-faced chef attempted to calm down and signalled for Martha to continue.

"It doesn't mean anything though, does it?" Chef was right, my old friend was a giant softy. "Just because she acted that way, it doesn't mean she could murder-" A nervous cry escaped as she was reminded of her boss's fate. "It doesn't mean Noémi would murder her mother."

I gave her a moment for the emotion to subside. Dean had been sitting quietly this whole time, listening to the details with the same serious expression on his face that he wore when discussing his work. He fished a clean cotton handkerchief from his pocket and offered it to our witness.

"Oh, you are kind, Mr Shipman," she said and almost broke into tears once more. "If it doesn't work out with that doctor of yours, Izzy, maybe you could…"

I smiled at Dean. "Thanks, Martha, but I think we both accept that ship has sailed."

I haven't! I still want you to get together with Dean so that we can live in his McMansion with its hot tubs and ice cream makers. That place is niiiiiiiiiiiiiiiice!

I pretended that thought hadn't just passed through my head and asked my next question. "Did you hear that there were only six people who could have been involved in the murder?" She nodded. "So, if it wasn't Elizabeth's children, who do you think the killer could be?"

Chef moved his chair a little closer. "It's obvious, isn't it?" No, it isn't! "Where do you think those kids got their savage nature?"

"The grandfather?" Dean tried.

"That's right, General Castleton of the tenth brigade of I don't know where."

Martha laughed a little. "Really, Ed. Half an hour ago, you were saying you thought the little Frenchman did it."

Ed took exception to that and made another dramatic hand gesture. It made me miss Ramesh. "I was only letting off steam. That Fabian is an interfering worm. He's always coming down here to the kitchen, telling me what to do. But he wouldn't gain much from her death, so I wasn't serious. It's the General you have to watch out for. Military man, no sense of humour, constantly barking at everyone, and he was never particularly nice to his daughter neither."

With every new accusation that Ed made, Martha looked more uncomfortable and less likely to tell us what we needed to know, but I tried to nudge her on. "Do you agree then, Martha?"

"Oh, I wouldn't say anything against the General. He might have a short temper, but I've known him a long time and I've never imagined him as the violent type. He's just at the age where a lot of things annoy him."

"Like what?" Dean asked.

"His grandchildren, for a start. He never had much patience with them, and he's been trying to get them to find work for a while now. Perhaps that's why…" Her explanation trailed off once more.

I squeezed her arm encouragingly. "You don't have to worry about anything. I'm not going to pass any of this onto the police unless I think it will lead to an arrest. I'm just trying to find out what happened. You know that my mum is one of the suspects, don't you?"

She nodded silently and pursed her lips together to avoid crying. "Perhaps the reason there's been so much tension between Elizabeth and her dad is that he was unhappy her children were still living here, still-"

"You can say it, Martha!" Chef stood up and grabbed our cups, though I hadn't managed to get the chocolatey bit off the bottom of mine and I almost cried out in agony as it was ripped from my grasp. "They're still leeching off their mother like damned... damned leeches."

Martha peered over at her colleague then turned back to us and, in the gentlest voice she could muster, said, "Yes, that's right. They're still not quite as independent as they could be."

"What about the knife?"

Ed returned and looked at me with one eyebrow raised. "What about the knife?"

"It was one of those chic, modern ones, made of a single piece of stainless steel, I thought it might have come from here."

"Like those?" He pointed across the kitchen to a magnetic strip on the wall which held a line of matching silver knives. I noticed there was a space in the middle of them. "Yeah, there's one missing, though it could have disappeared anytime since last night. I only just realised it was gone. I assumed the caterers had borrowed it, but maybe the killer popped down here sometime."

I let this revelation sink in, then nodded to them both. "Thank you so much for answering my questions. Oh, and did you spot anyone from the household down here since yesterday then?"

Ed had a think. "Just that Fabian, the General, Noémi and Elizabeth herself."

Feeling a tiny bit disappointed that he hadn't mentioned Bradley, I added a new note to the casebook in my head and stood up to leave. I thought about giving lovely Martha another hug, but I didn't want to smother the poor woman. I tried to look serious and professional as we left, but my brain had other ideas.

Quick, Izzy! It's not too late. Ask him to make lemon meringue pie for dessert tonight?

Chapter Seventeen

"That was interesting." Dean let out an impressed whistle as we went. "Hey, you don't suppose that chef bloke had something to do with the murder? He's definitely got the temper to be a killer."

I made a face to show how ridiculous he was being. "Nope, it's never the cook who turns out to be the killer. It's an unwritten rule."

"Izzy?" Martha called as we left the kitchen through a series of poky corridors. She caught up with us, then fell silent for a second. "Izzy, there's summat else I wanted to say." Another shy look, another pause, and it was hard to imagine this was the same ballsy woman who had terrified me with well-acted promises of a cane to my behind on our first meeting. "If you're right about this and the family are involved-"

I felt I had to explain myself. "I never said they were for sure. We just have to be open to the possibility."

She was agitated again, waving her hands and shaking her head as she replied. "Oh, I know, darling. I know you didn't. But, either way, it might be worth looking in the history room. It's up on the first floor, right next to madam's bedroom. It was a pet project of hers, you see. Family history and all that, not just ancient times but today as well. There're all sorts in there about her husband and... Well, you'll see why it's useful when you get up there. I'd show you myself, only it's not long till dinner."

"Thanks for letting me know." She nodded rather formally, so I said it again. "No, I mean it, Martha. Thank you so much for talking to us."

She blushed then and shot off back to the kitchen.

"She is so nice." I was glad that Dean decided to say this so that I didn't have to. "You don't think it's all just an-"

"No, Dean. No, I don't."

We got a bit lost in those labyrinthine halls, before finally emerging in the dining room. The police were still milling about, but I was impressed to see how quickly the catering staff had removed all traces of the party that had been in swing just hours earlier, and then themselves. I had to hope that the officers had taken down everyone's name and address for future reference.

We returned to the front parlour and scaled the immense staircase. The grandeur of the place overwhelmed me once more and I felt like Little Orphan Annie arriving at Daddy Warbucks' mansion for the first time. It reminded me of Elizabeth descending to greet her guests that afternoon. She'd waited until everyone had arrived so that her appearance would have the biggest impact. Her appearance in more sense than one of course, as she was revealing her dramatic new look to the family for the first time.

Something about it didn't feel right. The whole scene was a performance. She'd worn that lurid dress to be noticed; as if she were saying, I'm here and I'm not afraid. It was a red flag – well a purple one – intentionally waved to a bull. Perhaps she knew who her killer would be and wasn't afraid of death.

We navigated the main apartments in search of the history room that Martha had told us about. Dean was happy to remain silent as we peeked in doors and found ourselves in dead end corridors. It's in quiet moments like this that a death normally sinks in. Elizabeth's presence was everywhere we went. She'd been the lady of the manor for thirty years, she oversaw redecoration and renovation. Her photograph peered out at us from countless frames, but her occupancy of Castleton Square Manor had expired.

"This looks like her room," Dean told me, and he opened a door wider to show me the large suite.

There were a number of long colourful party dresses strewn across the bed – which it seemed unlikely that Noémi would have chosen – and a single family photo on the bedstand. Apart from that, the space was remarkably impersonal; a dark, drab internal shell and quite the least luxurious area of the upstairs world of the house.

It felt wrong somehow to step inside and, just then, Dean located the room we were looking for. He led me through the opposite door and we found ourselves in a museum devoted to the Castleton family. It was a long, bright room with several large windows on the exterior wall and old portraits between each of them of austere gentlemen in military uniforms and plump women with green eyes. But this was just the starting point.

On the left-hand wall, there were shelves holding photo albums, artefacts from centuries past, and long-deceased ancestors' diaries.

Close to the door, large sheets with an extended family tree and endless biographical details were held within metal housings, like timetables in a railway station waiting room. There was even a visitors' book.

"Funny sort of hobby," Dean muttered as we took a solemn turn of the room.

I noticed that there was no explanation of how the family had made their money in the first place. The Castletons had traded slaves between Africa and Europe, but that wasn't mentioned in the long introductory plaque by the door.

But then, this museum hadn't been designed to provide an overview of the family's history. It was a tribute which heavily focused on the last century and, in particular, on Elizabeth's deceased husband, Matthew. Fifty different versions of him were displayed around the room, his cool gaze and unsmiling features impossible to avoid. It was as though he was following me and it gave me the creeps.

"It's like a shrine," I said, drawing alongside my friend as he examined the largest print of Matthew Ogilvie.

"Or a tomb," Dean suggested with a shudder of his own. The temperature in the room felt about ten degrees cooler than anywhere else in the house. "How did he die anyway?"

I thought for a moment, to recall the circumstances when I was six or seven years old. "I can't really say for sure. I know that he got ill quite suddenly. He died a few years after Tedwin was born. He was a bit of a cold fish. We used to see them at family functions when I was really little, but Elizabeth stopped coming after he died."

"So, who was he, this Matthew bloke?" He pointed to a framed certificate from the company the dead man had owned. "Greybook Consulting, what was that?"

"He did something for the government and then became a private contractor. That's all I know. Mum would be able to tell you more."

Dean let out a cheerful snort. "Izzy are you serious?" I didn't understand what he was getting at and let him talk. "'He did something for the government before becoming a private contractor'? I'm pretty sure you just described a spy."

It was my turn to laugh. I was about to ask him what he knew about such things when I remembered that he owned a company that made spy gadgets. "Do you seriously think so?"

He paused and looked around at the photos. "Yes, actually, I do." He pointed at a small picture, high up on the wall. "You see that man on the left? That's Michael Howard, who was home secretary in the mid-nineties, and next to him is Sir David Spedding, the director general of MI6."

"Wait… mopey Matthew was MI6? *James Bond*, MI6? How is that possible? He always seemed so boring."

Dean's face grew sterner. "There are plenty of boring spies, Izzy. They're not all like James Bond. Plenty of them spend their lives in little offices, working with computers."

My voice was already shrill from surprise. "Hang on, you know what spies are like? You've met real life spies?"

It's hard to tell if he was doing it just to mess with me, but he looked around then in case someone was listening. "I might have."

"Who even are you!?"

"Concentrate, Izzy." He took a few steps around the room. "The chances are that he was a field agent though. Going by these photos, it looks like he travelled a lot in the eighties. Could all this have something to do with Elizabeth's death?"

I walked right up to the wall to be face to face with the man I hazily remembered seeing one Christmas at my grandparents' house and who made a brief appearance at my great-aunt's seventieth birthday. "I haven't a clue! This is way out of my genre. I'm more used to cheerful old maids and swaggering rascals. I don't know the first thing about espionage."

Not true. You started reading a John le Carré book once. It was pretty good until you left it on the bus.

Dean turned around and, tipping his head forward like what he was about to say was deadly serious, he said, "I think this is why Martha wanted us to come up here. She was too shy to say it directly, but she must have cleaned this room a thousand times and worked out the same thing that I did. Elizabeth's dead husband was a spy."

Chapter Eighteen

Well, what good did that do me? Did it get me any closer to working out who the killer was? No. Did it help me to see which of our suspects would have wanted Elizabeth out of the picture? Not at all. And did I give it another thought after I left Dean behind to scour the room for evidence? Nope, not really.

I could only stick to my plan which, at that point, was to wait for dinner as I was getting hungry. I wasn't sure where we'd be eating or whether we'd even be all together, but I knew that Mum would soon fill me in.

It took me a while to find her as she was downstairs in one of the immense lounges. It looked a bit like a furniture showroom, with sofas and armchairs organised in clusters across the elegant space. It had tall windows looking on to the gardens and the sun was going down to lend a pinkish hue to the walls.

My quietly mourning mother was playing cards with her husband and nephew. Bradley was there too, laid out on a sofa looking very sheepish and probably still nursing a sore head.

"Hello, Izzy," my uncle said, apparently unable to make eye contact but doing his best impression of a human being. "Is your chin okay?"

"Fine thanks." I wanted to talk to the others and not get stuck with him, though he was clearly eager to speak to me. "I like your plaster. Very… girly."

I suppose he thought this was a compliment, but pretty much everything that came out of his mouth sounded like a poorly veiled insult.

"Bradley, is there something you want to say?"

His eyes dipped lower still. "There is." He stood shuffling his feet like a little boy who'd been caught stealing sweets. "I need to tell you that I didn't have anything to do with Lizzie's death. You do believe that, don't you?"

I noticed my cousin peering over at us from the card game, and so I decided to play the part of a trusting niece, at least until I could get Axel on his own.

"Of course I do, Uncle Bradley. You were passed out drunk at the time she was killed, right?"

A grin carved open his stubbly face. "That's my girl. I knew I could count on you."

Appeased and reassured, he plopped back down on the couch and closed his eyes.

"Come and join us for a game, Izzy dear," my mother called across the room, but I remembered what happened the last time we'd played cards together and didn't need hypercompetitive Izzy coming out just then.

"Thanks, Mum, but I'm busy looking for something."

"Oh yes?" Greg's curiosity was piqued. "What's that?"

"Elizabeth's killer, as it happens."

My parents both made low, apologetic mumbles, which made me feel bad for making them feel bad, so I sat down to wait for dinner. Greg immediately folded and Mum hustled her own nephew for the chocolate pieces they were playing for and then they started another game to do it all over again.

"Tedwin was here a minute ago," my mother explained between sly glances at her cards. "He seems like such a nice boy. I don't know why you made such a fuss about them being the incarnation of evil on earth. They've both grown up to be such cheerful souls." She continued before I could correct her. "He said it will only be fifteen minutes until we can eat dinner in the evening room. Sounds like they'll be joining us, despite everything."

"Perhaps it's good to have family around at a time like this," Greg suggested and then folded once more.

"Actually, Mum," I said, realising I was remiss in my duties as a detective, "I should probably ask you something. You didn't kill Elizabeth, did you? I mean, it is safe for me to rule you out of the enquiry?"

She laughed a little too broadly, then sighed a happy sigh. "Of course it is, darling. I can promise you that I would never kill a living soul, especially not my cousin. We were very close growing up, remember."

A hush fell then as both Greg and Axel shot her shifting glances and she eventually had to address their smirks. "What? What are you looking at me like that for?"

Greg was the first to answer. "It's just… Well, you told me that the two of you were always competitive."

"Yes, Gregory, but two people can be both competitive and close friends. They're not mutually exclusive."

Axel was up next. "Maybe, Auntie Rosie, but Dad says that you and Elizabeth were like hellcats when you were kids. Didn't she pull your hair when you were teenagers only for you to vow revenge?"

Mum looked outraged. "Axel, my dear boy, I can promise that was all water under the bridge. My cousin and I got on very well indeed."

There were a few moments of silent play before Greg let out a *hmmm* and Mother took exception to it.

"Yes, Gregory? Is there something you'd like to say?"

"No, my love."

"So what was that *hmmm* for?"

Greg looked like he'd been found out. "I was just saying *hmmm* because…" his voice had grown fainter and we could barely make out the words.

"Because?" Mum was as angry as Miss Piggy – who, now that I come to think of it, was surely a major influence on her fashion sense.

Greg was reluctant to answer but, when the words finally came, they rushed out in one go like a burst water bomb. "Because you hadn't visited her for twenty years and have often claimed that, if anyone ever speaks to your daughter the way that Elizabeth did, you'll remove their intestines to make sausages."

Mum retreated down into her chair and held her cards in front of her face to hide how red she had become. "Well, I didn't kill her and I'm disappointed that no one believes me." She looked all pouty, until Greg and Axel started laughing.

"Oh, we got you there!" her husband cawed.

"Sorry, Auntie, but you are just too easy to wind up." Axel's giggle was a little more discreet.

I didn't like to spoil the fun, but I wasn't quite finished. "Only… what about the blood?" They stopped laughing and all three turned to look at me. "Elizabeth had cuts on her hands and the wound was deep enough that there should have been blood spray, but, by the time I got there, all our suspects were clean."

Greg and Axel cast their judgemental gaze back over my mother, who was starting to look worried. "I was in the bathroom the whole time. I left you on the balcony and, five minutes later, she was dead."

"Exactly, Mum. You were in the bathroom, you could easily have killed Elizabeth, washed any stains off your hands and then come to find the rest of us as though you knew nothing about the murder."

Mum froze for five long seconds before her face crumpled up with laughter. "Ha! Nice, try, Isobel. But you know that I deplore violence. I can't even bring myself to watch 'Babe 2: Pig in the City' after that horrific scene with the duck in the first movie."

The boys joined in with the giggling and Greg had to dry his tears with a handkerchief.

"You're all cruel and I don't like you." Mum was still smiling, so I think she'd forgiven us.

"How can you act that way on a day like this?" Fabian did not sound impressed as he shouted in from the hall. "It isn't funny! A member of your own family is dead."

We all fell serious again and Mum answered on our behalf. "You're right, Monsieur. She was my cousin and I feel terrible about what happened. But if we weren't laughing and distracting ourselves right now, I'd be up on my bed crying my eyes out." She rose and walked over to him. "I don't think Elizabeth would want a shadow to fall over this house forevermore. Would she?"

The Frenchman held my mother's gaze for a moment before it got too much for him. She held her arms out sympathetically and he soon began to cry on her shoulder.

"He's got killer written all over him." Axel sounded pretty sure of himself.

"Don't be ridiculous," Greg replied in a demure tone. "In French it's *assassin.*"

I felt I should intervene before their giggling got out of hand again. "I'm hungry. We might as well begin the search for the evening room. It takes so long to get anywhere here that I'm starting to miss our tiny house."

Axel had a quick peek at Mum's cards and looked annoyed that he'd been tricked by another of her bluffs. We told her where we were off to and left poor Fabian in the capable arms of counsellor Rosemarie Palmer.

On the way, I texted Dean to tell him about dinner. I was a bit worried he'd get lost and we'd never see him again, but, Knowing Dean, he probably had some kind of GPS radar location triangulation device and the plans of the house downloaded to his phone. He'd probably already hacked the mainframe, whatever that might mean.

There weren't nearly as many members of staff around as there'd been that afternoon. I was coming to realise that the platoon of butlers and maids that had run the house on my first visit had been slimmed down to a mere posse. When we arrived at the smallest of Castleton's dining rooms, the head butler was waiting to serve us and only Martha popped in and out.

Despite the room being comparatively minute to the space we'd enjoyed at lunch, it was still quite grand. The windows offered a view of the grand lawn and, between each, a dramatic biblical scene had been painted, complete with martyrs, angels and the odd demon.

Greg and Axel sat in awkward silence, and I felt as though we were hijacking someone else's dinner party. Fortunately, that sense of unease was soon relieved when Noémi rampaged into the room, screaming at her brother.

"You little backstabber!"

"What an appropriate choice of words," Tedwin spat back, as the two of them crashed down at the table without a glance in our direction. "But then you've never been the sensitive type."

Her anger gave way to a look of shock. "And what's that supposed to mean?"

"I mean, our mother's only been dead for a few hours and you're already planning on redecorating her bedroom. Why don't you admit you killed her and spare the police the trouble of investigating?"

This was the tipping point for Noémi. She seized the nearest object and sent it flying across the table.

Tedwin moved his head out of the way and smiled. "Barrington?" He turned to address the butler. "My sister will need a new soup spoon."

Chapter Nineteen

I know I should probably describe what happened next, but can I just take a moment to mention how incredible the food was that evening?

Yes, you can!

Oh my goodness! It made the lunch we'd eaten look like a McDonalds Happy Meal and I had to conclude that they'd been keeping the really good stuff for when the bulk of the guests had gone home. Speaking of which, I didn't get to say goodbye to Granny and Grampa. Oh well, back to the food.

There was an amuse-bouche of oyster foam. The starter was a mille-feuille of horseradish and artichoke hearts – which doesn't sound great, but was like a unique and delicious mini lasagne landing in my mouth. The main course was slow-roast French lamb served with a terrine of dauphinoise potatoes, shaped with their own battlements like miniature castles. And there was a saffron and Bordeaux wine gravy, which I would have happily gone swimming in.

For goodness' sake, Izzy. Would you get on with it? There are more important things to be thinking about than lamb and fake lasagne! Tell them about the dessert!

Oh, yes! And dessert was, wait for it… tarte au citron meringuée! That's right; lemon meringue pie! It was as if Chef Ed was psychic and he could sense exactly what his diners most wanted.

Or because lemon meringue pie is a really common dessert and it's just a coincidence?

That could explain it too.

I could talk all day about that dinner, but perhaps I should return to murder, intrigue, family infighting etc. After the spoon went flying across the dining table, the weirdest thing happened. Noémi and Tedwin laughed at one another.

"You've always been a bad thrower," the brother said, still looking cheerful after his sister's strop.

"And you've always been a snake." Their eyes were locked onto one another's and, despite the smiles on their faces, I could see their fight wasn't truly over.

Mum, Fabian and Uncle Bradley were standing shamefacedly in

the doorway. They cast their eyes around the room at us, trying to understand the weird atmosphere. Mum has never been embarrassed for more than ten seconds in her life and soon sat down by Greg at the end of the table.

I was surprised to see that Fabian joined them, which triggered an immediate response from Noémi.

"Are we seriously letting the servants sit down to eat with us these days?" She turned to the butler, who was pouring white wine to go with the starter. "Barrington, would you like to pull up a chair and join us too?"

Fabian instantly reacted. "I won't be your servant much longer."

"I invited Monsieur Montreux to have dinner with us." Mum puffed her chest out in defiance. "I imagine there's plenty of food to go around and the poor chap is feeling dreadfully sad about Elizabeth's death."

"Well, that was brazen of you." Noémi bared her teeth like a dog before it attacks. "This is my house, not yours, and you've no right to decide what goes on here."

Tedwin huffed out a weary breath. "Really, Noé? Must you be so disagreeable to everyone? Let the fellow eat his dinner. As he says, now that Mum's gone, this will be his last night. He was always very loyal to her."

I assumed that Noémi would bite her tongue then, but it wasn't her style. With a look of supreme distaste, she said, "Yes, he was so loyal to mother." Laser beams shot from her eyes, like a robot in a cheesy sci-fi movie. "But this is our house."

"Is it though?" Dean had arrived and his presence had a strange effect on the siblings. They seemed to be tranquilised by his voice. Perhaps it was their natural instinct around anyone richer than them.

No one spoke, so he sat down beside me and continued with his thought. "I mean, until we open the will on Monday, this place could belong to anyone. Elizabeth could have left it to Izzy even."

Briefly united against this potential horror, Noémi looked desperately at her brother. For once she was speechless, and it was down to Tedwin to reply.

"She never would. She loved us." He did not sound particularly confident, and he peered back at his sister in the hope she might have a better response.

Dean had set them up, and I would knock them down. "Did she though?" I let my words sink in before continuing. "Do you really think your mother loved you?" There was no humour in my voice, nor the faintest note of sarcasm.

I saw Noémi grip her fork a little tighter. "Of course she did. Why would you even say such a thing?"

"Oh, I don't know." I made them sweat for a moment. "Perhaps because you've spent the years since university trying to convince her what a wonderful person you are and, as soon as she was dead, dropped the act."

"I am a good person!" was her outraged response, but I could tell that even she didn't believe it. I also noticed that she was tucking into the meaty main course and, only hours before, had talked of the wonders of vegetarianism.

Every person in that room was watching me right then, waiting to discover what I would say next. I enjoyed the tension it brought, so I smiled and took my time before replying.

"You do realise that I talked to your mother today? She took me aside on two separate occasions, and I did not get the impression she was happy in life. At first, I thought it was guilt. She organised a family reunion to make up for lost time and her own mistakes. She specifically told me that she wanted me here to apologise for the way that her infernal children had behaved when I was eleven."

"Oh, come on, Izzy. We were tiny back then." Tedwin sounded quite genuine in his response. "You can't still hold that against us."

"I don't," I said, and realised that this was finally true. "But I could see in the way your mother spoke about you that Elizabeth did. Not just the time you tried to have me beaten and thrown out of your house, simply because I was poorer than you, but because of the things you've done since then."

Noémi shook her head disbelievingly, but said nothing. I thought that Dean or Mum might try to contribute. Apparently, they were happy to watch.

"I suggested to her that you'd grown up. That you were no longer the malicious characters that you had once been, but it was obvious she disagreed. She saw through your attempts to charm her, your game to see who would inherit this place when she was gone, but that wasn't all. When I went up to the east tower with her, it was clear that she was terrified. I couldn't have imagined then that it was her life she feared for, but that's the only thing that makes sense now. I believe that Elizabeth knew that someone wanted to kill her. I think she even planned to tell me, but something held her back and now she's dead."

You could have cut the atmosphere with a piece of paper it was so tense. I don't think that anyone took a breath for a whole minute as the inevitable flicking of eyes occurred. Noémi turned to look at my uncle, Fabian glared at Tedwin, Mum considered her cousin's children equally and Bradley glanced back at his food. My uncle aside, this at least gave me a clue as to who thought who was guilty. I made careful note of the fact that Tedwin kept his eyes locked on his big sister.

Such silence never holds for long and, when it finally broke, it did so with style.

"You odious witch!" Guess who this was from? "I should throw you out of the house this minute for saying such terrible things."

I smiled at Noémi and took a sip of wine. "But you won't."

"Don't be so sure of yourself, Palmer. You're not so impressive, you know. So what if you've been on TV and met the Queen or whoever?"

I pretended to be upset. "But… but you said you were a fan!"

My cynical reply really got to her. "No one cares about you, cousin. You're just a geeky little girl who never grew out of trashy novels."

"Go on then, throw me out!" It didn't sound like me. I was confident, strong, aggressive even. I couldn't have imagined myself saying such a thing a few months earlier and now here I was, staring down a potential murderer.

Noémi's only response was to let out an exasperated breath and turn away.

"That's right. You won't throw me out because, either you killed your mother and you don't want to look guilty, or you're innocent and you know that I'm your best hope of finding the killer."

Greg, Dean and Axel, who were the only real onlookers to the drama, being neither closely related to the victim nor potential suspects, let out an impressed, *oooh!*

"So you do accept the possibility I might be innocent?" Noémi had changed her tone to play the martyr. Poor thing. She wasn't very convincing.

"Anything's possible." Despite her ballsy demeanour and total lack of tears over her mother's brutal demise, I still had no specific evidence to link Noémi to the crime. "But perhaps you could tell me what you did after you followed your mother upstairs this afternoon."

She seemed to shrink from the question and became defensive again. "I never went upstairs with her. What are you talking about?"

I paused to make sense of her reaction. "We all saw you. You ran after her when Bradley nearly mauled me."

The fear faded from her face. "Oh, then. Why didn't you say?" She sat up straighter and looked down at her well-manicured nails. "When everyone else left, I stayed to make sure Bradley wouldn't swallow his own tongue and die."

"How selfless of you."

"Not selfless," she was quick to correct me. "I just didn't want my family to be responsible for a drunken idiot's death." My uncle winced at that, but he deserved every word of it. "What about you?" she asked, turning to her brother. "You disappeared rather quickly, if I remember correctly."

Tedwin looked far more nervous than when I'd asked him the same question.

"You were on the phone, weren't you?" I, for some reason, felt the need to help him in the face of his sister's persistent aggression.

"That's right." He didn't look at me as he replied.

Noémi wasn't backing down. "Who to?"

He turned to look at the dying light through the window. "To my girlfriend."

"What girlfriend? You never have *girlfriends.* You barely have any friends."

His head snapped in her direction like the hand of a clock. "I was out with her in town last night. You don't know everything about me, Noé, but I'm sure there are a few little secrets that you wouldn't want getting out."

His sister's voice was a low, lupine growl and her gaze seemed to lunge towards him. "Do your worst, little brother. See if I care!"

"Oh, don't tempt me." Tedwin slammed his fist down on the table so that the crockery shuddered. "Seriously, don't tempt me."

"Stop this!" The words echoed about the room and we turned to see a desolate figure standing in the shadows. “We mustn’t fight between ourselves. Stop it this instant.”

Chapter Twenty

"Stop your arguing and treat one another like family." The General sounded like an enraged priest, barking in at us from his pulpit by the door. "Arguing is what got us here in the first place. We've spent the last ten years shouting our heads off at one another and laying blame. Maybe that's what got Elizabeth killed."

His appeal for peace was undermined by the fact that he'd just accused his family of murder. Noémi saw this chink in his argument and leapt on it.

"Says the man who was just taken away for questioning. How was it, Grandad? Does Castleton police station put on a good spread?"

The General didn't rise to the bait, but crashed down in the free seat next to Axel. My cousin and the other neutrals were still watching, like spectators at a Roman coliseum, thrilled by every blow the gladiators could land.

"I had nothing to tell them. Elizabeth was alive when I went downstairs to the party and dead when I returned ten minutes later." Without looking, he motioned in my direction. "You saw me leave. I couldn't have killed her."

I thought for a moment before replying. "Well, you could have actually. The way I see it, There's nothing to rule out any one of you from having committed the crime."

"Now steady on," Tedwin said in his poshest voice, as though such an accusation was below the belt.

I kept on regardless. "Though the General had less time than the rest of you, you all had the opportunity to follow Elizabeth up to the east tower to attack her."

"I was wearing a rather stunning silver dress with no sleeves, straps or pockets," Noémi pointed out. "Where exactly do you suggest I concealed the knife?"

"You didn't have to carry it with you. You could have stashed it up there earlier." She looked vexed by my reasoning, but didn't answer back. "No one saw Elizabeth head to the reading room except her father who, for all we know, murdered her and returned to the party to make it seem as though he hadn't had time to do any such thing."

"This is preposterous," the stuffy old chap declared.

"Ha, you don't like it when the worm turns, do you, Grandpapa?" Noémi enjoyed her moment, then turned to me with a smug grin. "No offence, Izzy."

I didn't let them break my stride. "The fact that you were on the phone, Tedwin, is not an alibi. You could have called and left the line open to suggest you were talking to this girlfriend of yours. Or perhaps she's in on it. The police will have no trouble checking the truth of your claim, but it still isn't enough to rule you out. Did you see anyone after you left Bradley's room?"

"No." His answer was confident and direct.

"So no one can attest to where you were?"

"No."

"I can," my mother said. "I saw Tedwin at the far end of the corridor when I went to the bathroom. He did have his phone in his hand."

A smile brightened up the poor man's face. "That's right. I'd completely forgotten. I was sitting on the old chest there and you came in. Thank you so much, Rosie, for confirming my story."

I felt a bit guilty to disillusion him. "She hasn't. All it proves is that you were there five minutes before we discovered the body. You had plenty of time before then to carry out the murder. If anything, you've just proven that my mother wasn't involved. She left me, walked past the detective library, then turned right towards her bedroom. Unless you saw her leave again, she can't be the killer."

I drew a mental map of the east wing corridor to position everyone where they claimed to be. It felt a bit like a game of chess with the various figures roaming about.

More like Cluedo, no?

Nah, that's too.... On the nose.

I'm sorry to disappoint anyone who hoped that the big reveal at the end of the mystery would be that my all-singing mother was a crazed killer, but that was never going to happen.

Would have made a good twist, though. I can just imagine the headline. 'Bu-Bu banged up! From West End star to Downview Prison inmate.'

"Who else can you rule out?" the General asked with renewed energy.

"Well, let's think about it." I was on a high from successfully clearing my mother of murder – which would surely win me some brownie points when we got home. "Noémi, you say that you stayed in Bradley's bedroom. Was that right up until you heard your grandfather calling out in the hallway?"

She smiled, perhaps thinking she'd be the next off the hook. "Yes, it was."

"So, you're providing Bradley with an alibi?"

Her smile instantly faded and she knew I'd got her. "Wait, well..." She looked around the table, presumably totting up the other suspects and wondering what this admission might mean to her own chances of getting locked away. "Yes, he was there the whole time."

As Barrington arrived with the main course, I relaxed back into my seat. Every person in that room was playing the game. The stakes were different for each of them, but they were all desperate to find out what came next. Dean looked at me in that sullen yet approving way of his; smiling without having to smile.

I kept my focus on Noémi. "So, if you're telling the truth, that means neither you nor Bradley could be the killers."

She performed her mental gymnastics once more, but no longer sounded so sure of herself. "I... that's right, yes."

"Of course, as Bradley was unconscious, no one can confirm that you were there with him."

She risked a quick look at her grandfather and brother before answering. "I suppose not."

"That's a shame, as it doesn't really help us. You could be using Bradley as an alibi, knowing that he can't contradict you." I couldn't bear another of her indignant interventions, so I kept talking. "But let's take it for granted that you're telling the truth, what would that mean?"

It was supposed to be a rhetorical question, but my parents can never resist a chance to pile in with their ideas. "It means that Tedwin was lying about the phone call and he was really upstairs-" My stepdad replied, a little too bloodthirstily, so I cut him off.

"No, it doesn't. I was-"

Mum was up next. "It means that they were all in it together. It's a bit too convenient that they ended up scattered about the same wing at the same time. No one can provide an alibi, and no one can prove who was guilty."

I shot her an unimpressed look across the table. "So does that include your brother?"

Unwilling to back down, she nodded. "Yep, every last one of them."

As much as I liked the idea of my uncle going to jail for a long stretch, I had to set her straight. "Nice try, but, if we believe Noémi and Tedwin, and we already know where the General was for most of the time before Elizabeth was found, that only leaves one question mark."

Eight heads swung to look at our grief-stricken continental representative.

"Why are you all looking at me?" Fabian's tone was typically disdainful. "I had nothing to do with her death."

"So where were you when she was killed?"

He kept opening and closing his mouth like a singing fish pinned to a wall.

When it was clear he couldn't come up with an answer, I looked around at the other suspects. "Can anyone tell me where Fabian was? He seems to have forgotten."

The General took the measure of the room and quickly bellowed at the poor man. "I'll tell you where he was. He followed Elizabeth and me out of Bradley's bedroom, waited until I'd left and went up the east tower to murder her."

It was probably a bit mean of me to paint him as the main suspect when they were all just as likely to have been involved, but I needed to shake things up. The bristling looks that were exchanged just then were far more valuable than the half-truths they'd been trading in all afternoon. Fabian was just the bait.

I addressed the General. "Did you see where he went after Elizabeth left you?"

"Well… No, but-" That was enough for me and I interrupted him.

"Did anyone?"

There was silence. The only people there who didn't look entirely dumbstruck by the twists and machinations we were dealing with were Dean and Axel. To be honest, they were enjoying themselves far too much as they awaited the next revelation. The upshot of this was that I could now fill in the diagram in my head and, even if not everything they'd told me was true, I had a clearer sense of what had happened up in the east wing in those final moments before Elizabeth died.

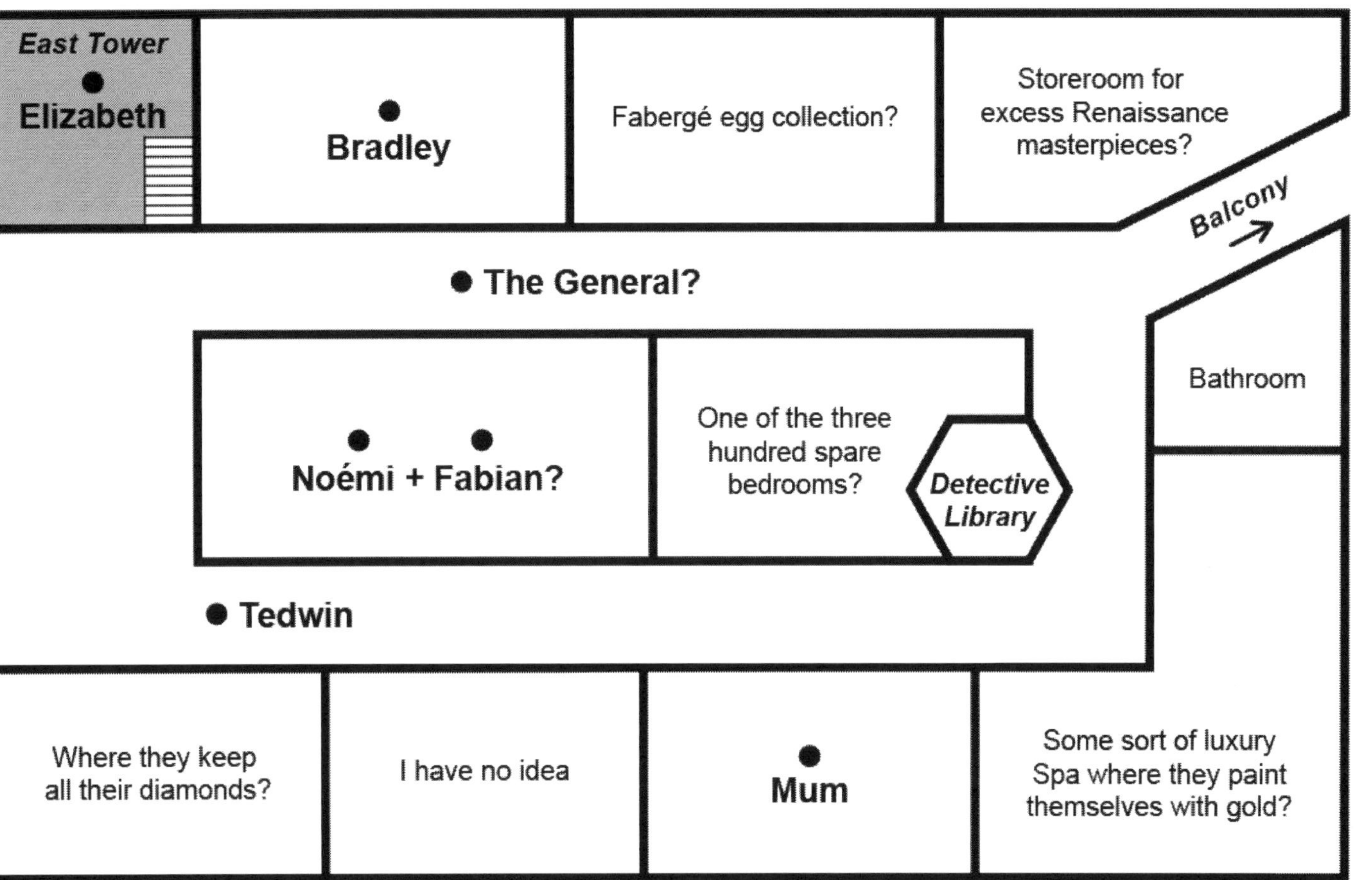
East Tower
Elizabeth
Bradley
Fabergé egg collection?
Storeroom for excess Renaissance masterpieces?
Balcony
The General?
Bathroom
Noémi + Fabian?
One of the three hundred spare bedrooms?
Detective Library
Tedwin
Where they keep all their diamonds?
I have no idea
Mum
Some sort of luxury Spa where they paint themselves with gold?

Chapter Twenty-One

After the remaining courses of that frosty but delicious dinner had been consumed, it was the General I hoped to speak to. I'd let him off the hook in front of his family, and I wasn't entirely sure why. He had a special way about him that made even the least reverential listeners fall into line. I suppose it was his time in the army that had taught him such a skill, but it would certainly come in handy if he decided to try his hand at murder.

Sadly, Noémi claimed me before I could get to her grandfather. "Izzy, I need to speak to you." She didn't wait for an answer, but sprinted from the room, expecting me to follow.

I dare you not to.

I lasted about three seconds before I gave in.

You're such a sheep.

Noémi had run off to the empty ballroom. She hadn't turned the lights on, but stood waiting for me in a pool of moonlight. She'd got changed before dinner and wore a loose-fitting, red cotton dress. There was something plain and old-fashioned about it. She could have passed for a virtuous puritan, but would have made a good Hester Prynne.

"I want you to know that I loved my mother." This felt like a negotiation already, so I decided to let her talk. "I know I act tough, but I'm not like most people. I'm not afraid to speak my mind or shock those around me – it doesn't make me a killer though."

As she hadn't asked a question, I figured I might as well. "Would you say that I've singled you out?"

She didn't answer, but peered around the gigantic space as though she were a visitor on a guided tour. "It was pretty weird growing up here. I barely remember my father, and he wasn't exactly a normal chap." She paused tellingly. "He was a spy, I bet you didn't know that." She laughed her self-important laugh and I couldn't resist.

"I did actually. Dean and I took a visit to your family museum and we joined the dots."

"Oh, how disappointing." That wiped the smile from her face. "Well, anyway, Daddy worked for the government, doing something even I don't know, in foreign countries where he wasn't officially supposed to be. He was wounded on a mission to some tinpot dictatorship and, by the time his plane landed in Britain, he was already dead. Mummy didn't tell us any of that for years, of course, and I can barely remember him being here, but something of his duplicity seeped into our family."

I was surprised how chatty she was and had to assume that the show she was putting on was for her own benefit as much as mine.

She swayed a little as she stood there. "Mother pretended that we were perfect little children, and I did everything I could to prove her wrong. That's why you were our victim, I'm afraid. It had nothing to do with you or how much money you didn't have. We just needed to find a new way to shock dear Mummy. Well, I did. Tedwin has always been a disappointment to me. He doesn't have that killer instinct."

"Are you trying to confess something, Noémi?"

She rolled her eyes and clapped her hand together. "No, Izzy. That's not why I called you here. I wanted to talk to you because I think you need to understand all this if you're going to work out who killed my mother. And I genuinely want you to find the person responsible."

There was an intensity to everything she said. I'd got lost in her words, so that, instead of responding, I allowed silence to consume the space between us.

She reached into an imaginary pocket on her dress to remove an imaginary cigarette, which she lit with an imaginary lighter. "Sorry, but I'm trying to give up smoking and this is supposed to help." She savoured the flavour of the pretend smoke billowing into her lungs as her neon green eyes caught the light. "I wanted to talk to you because I think my brother was involved."

I'd been waiting for some accusation to cut through her speech, but decided not to give her what she wanted just yet. "It's a strange expression 'involved'. You think your brother was involved in a murder the way some people are involved in their local scout group or my grandmother gets involved in church cake sales."

She refused to be distracted. "Think about it, who are the suspects? A foreigner with no connection to the family before last year. A decrepit old man who willingly gave up this house to his daughter decades ago, a drunken idiot who really was passed out during the time Mum was murdered, and my brother. My brother, who can offer no good excuse for where he was, has lied about who he was on the phone to and, if the police were at all competent, should be in a cell right now."

I walked a few steps closer as a cloud passed over the moon and the dim room fell dark. "It's a believable theory. But you're conveniently overlooking one important suspect."

"Your mother? I thought we'd already-"

"No, not my mother. You." I was only a few feet away from her and pressed my advantage. "You and Tedwin are two peas in a pod, two sides of the same coin, two…" I'd run out of clichés. "You're quite alike, but you said it yourself, Tedwin lacks the killer instinct that you have. When we were children, Tedwin used to follow you everywhere, but not anymore. And now you both think the other one is guilty."

She was frozen in place as she waited for me to pull her argument apart.

"I could take it as a sign that you're both innocent, that you're working together, or that one of you is trying to shift the blame. After all, you say that Tedwin's alibi doesn't hold up, but where were you when your mother was murdered?"

My words broke the spell and she drifted across the dance floor to sit on the broad windowsill looking over the garden. "We've been through all this."

I had to shout now and my voice echoed back to me. It was dramatic and I kind of liked it. "You were with Bradley."

"That's right."

"Not in my room with Fabian?"

"No, Izzy. He wasn't-" She soon abandoned her defence. "Fine, how did you know?"

Ha, got her!

"I was watching you both over dinner. As you laid out your alibi, his face fell. By the end, I thought he might cry. You were sacrificing him to save yourself. Add that to Fabian's completely over-the-top reaction, your less than convincing acting when he came to sit down with us for dinner, and the fact that you left my bedsheets a mess and it didn't take a genius to work out what was happening."

"That's lucky, as you won't find any geniuses around here."

"Hilarious." I had something better than insults to answer with. "What I don't understand is why you didn't just confess that he was in the room with you and provide yourselves with an alibi."

Though still facing me, she turned to look back over her shoulder at the gardens below. "Fabian and I have been pretending to hate one another for months. We knew that mother wouldn't like us being a couple and so we acted as though we weren't. If we'd suddenly shacked up on the same day that she died, it would have made us look rather suspicious, don't you think?"

"And running through the house, hungrily searching out her will didn't already do that?"

Half of her face was in shadow then. All I could see of it was a faint glimmer where her left eye should be. "Oh well, maybe I got a little carried away when I thought that grandfather was responsible. The police had just arrested him and I figured that meant the path to my inheritance would be a clear one."

"Yours and Tedwin's?"

She smiled like she knew something that I wasn't privy to. "Yes, but Mother changed her will; I don't really think for a second that my brother charmed her enough to get much. Whereas I have worked supremely hard over the last few years and our beloved matriarch just ate it up."

She made it sound like she'd been kissing up to her boss for a promotion. I can't say that I believed a word she was saying. Right on time, I spotted another hole in her argument. "So far today, you've blamed Bradley, Fabian and your own grandfather for the murder. Why should I believe a word you say?"

She was one of those people who live with the comforting belief that they are far cleverer than everyone around them. Every move she made was carefully calculated, but sadly for her, every move she made was the wrong one.

"Oh, I thought you'd worked that out already. I only said I was with Bradley to hide where I really was and blamed Fabian to throw you off the scent. After we left your uncle in his room, Fabian pulled me across the hall. I've no idea what Bradley was really up to. He might well have faked the drunkenness as an alibi."

It felt like I was going round in circles. "Okay. Well, you've been very helpful, but I think I should go to bed."

"No, you're still not listening to what I wanted to tell you." She got all agitated, throwing her arms out in front of her like an overstressed teacher. "I'm saying that I'm relying on you, Izzy. I'm an orphan now, practically alone in the world, and I need you to work out who killed my mother."

"So that you can inherit Castleton Square Manor?"

"No, because it's the right thing to do. Mummy wasn't a bad person. She was lonely and fragile and didn't deserve to die like that." She paused then to assess the impact of her words. "Maybe whoever killed her didn't care in the slightest about this place. Maybe she said the wrong thing to the wrong person and ended up dead because of it. It's down to you to work the rest out."

She nodded, as though happy with how that sounded, then, with the slinky self-confidence of a tiger in the jungle, strutted from the room.

"You can come out now, Dean," I said when Noémi had mounted the stairs and disappeared into the west wing.

"How did you know I was here?" Sounding disgruntled, he stepped from the shadows by the door.

"I could hear your heavy breathing. You'd make a great stalker, but a terrible spy."

"We never had that dance." There was a laugh in his voice, and it was obvious he was enjoying his weekend away. In fact, for Dean, this was a proper holiday. One of those murder-mystery breaks for hotel guests to work out which of the actors murdered the imaginary victim. For me, this was a busman's holiday.

"May I have the honour?" I held my hand out to him and he took it and spun me under his arm, so that we ended up cheek to cheek. "Did you hear what Noémi had to say for herself?"

"Most of it."

I'm certainly not a natural dancer, but Dean tugged me along after him and I noticed that he was following the same neat pattern with his feet time and again. He spun me out and back in before continuing the conversation.

"Can you cross her and Fabian off your list if they were together?"

"No, of course not." I was surprised he would suggest such a simple course of action. "She could be lying. He hasn't even backed up her version of events yet, and there's something I still don't trust about him."

"She's an odd one too, don't you think? Quite seductive in her way, but prickly." It was clear that Noémi's charms were starting to work on Dean.

"I prefer the term, raging psychopath, but prickly is fine I suppose."

He laughed. "Oh, come on, Iz. You don't really think she'd kill her own mother just for the inheritance? She's already rich, what would be the point?"

I sighed before responding. "I don't know, what's the point of anything to these people? Perhaps she wanted more independence, or knew that her mother wouldn't allow her to marry one of the servants. Noémi freely admits that she had a bizarre upbringing, I can only imagine that her absentee spy father and uptight mother did a real job on her. Perhaps living in a palace and having everything you could ever dream of is not the key to happiness after all."

"Oh, I don't know." His smile engulfed his normally crumpled face, ironing the creases quite flat. "I'm getting rather used to it."

I poked him in the ribs, and our dance came to a stop. "Dean…" I began but wasn't sure I wanted to continue the sentence. "You don't fancy me, do you?"

He full on laughed at me then. "Nope, not really. And you don't fancy me either. It's great."

I was tired, so I put my head on his shoulder and we swayed a little longer. "Yep, it really is. Thanks for coming this weekend and doing your best to make my awful family see me in a good light for once. And thanks for being my friend too. I don't know what I'd do without you."

He would have probably made fun of me then for being soppy, but we both felt his phone buzz in his inside pocket and he pulled it out to answer. "Good evening, Fiona. I'm dancing with a beautiful lady in an ancient ballroom, with only the moon to light our steps."

There was a pause at the other end of the line and then I heard his girlfriend's warm laughter come back.

"Yeah, it's only Izzy. She's a terrible dancer, and she just told me she doesn't fancy me, so I couldn't make you jealous even if I tried."

I liked seeing his face light up whenever they were together and the same thing happened now. He was missing her and it made me miss Danny too. Having a fake boyfriend had reminded me just how nice it would be to have my real one there with me.

"Well, we're going upstairs together now and there's only one double bed in our room so you should be jealous." He pointed at the phone and then up the stairs as he chatted away to his kind, gorgeous and clearly very trusting girlfriend.

I watched him go before going hunting for my mobile in the depths of my trouser pockets. I hadn't looked at the thing for hours.

If you happen to be having boyfriend problems, may I recommend investigating a murder? It's the perfect antidote to all that pensive brooding. I'd clean forgotten about Danny for an afternoon and was briefly plunged into a pit of despair as I questioned what this said about our relationship and whether I could repair the damage I'd done by hanging up on him days earlier and not replying to his messages since. Which didn't even cover the fact that, whether he'd heard it or not, I'd asked him to marry me.

My head was a mess and the last thing I needed was to jump back into all that drama, but I figured I owed him a text at least. There were countless missed calls from Ramesh on my phone too, and a ton of messages, many of which simply read "**Industrial Strength Bleach!?**" but I ignored them and opened Danny's window. Seeing his picture filled me with hope and calm and made all the horrors of Castleton Square Manor feel small and far away. I wrote,

Sorry I haven't been in touch since Wednesday. We're away for the weekend at a family reunion/murder investigation and I just realised how much I miss you. Let's call when I get back home in a couple of days. I'm really sorry that I'm such a weirdo and don't know how to talk on the phone like a normal human. You'll just have to put up with me talking about baked beans and the best kind of wood glue until you finish your job. It's your fault for going out with an idiot. I love you, Danny Fields. I have since the very first day we met.

I pressed send and was about to put the phone away and go to bed when a message came back to me.

You're not an idiot, Izzy. You're the most brilliant person I know. Now, on the topic of wood glue, I've personally always been a fan of ExoStick. And while I might be able to tolerate any number of boring phone calls, I don't see much future for us if we can't agree on our favourite wood glue.

I sent a *phew!* emoticon back to him.

EXOSTICK!! That's exactly the one I always go for.

Well, that is a relief.

We might have enjoyed some flirty texting that night, before I fell asleep with thoughts of Star Wars, dead cousins, wood glue and baked beans in my head.

Chapter Twenty-Two

I was woken by my phone vibrating under my face. I'd apparently fallen asleep on top of it.

"Izzy, I know you say I use the word emergency far too often, but this is an emergency." It was Ramesh, I'd like to say he sounded more worked up than usual but I reckon this was pretty much his standard level of agitation.

"What do you need now?"

"I've run out of gold paint and the shop I need in West Wickham is closed on Sunday. If I don't get any soon, the whole project will be ruined."

For once, I was able to help him. "Just go into Greg's studio at the back of the garden and see what he's got."

"Why didn't I think of that?"

"Morning, Izzy!" My father shouted in the background. "We haven't had a wink of sleep, but we're really motoring now. Ramesh's plans are something else and, though it was difficult to bend the sheet of wood into the exact shape we needed, I think we're on the home stretch."

I was still waking up and this was all too much to process at seven thirty in the morning. "I have no idea what you're talking about, but I'm glad you both sound so happy."

Ramesh pulled the phone back. "Yeah, we've had quite a lot of energy drinks, Iz. Have you tried them?" He didn't wait for an answer. "They're amazing! Anyway, good luck with the murder. Your dad filled me in on your family dynamics up there and if you'd like my opinion, I reckon that this Tedwin bloke was having a secret affair with-"

"Thanks, Ra. I think I've got it covered."

He smiled down the phone. "Great, but you can ring me if you need anything."

"I won't! Byeeeeeee!"

Dean was still snoring next to me. As he'd spent a good ten minutes the night before making fun of me for wearing my favourite purple cat onesie, I didn't think there was much risk of him getting the wrong idea about us sharing a bed – plus the floor didn't look very comfy.

I got dressed as quietly as I could and slipped out. Sometimes a good night's sleep is just what I need and, with the chance to think carefully about all the different elements to the case, a picture was forming in my head. I couldn't see the face of the killer just yet, but I knew it wouldn't take much more to get me there.

On my way down to breakfast, I prepared my lists in my head. The suspects were nailed down already, the terrible twins, Lord General McGeneralson, Uncle Berk, Fabian the Frenchman and my dear old mum. I'd read too many Christies to rule her out entirely, and besides, I've always considered an interest in musical theatre to be sure-fire proof of an evil mind. She and Ramesh could rip your guts out in the time it takes to say, "Andrew Lloyd Webber is an undersung genius."

The clues I'd discovered felt clear and concrete for once. There was the putty on the victim's fingers, the letter and spilt ink on her desk, the key in the lock and the knife in her back. I'd compiled a bunch of secondary evidence which might or might not be relevant too. The will would no doubt prove revealing, but there was also the dead spy Matthew Ogilivie's complicated past, The General's bad mood when we arrived for the party and Uncle Bradley's trip upstairs to see our victim before she died. If I could get my hands on them, I also wondered whether the photographs Fabian had taken would help me see things more clearly.

For once I felt confident about my chances of getting to the truth. So you can imagine my disappointment when I went downstairs and found that the foundations that I'd built for the case were already in ruins.

I found them on the floor of the breakfast room. Tedwin had his body over his sister's, as though to protect her from the blows that had rained down upon them, and Noémi held her hands to her face. They couldn't have been there long either, as someone must have set the food on the table that morning before we got up. There were croissants and pastries, cold meats and-

Just for once, I'm going to suggest that this is not the moment to be thinking about food.

The pair looked like the embracing figures at Pompei, and it was still a shock for me to see young people cut down like that. Though they were not my first and, if Dean's *murder magnet* theory was true, wouldn't be my last, I had to take in a sharp breath to process what I was seeing. The glistening knife had been discarded not far from

Noémi, but Tedwin appeared to have the more serious wounds. There was so much blood that I didn't consider checking for a pulse at first. It was only when Martha entered the room that I came back to life.

"Oh goodness." She let out a shriek as soon as she arrived. "Are they dead?"

"Ambulance, Martha. Quick." I ran over and was relieved to discover they still had some life left in them. Noémi was unconscious, but Tedwin opened his eyes a tiny bit to murmur at me. I couldn't work out what he was saying and pushed him on to his side to check where the blood was coming from. He had long gashes across his chest but they were only superficial and the worst I could find was a nasty wound on his shoulder where he must have put himself in the way of the killer's knife to protect his sister.

Noémi appeared to have got off lightly. She had a nasty bruise on her face, which must have knocked her to the floor and out of consciousness. As far as I could tell, most of the blood belonged to her brother though.

I tore strips from Tedwin's already ripped shirt and the butler Barrington turned up soon after to help me tie off the cuts as best we could. Tedwin had lost too much blood and passed out, but, when the ambulance arrived fifteen minutes later, neither of the siblings had left us completely.

"Perhaps I should have taken you in for questioning yesterday." D.S. Osborne was back with his stupid theories. Luckily, his boss had come along too.

"Don't be absurd, man," D.I. Fincher instantly reprimanded him. "She saved their lives. Just go and talk to the staff and find out who was here this morning."

Fincher waited for Osborne to wander off before letting out a frustrated cry. "The man's an imbecile. It's like working with a four-year-old. He couldn't solve a murder investigation if he had a signed confession in his hand and the killer in handcuffs." I thought he'd run out of steam, but he still had one last insult in him. "Osborne has probably caused more murders than he's solved."

I could only sympathise with him, but had my own grievances to address. "This shouldn't have happened. We should have found the killer already. There are so few possible suspects. Between the two of us, we must be able to come up with the right answer."

P.C. Chandra had been setting up a perimeter and came over to appeal to the senior investigating officer. "I know it's not standard practice, sir, but it might be worth considering. She's a smart lass, maybe she's right. Maybe we'll get this done faster with her help."

Fincher was conflicted but nodded and pulled me to the side of the room where a line of chairs was arranged by the windowsill. He pushed me down into one like he was forcing me into the back of a police car.

"All I can give you is a bunch of leads that turned out to be dead ends." He had a quick look around in case the other officers were listening. "We've got no clear forensic evidence to suggest who's responsible. No fingerprints to give the game away. I interviewed the six suspects yesterday and couldn't spot any glaring discrepancies in any of their stories."

He had a matter-of-fact manner that made following the details quite simple. "For the time before Elizabeth Castleton was murdered, no one had a definite alibi, but I didn't feel that anyone was obviously lying either. The victim doesn't appear to have had any particular enemies, though she spent a lot of money on this place recently and her father did not seem happy about it. They'd been arguing about their finances before she was killed."

"What about my uncle Bradley? He went up to see Elizabeth about an hour before it happened. He also said that this place is like a 'home from home' to him, which I found odd as our family has never been particularly close to the Castletons."

Fincher sat down beside me, looking both exhausted and troubled by what I'd said. "Bradley Gibbs? He didn't tell us any of that. Just told us how much drink he'd consumed and that he could barely remember a thing that had gone on all day."

I'd been willing to dismiss my uncle as a serious suspect at one point yesterday, but, with Tedwin and Noémi apparently out of the picture, he was emerging once more as a potential culprit.

"There was the putty that we found too," I pointed out. "If it's the same substance that was under Elizabeth's fingernails-"

"We had the results back," he interrupted. "The two substances are the same."

"Well, then that could link back to Bradley. Though I don't see why he'd have thrown it outside."

Fincher suited his name. He was petite and exact, his arms folded into his sides like the wings of a tiny bird. "To throw us off the scent somehow? To make it look as though someone else had been using putty on the property, which would explain how it ended up on the victim."

"No, that doesn't add up. He'd have had to take a handful of the stuff upstairs for no real reason. That sounds a little ridiculous."

He swayed side to side then, as though he'd taken the comment personally. "Alright then, what have you found out?"

"Noémi and Fabian are having an affair. She says they were in my room together before Elizabeth was murdered and, at the very least, I can confirm that the sheets were messed up when I went in there later that afternoon."

"That doesn't prove much. One of them could have tussled the sheets while the other went to kill the mother." He was quick witted; just the kind of person it was good to bounce ideas off.

"I thought the exact same thing until this morning. But after this attack, it might suggest that Noémi was telling the truth."

He shook his head, unimpressed. "It's just as likely that the brother, the sister and her lover were all involved in the murder. They had an argument this morning, and the Frenchman stabbed his two accomplices."

As much as Noémi's horrendous personality and transparent greed made me want to believe she was the killer, it no longer seemed so likely. "Well, if you're right, you'll find Fabian somewhere here covered in blood. I don't see how he could have carried out such a violent attack without there being traces all over him."

He looked over at his uniformed colleagues. "Chandra, Lowe, find the French chap. He must have a bedroom down in the servants' quarters."

"No, sir," the constable who had shown such common sense the day before corrected him. "P.C. Powell spoke to him yesterday. Fabian Montreux has a room upstairs with the family."

Fincher and I looked at one another. It was an unlikely revelation. Fabian might not have been a maid or footman, but he was still an employee, so why had Elizabeth kept the man so close to her?

"There's nothing certain with this case." Fincher let out another puff of despondent breath. "Nothing to get my hands on."

The sirens must have woken up the rest of the house as the General appeared just then with an anguished look sculpted onto his face. "I saw the ambulance driving off…" His eyes landed on the stains on the heavily patterned carpet. "Whose blood is that?"

Fincher looked at me again to suggest I should be the one to break the news, so I stepped forward to steer my great-uncle from the room. A few doors down that long corridor was a small lounge which might once have been used by servants for polishing silver or preparing drinks and now existed without any clear purpose. It had two armchairs in, which was all we needed.

"It's Tedwin and Noémi, they've been attacked. The police are looking into what happened, but we have to assume that it was the same person who killed Elizabeth."

He was crying before I'd finished speaking. I'd never seen the man as anything but a robot before. To see him there, with the tears running down his reddening cheeks, felt paradoxical. It was like discovering that my freezer could tap dance or my wardrobe could paint.

I put my hand out to comfort him. "They're both alive, and the wounds didn't look too deep. They were very erratic; as though whoever was responsible didn't know what they were doing."

Or they were drunk? What if Bradley hit the bottle and made a night of it? He came across them this morning, there was an argument and he went for a knife. Did you see the joint of beef on the breakfast table? That must be where he got it from.

And why would he bother?

My brain didn't have time to reply before the General spoke again. "Were you the one who found them?"

"That's right." I was trying to be careful with my words. The man was either a Lawrence-Olivier-calibre actor or he was genuinely suffering at the knowledge of this fresh assault on his already depleted family. "I came down to breakfast, and they were there."

He started speaking very quickly then, as though he needed to get all his thoughts out in one go. "You have to stop this, Isobel. You have to find whoever's brought about such wickedness."

"I'll try," I replied, and felt more like a counsellor than a detective. "But I'm going to need your help, General."

"Francis." He looked at me like I'd offended him, then shook his head sadly. "I'm your great-uncle and you don't even know my name. I suppose that's my fault as well. It speaks for all that's wrong with this family. Whatever you discover, I have no doubt that I'm the one who's most to blame."

I was about to sympathise and tell him that it didn't make sense to be so hard on himself. He raised one hand in his usual authoritative manner and I fell silent before I could utter a sound.

"I'll tell you whatever you need to know. Anything at all. I'm an open book now."

Chapter Twenty-Three

There were more police there than the day before. Teams of uniformed officers roamed the halls, but I could tell that they were as confused by the sheer scale of the place as I was. I felt lucky not to have to direct anyone about the enormous house, and I could only imagine what Fincher was going through.

As they conducted the investigation at their own pace, General Francis Castleton, my mother's uncle and the former owner of the estate, took me to the third great hall on the property. It was known by the family, rather appropriately, as the great hall.

I had a question for him that had been weighing on my mind since I'd arrived. "Why did you sign the house over to Elizabeth and Matthew?"

He wandered purposefully alongside me as we took a turn around the gigantic space, which was lined with old family portraits. "I was a serving officer when my father died and I thought that Elizabeth and her family would get more use of the place than I ever could. My wife was on her last legs back then too, so it seemed like the right thing to do. No point living in the past these days, is there?"

He spoke with all the hardy resolve of his generation. He couldn't have been less than eighty and I calculated that he would have lived through the second world war, the cold war and 1980s hairstyles. Clearly, he knew the meaning of resilience.

There was a grand piano at the far end of the room and rows of chairs laid out for a concert, but the carpet of dust underneath them told me that it had been a while since anyone had put on a show there, or even given it a clean.

"There he is." The General pointed up to the largest portrait in the room. It showed a man dressed in a scarlet military uniform, which was not so very different from his own. "It's my father, your great-grandfather, Field Marshal Henry Castleton. Have you heard of him?"

I thought back to the old stories my grandmother had told me as a child. "I think so. He won a bunch of medals, didn't he?"

There was a note of amusement in his voice. "Well, you can work that much out from the portrait, but yes, he was quite the soldier. Did all sorts of wonderful things during the second world war. Led platoons of men to glory, overturned unwinnable battles and was admired the nation over. He was also a sadist, a braggart and a sorry excuse for a human being." All that levity disappeared, and he fixed on the distinguished gentleman in front of us with a look of pure wrath.

"If he was here today, I'd tell him exactly what I thought of him, and quite possibly punch him on the nose."

Something about the way he said this made me laugh. It was hard to imagine that the old chap in the portrait – with his lambchop sideburns and tufty whiskers – was a sadist.

"What did he do to you?"

The General looked at me side on for a moment, as though deciding whether I deserved to know. "Not just to me, but to every last one of us. Your children themselves may suffer because of that insufferable man, and I know that my Elizabeth did."

He ran out of words for a moment, and I thought he might spit at the portrait. "I was the eldest of his ten offspring and your grandmother was the youngest, but he treated us all the same. We were a nuisance that he felt needed to be corrected, and his only didactic apparatus was to take us over his knee and thrash the living hell out of us. I have no doubt that his own father had treated him the same way and his grandfather before him, and so on and so forth back through time. But the celebrated Field Marshal Henry Castleton took pleasure in the punishment he doled out. He took pleasure in seeing his own children in pain."

As the sound of this sad confession died away, it amazed me that I could live with such misconceptions. Both my mother and I had dismissed the General as a cold-hearted snob, but we were way off. He didn't act like that because he was distant or disinterested, Francis Castleton was a survivor.

When my reply finally came, it was oddly brittle. "I'm so sorry, I don't know what else to say. I have three fathers and they've always treated me with kindness. I can't imagine what it was like to grow up with such a man."

New ideas about my family clicked into place to replace the old ones. The female line's insistence on marrying loud, domineering men suddenly made sense; along with my grandmother's quiet fear of the world around her. And something else changed too. I suddenly found more respect for my mother. Mum had broken the chain and made a very different life for herself from the generations before her.

My hand had come to rest on my great-uncle's shoulder and he took it affectionately in his own. "Thank you, my dear, but you've no need to feel sorry for me. This was all many years ago. Though men like my father cast a long shadow, my own wounds have healed."

I was about to ask him why he was telling me these things, but he anticipated the question. "What I feel you ought to know is why Elizabeth was the way she was. You see, I'm not blind. My daughter was a strange person and always had been. As a child, we called her eccentric. She could be detached or delightful, full of love or cold as a Scottish winter. And that has to be down to me. I couldn't give her the affection a child requires, because the very concept seemed so foreign."

I knew that he needed to get his story out, so I let him continue without interruption.

"I was the one who introduced her to her husband. Matthew had worked under me in intelligence before joining the secret service, and he had a rather spiky personality that I thought would fit perfectly with Elizabeth's. They were two misfits who happened to click together rather nicely. During the time they were married, I believe they were very happy. Of course, he went off to Eritrea and got himself killed and Elizabeth reverted to her strange old self."

He had to breathe for a moment, as though he'd run out of air. "The children were tiny back then, and they became dolls to her. She dressed them up like Victorians and talked constantly about them, as though they were perfect, humanitarian geniuses. Whenever I was here, I could see that the more she adored them, the more devilish those two children became. I didn't have the tools to do anything about it though, and my wife wasn't alive to help, so it continued like that for the next fifteen years."

His eyes had drifted away from the portrait and were fixed on a point through the window. The sky was brighter than the day before. It was that sunny kind of overcast that I can't imagine exists outside of Britain. It tells us that there's a blue sky just above the clouds and it will be along eventually, we just have to be patient. I doubt that the General was thinking anything so optimistic as he continued his sad tale.

"Tedwin told me some years ago about the time you came to visit. That was just one example of the cruelty that my grandchildren could achieve when they put their minds to it. It was only when Noémi left for university that my daughter seemed to accept that her two little darlings weren't the angels she'd imagined them to be. But Elizabeth's only solution was to go to the other extreme. All of a sudden she viewed Tedwin and Noémi as the root of her problems."

I was trying to process everything he was telling me, but the image of the wounded brother and sister being taken away by the paramedics kept spiking through my thoughts. "Noémi seemed to think that she had her mother wrapped around her finger."

The old man let out a cold, disbelieving laugh. "Sometimes Noémi's view of the world is just as far from reality as her mother's was." He frowned then, as if the clash of present and past verbs was too much for him to bear. "When Elizabeth gave up on her children, she threw herself into other things. First it was her charity work and then her appearance. We never talked about the cosmetic surgery, but it was almost as if she was attempting to replace herself. I found it quite sad."

"When did all that start? The surgery, I mean. It looked like she'd had a lot done."

"Yes, she'd spent hundreds of thousands over the last few years but promised me that it was over. That's what the party was for; her coming out to the world as this new person." He sighed, then gave one last bitter glance towards his father's portrait and continued on around the room. "She died pretty, I suppose. She'd fought back old age only to be slaughtered in her own home before she could enjoy it."

He fell silent, and I already regretted what I had to ask next. "I saw you arguing with your daughter at the party. You were unhappy with her. Can you tell me why that was?"

He didn't look at me, but kept his eyes on the pine floor. "I'll tell you, though I wish I hadn't said anything. If I'd known that she would…" He couldn't bring himself to finish that sentence. "It was about the money for the party. The way she'd been spending over the last couple of years was out of control. Not just the surgery but all the money she gave to her charities and the work she did on the grounds – a swimming pool that it's only warm enough to use three days a year, and tennis courts that no one is interested in playing on. I fear she would have bankrupted us, and that assistant of hers didn't come cheap either."

His mouth pursed closed and so I prodded him on. "Fabian?"

"Yes, that French fancy of hers. Elizabeth had never been one for silly trinkets and fashions, but she suddenly had to have all the finest clothes and accessories and I think that he was the most expensive of the lot. I have no idea what he actually organised for her, but she liked to be seen with him at the functions she attended."

"Do you mean they were in some kind of romantic relationship?"

The General cocked his head back like a startled cockerel. "Good lord. I hadn't thought of that. I damned well hope not."

"I only ask because… well, Fabian's room isn't downstairs in the staff quarters, but up in the west wing with the rest of the family. I wondered if that meant-"

"Oh, no, no," he blustered. "Nothing like that, I'm sure. That was just convenient for Elizabeth when she worked in her room in the mornings. She was forever planning some fundraiser or gala. I can't say I paid the man much attention until this weekend though. Bit of a spider, if you ask me, lurking about in the background, waiting for a scrap to pounce on."

"And if you had to choose a likely killer from the other suspects, who do you think it would be?"

Perhaps finally overwhelmed by the events of the weekend, his legs buckled beneath him. I supported his arm and helped him to one of the chairs in the centre of the room.

"I'm sorry, but it's a difficult question to hear," he explained once he'd recovered his energy. "And yet more difficult to answer. I have to say that I can't completely rule out my granddaughter, even now."

This was interesting to me. "So you'd suspect Noémi over Tedwin?"

"Oh, yes, very much. Though he's always gone along with his sister's plans, I don't think that boy has the same lust for cruelty as his sister. There have been times when she reminded me of my father."

"Did she have any particular falling out with Elizabeth recently?"

He looked up at me, rather surprised. "More than normal, you mean? They were always fighting about something. Elizabeth forced Noé to come back from her gap year in Paris and wanted her to get a job. Noé wanted her mother to buy her a flat in London. There was a constant back and forth between them."

"So nothing out of the ordinary?"

His hands together in his lap, he looked towards the immense piano. "Wait, there was something. On the night before the party – Friday, wasn't it? Noémi threw a real tantrum. She was furious with her mother and threatened not to show her face. To be honest, I was surprised when I saw she was mixing with everyone so sweetly yesterday. She'd been out on the lawn shooting all morning, and I wondered if she'd ever come in."

"Do you know what the argument was about?"

He turned back to me and, with an amused wink, said, "You, Izzy. Noémi wasn't happy that her mother had invited you."

I felt a bit defensive then and, like every good teenager in the history of time, said, "Me? What did I do?"

"Oh, don't worry about it. My granddaughter is a terrible brat and I'm sure she was simply afraid of you upstaging her. Remember that the last time you came here, she did everything she could to make you feel insignificant, but now you're a famous detective and what has she achieved with her life?"

Wow! I was not expecting the General of all people to give me a confidence boost that weekend. But he was right. I'd accomplished far more than spoilt little Noémi had. She was rich and set to inherit a fortune, but I'd built a life for myself through my own hard work.

Yeah, yeah. Don't get a big head.

"What did she say was the reason she didn't want me to come?"

He shook his head a little, as though the whole thing was irrelevant. "She didn't like the fact that her mother had changed the guest list at the last minute. They'd been planning this party for months, but, Elizabeth only invited you a few days ago. Noé made it sound like her mother had done it to spite her. She thought she was being punished by dragging up her past offences."

Of all the witnesses I'd spoken to that weekend, the General was not just the most knowledgeable about the family, he was the most forthcoming with his evidence. Even my mother had lied to suggest that she and Elizabeth had never been rivals. Great-uncle Francis was serving up the truth, warts and all.

"You have to understand," he continued, "she's spent the last five years trying to prove to her mother just how sweet she is. So, to let her guard down like that, something must have really upset her."

I wasn't sure how to phrase my next question and ended up going with, "You honestly think she's the most likely killer?"

I saw his uncertainty ripple across his face then. He fought a battle between his loyalty to his deceased daughter and the girl on her way to the hospital and finally chose the middle ground.

"I didn't say she was the killer; I said that I couldn't rule out the possibility. But after this morning, perhaps I was too hasty. If you want an obvious choice, then your uncle would be next on my list."

"Bradley?"

"That's right. He's another spider. Another hanger-on who'd tried his luck with my poor Elizabeth. You know, we didn't hear from him for decades until he turned up here one sunny Sunday afternoon acting like we were all bosom pals. I'd have sent him packing, but Elizabeth was in that charitable mood of hers."

I thought about my headache of an uncle. "He told me that he was fond of the place. I assumed he was just showing off. What did he want from her?"

The General looked up at me like I was foolish to ask. "What do you think he wanted, Isobel? He wanted her money."

Chapter Twenty-Four

I'm not going to lie. I would love it if Bradley turns out to be the killer and gets sent to prison for life. I believe the word for that would be karma.

I was going to say exactly the same thing!

I left the General with all those mouldy ghosts in the great hall. They were my distant relatives too of course – pinned and framed to the wall – but they meant nothing to me. My mother had escaped from that side of her life when she'd moved down to London in her twenties to become a teacher. She'd lost her Derby accent, just like she'd shed her connection to her family's historic wealth. Though my great-uncle was still haunted by his father and all those stuffy old figures who surrounded him, I'm happy to say that my own little wing of the family had long since broken free.

Unlike us, Bradley had sought to align himself with the Castletons, but could his need for money have driven him to kill his own cousin? It's not always the reprehensible characters who end up being the killers. If solving crimes was that easy, a quick chat with all the suspects would be enough to spot the guilty party.

Still, my uncle's horrendous personality certainly didn't rule him out and there was plenty of circumstantial evidence against him. There was the putty beneath Elizabeth's fingernails and on the ground below her window. His gloomy visit to the east tower – which in itself could have been engineered to account for any forensic evidence found at the scene. And now there was money in the picture, which is surely the number one motive for murder since time began.

My brain was an electric circuit working on overdrive. I was trying to put together a case against Bradley, but kept landing on new questions that needed answers. I thought about going straight to him for another interview, then had a better idea.

The whole house was awake, though our numbers were depleted. In fact, as the General would soon head off to the hospital to check on his grandchildren, there would not be a Castleton left in the place before long. Martha had relocated the breakfast to yet another dining room, so it took me another five minutes to find everyone.

"Tragedy," Bradley said when he saw me, and I was rather glad that he didn't break out into the Bee Gees song. "If you're not safe in your own home, where are you safe?"

Oddly, he sounded like he was expecting an answer so I landed on, "Prison? At least behind bars none of your family can get you."

He looked puzzled for a moment, then nodded. "Well, yes, it does have that benefit. Though I can't imagine the food is as good as this."

He seemed to have got over his shock at the second attack in the family in less than a day and continued to fill his mouth with fancy pastries. His son was with him, looking as downtrodden as ever, and he was the one I wanted to talk to. Dean looked sleepy, Mum and Greg were chipper and there was no sign of Fabian.

I was about to negotiate a private audience with Axel when the police arrived.

"Now listen up," the half-man, half-amoeba D.S. Osborne said. "We're going to arrest every last one of you. That's the only way we can be sure that no one else gets-"

"That won't be necessary, thank you, Sergeant," Fincher interrupted him, sounding just as stressed as before. "But we will need to talk to you one by one and, it's possible that you'll have to go down to the station for a more formal interview."

"A more formal interview!" Osborne reiterated, like a backing singer in a really dreadful band. "So no talking to one another. No changing your clothes and definitely no hanky panky."

It was hard to make sense of what he was talking about, so we ignored him and waited for Fincher to deliver more rational instructions.

"Bradley Gibbs." Fincher nodded to my uncle. "You were one of the closest here to the victims; perhaps we could talk to you first."

Bradley looked horrified, though I'm pretty sure it was the idea of missing out on breakfast more than any fear he had of talking to the police. "Seriously? But I just ordered some eggs."

He huffed and puffed, but Fincher wouldn't be blown over by his arguments and waited for the miserable character to leave the room with D.S. Osborne.

"Did you find Fabian?" I whispered to the more intelligent of the two officers, before he could head out himself.

"Yes, he was still in his room. No sign of any blood, or evidence that he'd done anything to get clean this morning. I don't think he was involved. It's not looking good right now. We just have to hope that the younger Castletons recover and tell us what the hell has been going on here."

"I might be able to help with that, but I need some more time first."

"Very well." He moved to leave, before tossing another comment over his shoulder. "Keep me informed."

"Darling, come and have a toasted cheese sandwich," my mother called. "The melted gruyere is heavenly."

"Sorry, Mum. I'm a bit busy right now." The police intervention had cleared my path. With Bradley gone, I didn't have to find any pretence to speak to his son. "Axel, could we talk for a minute?"

He looked down at his very full plate and I realised that he did have some things in common with his father after all. "Can I bring my bacon sandwiches?"

We went for a walk in the garden to avoid Axel dripping ketchup over anything stainable. There were six police cars out on the front drive this time, as we walked towards the wildest part of the estate where the neat lawns gave way to woodland.

"Dad's been coming out here at the weekend for a few years, but he only brought me a couple of times."

"Do you know why he came?"

I had to wait for him to swallow a mouthful of toast before he could continue. "Pretty obvious, really. My dad's only motivated by three things; food, money and women. I don't think that even he would stoop to romancing his cousin though, so I suppose he came for the first two."

"Did he bring his fiancée?"

A look of true misery consumed my poor cousin right then. "Deidre? No, not even she was allowed to join him for his 'special afternoons with the Castletons.'"

I couldn't resist asking, "What's your future stepmother like?"

"She's the human equivalent of a piece of toilet paper that gets stuck to your shoe. Dad met her in an STD clinic where they were both getting tested to confirm how terrible they are as people." His voice soared higher. "I'm not even making that up. Dad hit on her while she was waiting for a chlamydia test."

"Ahh, how romantic." I let out a tiny laugh.

"She hardly ever wears clothes about the house and calls me her baby. She's only about ten years older than me. She's not old enough to be my mother, and yet she's going to be my mother."

I really didn't have the words to respond to any of that ickiness, so I changed the subject to something safer. "Okay, your Dad comes here for food and money. So he had a loan from Elizabeth?"

He stepped over a fallen tree and put his hand out to help me do the same. I have to say, of all my relatives there that weekend, I like Axel best. Even though there's ten years between us, he fulfils the role in his family that I do in mine. We both even have a collection of step-parents!

"Yeah, six months ago now. She gave him fifty grand to invest in his business, but he kept all the money for himself. Spent most of it on planning his wedding." He had to steady himself then at the thought of it. "Urgh, Izzy, you should think yourself lucky that they're getting married on Bora Bora. I'm one of only eight people invited and they've already given me a sneak preview of the first dance. It makes 'Dirty Dancing' look like a Jane Austen society ball."

I always enjoyed hearing Axel's horror stories and hated to move the discussion on. "How did Elizabeth react? Do you think she knew about the wedding?"

Leaning against the trunk of an ancient oak, he considered the question before replying. "Yeah. Dad's only too desperate to show everyone photos of where they're holding the 'love ceremony'. It must have got back to her. Noémi would have made sure of that. She's like a detective herself that girl. She's always checking up on everybody and listening at keyholes."

"So, what happened? Did Elizabeth ask for the money back? Was she angry?"

We walked on along the path through the trees. "Dad likes to imagine he could charm a banana from a monkey, but he's really not as smooth as he thinks. He came back a second time to beg for more money and old Lizzie threw him out."

There aren't many people I trust in the world to tell me the straight-up truth, but this was solid evidence coming from one of them.

"When was that?"

He squished his lips together, as though questioning why such information might help me. "About a month ago, I guess."

"So after or before you were invited to the party?"

"After, I think. Why?"

I needed time to be sure of myself but, as we emerged from the copse of trees onto the open plains around the house, I felt confident enough to tell him. "Your dad went up to the east tower yesterday after lunch. I don't know what he and Elizabeth talked about, but when they came back down, they could barely look at one another and Bradley bolted away from us as fast as he could."

The memory came into focus in his mind. "At the photograph, right? Yeah, he was in a foul mood. Kept telling me off for not standing up straight enough, like he's some sort of military example."

It struck me then just how different our parents were. I had to fight the urge to run to Mum, Greg, Dad (and even my ex-stepdad Arthur down by the seaside) and give them all a massive hug.

I had no idea how to get the next question out. "Do you think… I mean, assuming he'd used the invitation as a way back in here to butter up Elizabeth… If she'd got angry with him and demanded the money back, could you imagine that your dad would be capable of killing her?"

He wasn't offended by the question, but took his time to answer. "I'm not the most impartial person to ask. I'd stand up in front of any judge and tell them my Dad's a savage killer if it means I don't have to see Deidre 'I'm not a nudist, I just like the feel of the air against my skin' Coombs again, but…" His voice died away for a moment and I wasn't sure he'd be able to continue. "But yeah, I reckon he has it in him. It's a sad thing to confess, but Dad's an absolute demon when he doesn't get his own way."

Chapter Twenty-Five

I spotted Bradley on the front steps, taking in the estate like he was lord of all he surveyed.

"Morning, Ian," he said, between puffs on a skinny cigar. "Back to boy's clothes today, I see."

Axel nodded a goodbye as we approached his unscrupulous father, then breezed right past without a word.

"What's wrong with him?" Bradley's voice became indignant. "Bloody wet blouse, making everyone around him miserable."

I'd been hoping to play it cool – to find out what he knew without alerting him to my suspicions – but, in the end, my subterfuge was forgotten and I kicked off the interview with a nice, subtle, "Did you kill Elizabeth? Did you attack her kids?"

He would have feigned shock right then, but he was halfway through a drag and had to let the smoke out first. "How could you accuse me of such a thing? I'm your own flesh and blood."

"And?"

"Izzy," he said, making the word sound somehow tragic. "I'm a plumber, not a fighter."

The rational part of my brain could see what a petty man he was, but that subservient instinct which had been handed down from my ancestors made me feel weak and incompetent around him. I balled my hands up and started over. "You owed her fifty thousand pounds, which you've wasted on an expensive wedding."

"Oh, come on, Izzy. It's not a waste. My beautiful bride has always wanted a Bahamian wedding, and it's going to be stunning."

"Bora Bora isn't in the Bahamas."

He looked around us then, in case his fiancée had popped by for breakfast. "Well, I know that, but don't tell Deidre. She's never been very good at geography and I got an excellent package deal."

We were getting off track. "The point is that you borrowed money from your cousin and, when she wanted it back, you killed her."

Not only is smoking a disgusting habit, it totally destroys the tension in an interrogation. He attempted a loose smoke ring this time, but ended up coughing his lungs out.

"I didn't kill anyone. I needed the money because I was trying to impress Deidre. You see, I might have made out that I was quite a bit wealthier than I actually am and… well, the tropical wedding was a deal-breaker for her."

"If she's so bad at geography, you should have booked a weekend in Bognor Regis."

"Oh, come on, Izzy. My Deidre's not stupid. She can tell the difference between an exotic paradise and an English seaside town."

"Though not between the northern and southern hemispheres, apparently."

You're getting distracted again.

I know I am! But it's his fault.

I perched on the great stone bannister that swept down from the entrance, took a deep breath and started the conversation for approximately the tenth time. "I saw you upstairs before the photograph. Were you scouting out the spot where you planned to kill her?"

He had a self-satisfied grin on his face that I couldn't make sense of. "I've just been through all this with the police. And, I'm not going to lie, I really thought I was in trouble after all the dodgy dealings I've got up to over the years. But all they wanted to know about was poor old Lizzie. I was passed out drunk when she was murdered, so there's nothing to worry about there."

It was difficult to say whether it was a clever ruse, or he was an out-and-out dimwit.

"When I spoke to you after the photograph, you'd sobered up. Half an hour later, you were barely able to stand, which is when you yanked me onto the floor and gave me the cut on my chin."

"Oh, come on, Ian. Surely you've got over that by now? It looks like it's healed up pretty well." He reached out to poke the scab, but I slapped his hand away.

"Stop interrupting." I was trying to sound tough. I don't think he realised. "You could have staged that whole scene to make everyone think you were drunker than you really were. You knew that Elizabeth would come to see what the problem was, and you were the one who suggested you needed a lie down upstairs."

"What are you saying?" I think he finally cottoned on to just how much evidence was stacked up against him.

"I'm saying that no one was with you for the fifteen minutes when she could have been killed. Once the General had gone down to the party, and the others had gone their separate ways, you could have asked Elizabeth for another little chat and followed her upstairs."

"Oh yeah?" That arrogant tone distorted his every word. "And where would I have got the knife from?"

I was focused now and my brain picked out an answer from the crisp air between us. "You could have gone to the kitchen when you arrived yesterday morning and stashed it in your room. You knew that Elizabeth wanted the money back. You knew she didn't want you visiting her anymore, but you came to the party anyway. Perhaps you even thought that she'd leave you something in her will. After all, you said this place was a 'home from home' for you; you must have been pretty close to your wealthy cousin. What would you have done to keep your Deidre in the manner she expects?"

When I've laid out such accusations to suspects in the past, I've witnessed any number of reactions. Some people appeal to my kinder nature to prove their innocence, others lose their temper. Bradley just laughed.

"Oh, that's a good one that is, Ian. You are a funny lass. Must be all them books you read." He paused and stubbed out the cigar on the balustrade. "You know what? If you can prove any of it, I'll give you whatever Elizabeth leaves me in the will."

He went fishing for a lighter and cigars in the pocket of his putty-and-grease-spotted workman's jacket. When he managed to extract one, I noticed a curious sight. His hands were shaking and he could only just get the lighter to spark. It took him three attempts to fire up the acrid, brown tube.

"You know what, Izzy? You've got me all wrong. Just because I've got a big mouth, that don't mean I'd murder someone for a few thousand quid. I came here yesterday to apologise to Lizzie for how things had gone between us. We used to have a laugh when I came here. And I can tell you, that woman needed it. Her kids are monsters. Even when that Noémi was acting all sugary sweet, she was still a conniving little-"

Maybe he'd remembered what had happened that morning, as he decided against finishing his sentence. "I'm telling the truth. I liked

Lizzie and I never would have leaned on her for the dough if I hadn't been desperate." His eyes fell down to the stone slabs beneath our feet. "You see, I might make myself out to be a big man, but my business has been tanking the last couple of years and Deidre wouldn't have looked twice at me if I couldn't splash the cash around. I'm a sixty-five-year-old man. She could have her pick, but she chose me."

His pleading tone was doing little to win me over. "You said yesterday that you were thinking of ending it with her because she was already too old for you."

He looked back up at me then. It was a swift, jerking movement, like he'd just had an electric shock. "I say a lot of things, Izzy. I shoot my mouth off before my brain can tell me not to. And yes, I told your ma that I was planning to leave Deidre, but only because I'm worried she'll do it first."

I suppose I should have had a smidge of sympathy for him, but nothing came. "Elizabeth had putty under her fingernails. How do you account for that?"

He looked desperate and practically took a bite out of the cigar. "That D.I. Fincher asked me the same thing. Said the boffins at their lab have identified it and, as I was the only manual labourer invited to the party yesterday, he asked me to explain how it got there."

"What did you say?"

Instead of the Jack-the-lad I was used to, he sounded scared. "I said I don't know how it got there, only it didn't have nothing to do with me. Except for a couple of pecks on the cheek, I hadn't touched Lizzie all day. Not so much as a handshake. And, that's what got me worried." His grey eyebrows shrank in towards one another. "What if someone is trying to set me up? I mean, I had a lot to drink, for sure, but I never normally crash out like that. What if someone spiked my Cuba Libre and that's why I made such a scene? It would explain why I was dead to the world while my poor cousin was being murdered a few metres away."

After his rapid shifts in defence over the last ten minutes, it was hard to believe a word he said. Then, for at least the third time that weekend, I heard the same plea.

"You have to find the real killer, Izzy. You have to find the fella what did this."

Don't fall for it, Iz. He's playing you.

I know that, but… "If you didn't do it, who do you think the killer is?"

He instantly perked up. "Has to be that French bloke, doesn't it? I never trust foreigners."

Ahhhhh! Make it stop!

"I'm not sure that argument would hold up in court. Did you see anything this morning around the time Tedwin and Noémi were attacked?"

"They were fine when I left them." This surprised me.

"So you were up early?"

"Oh yeah. I'm never a late sleeper, even when I've had a few the night before."

"So tell me exactly what happened."

He took a step up the staircase so that he was almost as tall as me. "Well, I went down to breakfast and they were digging away at one another like normal. She was saying that, if their mother had changed her will, it was only to cut him out of it and she wasn't worried. Then the boy said that she sounded awfully sure of herself and maybe she'd taken the copy that was supposed to be in the safe. It was the usual thing with them. Obsessed with money they are those two. Kinda sad really. I've brought Axel up to be interested in more metaphysical concepts than just wealth. You know, football, good food. Those kinds of things."

"So what happened when you went into the breakfast room?" I asked, as I really didn't need a lecture on what a good parent he was.

"Well, when they saw me, they put that same sweet act on. Noémi even offered to pour me some orange juice, but I decided to leave them to it and went down to the kitchen to ask whether they could make me a cheese omelette. By the time I got back, the police had turned up. Terrible business it was. Really terrible."

"So, you were the last person to see the two of them unharmed." I was still fixing him with a suspicious stare, as he'd basically just spelt out how easy it would have been for him to attack them.

"What are you looking at me like that for?" he asked, but I didn't say another word. "Hey, quit it." He was getting really worked up by now. "Seriously, stop eyeballing me. I didn't stab anyone and I'm not such a bad guy as everyone thinks."

Chapter Twenty-Six

I can't say I truly believed a word that Bradley had told me, though it would be easy enough to check with Ed the chef whether he'd made a trip to the kitchen. I had to assume that the police would be ahead of me on that score.

I left my uncle to smoke the rest of the pack of cigars and wandered back through the manor. The entrance parlour was deserted. There was no string quartet to serenade me or waiters to bring me drinks. In fact, the stillness of the house came as a shock. Was this how the estate would be from now on if the next generation of Castletons never made it back here? Would it lie dormant until the General died? Or be sold to some Russian oligarch or Qatari sheikh?

It was no business of mine what happened to the place, but the sensation of being all alone there gave me a clue as to how it must have felt for Elizabeth after her kids went off to university. One woman in such a gigantic space, even with a staff of servants to attend to her needs, it must have been terrifying. Her memory of the young children she'd worshipped would have haunted the place and I could see why their absence had served as a mental break in her attitude towards them.

I slowly climbed the marble staircase to the west wing, thinking of all I had learnt over the last day about the house and the oddball branch of my family who lived there. My great grandfather Henry Castleton had once been in charge and, as his son the General had explained, his cold treatment of the other members of the household had sent shock waves through time, right up until the present day.

I passed Noémi and Tedwin's bedrooms, which, like mine back in West Wickham, maintained their teenage décor. Noémi had photos of hunky boys and old friends above her bed, and it was hard to think of her as the cold-hearted, calculating person who had shown so little sorrow after her mother's death.

Elizabeth's room was just as drab and cold as it had been the day before. It was more a cell than a comfort. So dark and impersonal, it felt as though the place was a punishment. Perhaps she was paying the penalty for her offspring's crimes, or perhaps she only slept there and didn't particularly care what it looked like inside.

I peeked into the museum for another glimpse at the family spy. Fifty versions of Matthew looked down at me and I realised once again what a tribute this place was to him. He was another of the ghosts which haunted Castleton Square Manor. Perhaps if he hadn't gone off on a secret mission and ended up dead, things would have turned out differently. Perhaps his children wouldn't have been so monstrous and his wife would have discovered a happier fate.

There was always sadness to my investigations, but this one hit closer to home. Whoever the killer was, they'd changed the path that my family were on. Noémi and Tedwin had lost their mother and perhaps more. Noémi had called herself an orphan when I'd spoken to her the night before and I had to hope that she and her brother would survive their injuries, to at least hold on to one another.

I kept walking and came to Fabian's room. The scene of crime officers were combing the carpets and bedsheets, for signs of blood and other DNA, but the Frenchman was nowhere to be seen. He was the only suspect I hadn't had the chance to speak to, but no one had seriously put him forward as the culprit. And if Bradley wasn't responsible, then who was? I had no solid theories, no conclusive evidence and, from what Fincher had told me, the police weren't doing much better.

Perhaps I needed the urgency of a deadline to get my brain firing. I needed the pressure of a client breathing down my neck and demanding answers. But there was no client this time. My family were the only ones with any expectations, and I'd spent my life learning not to care what they thought. As I left the west wing, headed back across the ballroom balcony, I realised that this case had one advantage. Instead of returning to my bedroom for a lie down, I picked up the pace, jumping three stairs at a time to get to my family that much quicker.

I didn't have a clear idea who the killer was, but I had a plan to find out.

Returning to the makeshift breakfast room, I was pleased to see that all the people I was looking for were already there.

"Dean, I might need your help. Mum and Greg, I definitely need yours. I can't do this alone. Perhaps it's Ramesh I'm missing, or perhaps I'm simply not up to the task this time, but we have to find an empty room and preferably some sort of flip chart."

"On it," Dean said, as he pulled a small, futuristic box from his inside jacket pocket.

"I'm in too." Axel had been standing beside the tea urn, and I hadn't noticed him until now. "Wait, what are we doing?"

Mum was full of energy and rose from the table with a glass of orange juice in her hand as though she were about to make a toast. "We're going to solve the murder of Elizabeth Castleton."

"Then I'm definitely in," my cousin said, before adding, "Wait, how?"

"Don't worry about that. But I need you all there." I noticed that my stepfather was the only hold out. "Are you in Greg?"

With his usual careful consideration, he weighed up his options. "I'd love to help, Izzy. I really would, it's just…" Martha appeared at that moment with a steaming bowl of soup. "Ah, here she is now. Give me three minutes to wolf this down and I'm all yours."

A little longer than three minutes later, the four of us had relocated to a far more suitable space. The southern gallery of the house was perfect for an impromptu meeting of the Hawes Lane Crime Club for one very important reason; it had curtains, so Dean's fancy portable projector would be visible on the wall.

It was yet another huge space and, this time, there was a display of contemporary art on the walls. I'd even heard of a few of the names listed on the little plaques beneath each frame. There was a tiny Damien Hirst painting at one end of the room, a few sculptures by the Chapman brothers and plenty of big colourful designs by lesser-known artists. If I was planning to rob the place, I'd have started there.

"Are we all setup, Dean?" I asked, once Mum had arranged the room to her liking.

"Almost." He'd connected his phone to the projector and was doing all sorts of techy things I will never understand. With a few more taps on his screen, beams of lights sprung from three sides of the tiny machine. One of them projected a blank document split into three columns, while, on another wall, my most valued assistant Ramesh and my father Ted were looking back at us.

They both had oil stains on their faces, and Ramesh was wearing a welding helmet tipped back on the top of his head. He looked like a dancer in a pop music video, pretending to be a tough working man. Dad looked like his older, whiter boss.

Ramesh let out a happy, “Ahhhh! You couldn’t do it without me, could you, Iz?”

I ignored him and Dad piped up. “I’m just glad to be included again. Hello everyone!” His voice boomed out of a miniature Bluetooth speaker that Dean had set up. All these invisibly interconnected gadgets meant nothing to me. If Dean had told me he had magic powers, I would probably have believed him.

I wasn’t sure how our virtual guests could see us, though I suspected there was a small camera drone flying around somewhere. Either way, they managed to follow everything that was going on.

“Izzy!” a new voice cheered and, a moment later, Mum’s hairdresser Fernando appeared on the wall between a big splash of red paint and a photomontage of a pigeon in drag. “Your mum’s been keeping me abreast of developments. Sounds like an interesting case and I look forward to giving you my perspective.”

Of all of my regular helpers, Fernando of Penge was, oddly, the most insightful.

Because hairdressers are stupid, Izzy? Is that what you’re saying?

I was about to tell my brain that if it couldn’t think anything nice, it shouldn’t think anything at all, but I didn’t want to sound like Mum.

Instead, I brought our meeting to order. “We have a lot to get through but, by the end of this morning, I hope to be able to tell the police who the killer is.”

Chapter Twenty-Seven

"I have something I'd like to say," Ramesh interrupted.

Feeling like the presenter on a TV game show, I turned to his side of the room. "Yes?"

"I have a theory about why Elizabeth was killed." He said this very dramatically and several of my parents were taken in.

"How exciting," my mother cooed. "Now we're getting somewhere!"

It fell to me to be the calmer head. "Ra, you haven't actually heard the evidence yet. Don't you think you should wait?"

He considered this for a moment, conferred with my father in a whisper and then responded by saying, "Very good, you may continue."

"Thank you." I cleared my throat before getting down to work. "Yesterday afternoon at around five o'clock, Mum's cousin Elizabeth was murdered in the east tower of the stately home in which we now stand. At the time, there were six other people in the wing of the house immediately beneath the reading room where she was found."

Dean had shown me how to use the interactive whiteboard thingy he was projecting onto the wall and, in theory at least, if I held my hand at the correct angle, I could write or draw whenever I broke the projector's light beam. Except, of course, it wasn't working.

"Dean? A little help?"

He ran over to the projector and pressed a few buttons, then apologised under his breath. "It's a prototype I'm trialling for a friend. It hasn't had much real-world testing yet, so there's bound to be a few bugs. Tell you what; you talk and I'll write the notes."

This seemed like a fair compromise and would begin to make up for the years of pretty girls posing inanely beside men in suits on every game show in history. I nodded and, having fitted a white glove that covered only his fingertips, he was ready to write.

"Okay, we started off with six suspects. My mother, the dead woman's father, her assistant and two children, and, last but certainly least, Mum's brother Bradley."

Axel gave a pantomimish *boo!* Which Dad and Ramesh joined in with.

I continued undistracted. "To avoid any claims of nepotism, I'm going to start by ruling out my mother. Rosemarie Palmer only arrived in the east wing five minutes before we found Elizabeth bleeding to death upstairs. Tedwin spotted her entering her own bedroom, and she did not emerge again until after Elizabeth had died. So I think it is fair to say that it would have been impossible for Mum to be the killer."

I actually thought I'd managed to clear the matter up in a simple, straightforward manner without the need for contributions, when my stepfather spoke.

"Unless she was in league with Tedwin, of course." Greg sounded quite concerned about the possibility. "He claims that he saw Rosie enter our bedroom, but what if he's only saying that because he was working with her to kill his mother?"

"That's a very reasonable point," Fernando added.

"Is Tedwin even a real name?" My father had already got sidetracked by complete trivialities.

"I think it must be, but only for a very posh dog." Ramesh looked deep in thought, as if this was the mystery we should be focused on. "You wouldn't want to call an actual human Tedwin, would you?"

My mother was already worked up. "Gregory, are you seriously suggesting that I plotted to murder my cousin with a man I hadn't spoken to since he was six years old?"

Greg never gave anything away. His face fixed in a look of pure conviction, he said, "No, my darling. I'm only pulling your leg."

I clapped my hands together to get their attention. I was more like a nursery school teacher than a game show host. For a start, game show hosts can cut their contestants' mics when they get out of hand.

I checked to see that Dean was keeping up and, on the virtual screen on the wall, he'd written,

Suspects: ~~Rosie Palmer~~.

"Great, let's keep going then. From what I can tell, Elizabeth's assistant Fabian is unlikely to have gained from his boss's will, though he was having an affair with her daughter Noémi Castleton."

This garnered an *oooooooohhhhhhh!* from Ramesh and Dad and I had to worry about how my friend's eccentric personality was rubbing off on my susceptible father.

"In his favour, however, Fabian did get extremely upset over the death, to the extent that he was in tears when none of the rest of the family were. So it's fair to say that he and Elizabeth were somewhat close."

"Maybe he went for the full set." Ramesh sounded as if he was talking about a card game. "He could have slept with the mother and the daughter. And, when Noémi found out about it, she killed her mum in revenge."

Ramesh often has far-out ideas, but this one left me dumbfounded. "I don't know how to say this, Ra. But that is exactly what I was thinking."

He acted as though this was no big deal, just as Dad raised their hands in the air in victory.

I laid out the evidence. "When I went to see Elizabeth before she was murdered, there was a handwritten letter on her desk. I didn't see who it was addressed to, but it looked personal. It was there when I found the body, but gone when I returned to the crime scene with D.S. Osborne. One of our suspects must have taken it."

"Noémi obviously snatched it when she killed her mother, so as not to incriminate her boyfriend," Fernando suggested. "What's this Noémi like anyway?"

"Bit of a psycho." Dean broke the game show assistant's first rule. They should never speak without being spoken to. I shot him a disapproving look before, reluctantly, agreeing with him.

"Yep, that's a fair assessment. Growing up in a family like hers, she went to the dark side and I wouldn't have been surprised in the slightest if she turned out to be the killer. Of course, that was until I found her and her brother this morning covered in blood."

"Sorry, Iz." My glamourous assistant's interruptions were becoming a habit. "Can you say that again, the screen wasn't working." He was waving his hands about like an air traffic controller, but nothing was coming up on the wall behind him.

"Perhaps a pen and paper would do the job better?" As I said this, my head crossed the beam of light and left a big black mark which covered up half the notes that Dean had already written. "You know what, forget the technology and let's try to use our heads to remember what we're talking about like we did in the old days."

Dean looked sheepish and mumbled, "The good old days when we all lived in caves."

Mum was still focused on the case. "We haven't ruled Noémi out, it just means there are two killers. The Frenchie felt guilty for poor Elizabeth and did his girlfriend in." She paused to marvel at her own idea. "Think about it. It was the perfect way to complete their love triangle. Noémi killed her mother, so Fabian tried to kill her. Except, her brother got in the way and stopped him."

"Which would make sense if there was any forensic evidence on Fabian. You can't run around a house stabbing people without traces of fluid or fibres getting on you. Our killer is no ghost and, from what the police could see when they found him upstairs in bed, Fabian was clean."

"So it has to be my dad then," the only voice to remain quiet until now spoke up. "He owed Elizabeth money, has had a disastrous year with his business, and is engaged to a woman who thinks he's as rich as Elon Musk."

I looked at Dean for a translation.

"Elon Musk owns Tesla." This still didn't mean anything to me. "He's one of the richest men in the world?"

As I was busy pretending that *I knew that, thank you very much*, Mum held her hand up to speak, before struggling to find the right words.

"Well… I might be biased of course, but I can't believe that Bradley has it in him." I'd rarely heard her sound so hesitant. My mum was a woman of bold statements and even bolder outfits. Once again, the influence her brother held over her was plain to see.

"Bradley is another top suspect," I began, still not sure which side of the coin I'd finally landed on with my uncle. "Everything that Axel said is true and perhaps even more damning is the fact that Bradley was up early this morning. He actually admitted to speaking to Tedwin and Noémi before they were attacked."

This led to some breakaway discussions, with Axel and Fernando quickly teaming up and the other pairs already established.

"Surely the police would have checked him for forensics too?" Dean put forward. "They'd have his clothes off him and his room turned inside out."

"Dad has overalls and a mask in his van." Axel clearly had his heart set on the idea that his father was a murderer. "He could have put those on for the killings and stashed them away somewhere. This house is so big, the police would never find them."

"I think there's a simpler solution." I was just about to set out my grand theory when there was a knock on the door and D.I. Fincher came in.

"I wondered where you'd all got to." He looked around, a little puzzled as his eyes adjusted to the dim room. "Noémi Castleton has woken up in the hospital. She says it was her brother who attacked her."

Chapter Twenty-Eight

I'm no prima donna, but I still get annoyed when I commit all my time and mental energy to working out a mystery only for someone else to swan in and give the game away. It would be like popping into Leonardo da Vinci's studio and saying, 'Sorry, Leo, old pal. You didn't paint the Mona Lisa. That was me.'

Not a prima donna, but comparing yourself to da Vinci? You're right, Izzy. You're exceptionally down to earth.

Okay, fine. I'm a massive prima donna and I hate it when people upstage me. Happy now?

Once the impressed cooing at Fincher's news had subsided, I lodged my complaint. "I was literally about to say that! There was no forensic evidence because Noémi and Tedwin stabbed one another. I should have seen it instantly. They've been fighting the whole time we've been here over who would inherit what, and apparently such behaviour is pretty standard for them. But, when I found them cradling each other like that – Tedwin with his body in front of his sister's as if to protect her – they looked so sweet and I wanted to believe that they really did care for one another."

"Oh, Izzy." Ramesh was close to tears. "That is the nicest thing I've ever heard you say. I'm sorry, but I have to call my sister to tell her how much I love her."

Once my faithful friend had disappeared from his screen, D.I. Fincher had something to add. "I appreciate everyone's help with this, but it looks like we've got our man. D.S. Osborne is already at the hospital and I don't want him to mess anything up, so I'd better shoot off."

"Congratulations," my always respectful stepfather shouted over to the retreating officer. "You've done a fine job, no doubt."

I was the only one there who seemed uncertain. Though, to be fair, I don't think Dean was listening as he was busy trying to fix his space-age device.

"Wait," I shouted before Fincher could leave. "Why are you taking Noémi's word for it?"

He stopped by the door and straightened himself up to consider the point. "You mean she could be the killer and she's shifting the blame?"

I wasn't quite sure what I meant. I'd gone into that room to get things clear and ended up even more confused than before. I wanted to see all the evidence set out before me but, instead, there was a big black digital blob on the wall. I couldn't think fast enough to give him a definite answer, but I knew we shouldn't believe two-faced Noémi without examining the evidence.

"It's possible, yes. Perhaps Tedwin worked out what she'd done, so she attacked him with the knife from the breakfast table, but he fought her off. Neither of them would be entirely innocent, but his case would be a lot more sympathetic."

"It could just as easily be the other way around." As so many of us were now on our feet, and Mum hated to feel short, she stood up too. "Tedwin could be the killer."

I could see that Fincher was interested and he took a few steps back into the room. "I have to admit that we didn't find much to suggest any particular grievance between Tedwin and his mother. He's definitely the more tranquil of the two."

"That's hardly scientific reasoning," Fernando shouted down from the wall at the experienced police officer and there was an awkward silence which I attempted to fill.

"Oh, sorry, D.I. Fincher. This is my mum's hairdresser."

The two men waved politely at one another and then the inspector continued. "If you'd let me finish, I was going to say that Tedwin couldn't explain his actions in the period just before his mother was murdered. He claimed that he was on the phone but, when we looked into it, he hadn't made a call. As far as we can tell, he was just sitting in the hall in the east wing doing nothing."

"That doesn't make him a killer, does it?" My words came out far louder than I'd intended. I have to admit that I was defending Tedwin for the simple reason that I found his personality more palatable than his sister's.

"I'm sorry, Miss Palmer, but unless you can drum up some evidence to the contrary, as soon as Tedwin Castleton is in a fit state, we'll be charging him with the attack on his sister and, most likely, his mother's murder."

Fincher nodded civilly to my parents and left the room. Sensing that the jovial mood had disappeared, Dad attempted to turn the video feed off and failed. He managed to send a series of floating hearts across his screen though, which I have to say made me feel a bit better. Axel offered me a sympathetic frown before Dean shouted, "I've fixed it!" then turned around to realise that it really wasn't the moment. Axel and my parents were already getting up to leave.

"You can still do this, Izzy!" my mother told me, before shepherding the others towards the door, with a gesture that said, *quick, let's get back to eating. This girl hasn't got a clue what she's doing.*

Fernando's screen had frozen and, once the last of my fair-weather assistants had melted away, Dean and I were left alone.

"I don't see why you're getting so worked up," my friend told me. "We already knew that Tedwin was lying about the phone call to his imaginary girlfriend. It's not such a big deal that you failed to complete one murder enquiry. There'll be another along before you know it."

"It's a big deal to me. Just like it would be a big deal to you if a techy cyber gadget LED digital processor you'd invented didn't fulfil its..." I couldn't finish that sentence because I'd forgotten how it started.

"You've really got no idea what I do in my job, have you?" he replied a little wistfully.

"No, of course I haven't, but I know you take pride in it. And that's what I'm doing right now. So, if you've got that thing working, I want to see all the evidence we've accumulated laid out in columns on the wall with-"

He pressed a button on his phone and my wish was granted. "These are the notes I've been keeping as the weekend has progressed. I've divided them up into suspects, evidence and hypotheses, as your mum told me that was how you like to organise things."

"Perfect." I stood back to take in his handiwork, and he had a few thoughts of his own.

"We must be overlooking something major. There must be some big reason for why the killer locked the door after leaving."

"We discussed this. It was to make sure that Elizabeth couldn't crawl for help."

He was suddenly animated and leapt forward to wag his finger at the wall. "Yeah, but that doesn't make sense to me. She was already a flight of stairs away from everyone else, with a knife in her back. Locking the door feels more personal somehow. Like they were taunting her."

I considered another option but didn't see how it was possible. "It's a reverse locked room mystery. Elizabeth loved crime fiction almost as much as I did, so maybe the killer was playing a joke on her."

"What a sick mind." Dean sounded unusually disgusted right then, and I had to hope he was talking about the killer, not me.

"The letter is a major clue too. It has to be. One of our suspects removed it from the room with us all there. They were obviously scared that they'd get found out, but if that was the case, why didn't they take it when they stabbed her?"

"I guess…" Dean's voice faltered. "I guess they didn't notice it the first time."

I don't think either of us were particularly convinced by his idea. We stood staring at the list in the hope some bright spark of elucidation would jump out at us.

<u>Evidence</u>
Missing Letter
Key in door
Putty on fingers / outside window
Books on floor and upturned chair
Defensive marks on hands – presumably cause of blood spatter on desk
Spy husband - Important?

After three minutes of silence, Dean said what we were both thinking.

"We're not getting anywhere, are we?"

I sighed a tragic sigh. It was worthy of a heroine in a 1930s melodrama, but it didn't make me feel much better. "It doesn't look like it. There are plenty of reasons why each of our suspects would have killed her, but there simply isn't one all-encompassing explanation that fits all the clues."

Dean had been biting his lip so hard I could see small white marks on it. "And yet it feels like we're close."

"Or perhaps I want to be the one who solves the case so badly that I'm unwilling to accept that Tedwin is the killer. After all, he gains just as much as anyone else, lied about his alibi, and it looks like he just tried to murder his sister."

"Nope, I don't buy that either." There was something about Dean's grumpy manner that I always found reassuring. His thinking was resolute, unromantic and fact-based to balance out all the lovely drama queens in my life. Just as I felt like giving up altogether, he spoke again. "You said that the knife was on the floor and Noémi had very little blood on her, right?"

"Well, little of her own blood, yeah."

"So then it's unlikely that Tedwin attacked her with the knife. And if he didn't initiate the fight with his sister, there's no reason to think he killed their mum."

I was still staring at the lists projected on the wall, my eyes scanning the names of our suspects as I remembered the shape of the two siblings' bodies curled around one another.

"Don't give up, Izzy." Dean sounded a bit shy then. "I have faith in you."

"I'm not giving up." Now I was the confident one. "I never give up." I smiled at him as I turned to leave the room. "I just need a little inspiration."

I crossed the gallery, darting through the chairs and over to the door, as Ramesh reappeared in his illuminated box on the wall and said, "Oh, where's everyone gone?"

Chapter Twenty-Nine

Dean had mentioned something that I'd given very little weight to until then. Elizabeth was a fan of murder mysteries. She had a whole library devoted to them, which had been passed down through the generations from my great grandmother. We were a crime-fiction family, in fact, so that's where I went to have some time alone.

I sat cross-legged on the floor of that funny little hexagonal room which had been squished in between bedrooms. And to begin with, I didn't touch any of the books on the shelves, I just looked at their spines and tried to imagine Elizabeth going there each day to fish out a new mystery.

Some of them had been read so often that the titles had worn away or the covers had fallen off. Others looked as though no one had taken the time to crack them open. I have to admit that I got a little sidetracked from my own case for a couple of hours as I came across a collection of Agatha Christie's short stories that I hadn't read for years. In my defence, I was hoping that one of Poirot's cases might subconsciously trigger the solution to Elizabeth's death. Sadly, despite the fact it was a locked-room mystery, set in Derbyshire, 'The Mystery of Hunter's Lodge' failed to provide the key – unless one of my suspects had been in disguise. 'The Tragedy at Marsdon Manor' suggested insurance fraud could be the motive and, I'll be honest, I never expected 'The Jewel Robbery at the Grand Metropolitan Hotel' to serve up any clues – though it was great fun to accompany Poirot and Hastings on their weekend away at the seaside.

I finally extracted myself from that thrilling excursion, and my eyes roamed on across the shelves and through time. They made stops to read the titles of old favourites and novels I'd never heard of. At first, I assumed they were organised without care, neither by date nor alphabetically. It took me a few minutes, but I realised that they were arranged by something far more personal. Their haphazard grouping was surely a snapshot of the order in which Elizabeth had read them.

My idea was confirmed by the fact that, in the bottom corner of the right-hand bookshelf from where I was sitting, was an eye-catching edition of Edgar Allan Poe's 'Tales'. It was one of the books she had mentioned purchasing before she was killed. As I pulled it free from its slot, I could see just how old it was and wondered whether I should have been touching it at all.

The cover was like some occult bible. The black leather Morocco binding displayed golden spider's webs, stars and winged beetles, and there was a skull motif on the front cover just to make things cosier. It was printed in 1845, a few years before Poe had died and, as the title page informed me that it was a first edition, I had to assume it was the most valuable item in the library. It spoke to the wealth which the Castletons possessed that it could be dumped in with a bunch of cheap paperbacks.

I turned to the index to find the usual selection of Poe's proto-detective stories and tales of the grotesque, but that wasn't all. A letter tumbled into my lap. It was neatly folded in quarters, the creases military straight. I was torn between wanting it to be a handwritten note from the author or a clue to the case.

> ***My dear Elizabeth,***
>
> ***I know it may be old fashioned to write to you like this, but then our situation is an old-fashioned one. I am close to you each day, yet feel a million miles away and it destroys me. I can only take succour from the fact that, throughout history, countless romantic figures like myself have endured such hardships.***
>
> ***And so, as you will not listen to me in person, I write to set my feelings down on paper. I write in the hope you might find some shred of mercy within you. I write to beg you to love me.***

The letter went on like that for pages. It was needy, hard done by and reflected all the author's problems onto the object of his supposed affection. There was something cruel about the language as well. It did not read as a confession of love so much as an accusation of mistreatment. It was signed *Your Fabian,* but it was very hard for me to imagine the teary Frenchman having written it. I could tell it was only part of a longer chain of correspondence and searched the subsequent books for the next in the series.

If anything, my search was too easy. Every book in the bottom shelf, from Poe onwards, contained a love letter. They were all written in the same neat hand and folded into a tight square, like a child's paper fortune teller. They charted a short, tempestuous fling that had taken place between boss and assistant. I learnt from the letters of their first kiss, subsequent happiness and the abrupt fashion in which Elizabeth had called off the relationship.

I sat on the floor, surrounded by discarded books and the small pile of letters, trying to join up the dots. Was my discovery enough to account for a man taking a knife to his former lover? It would mean that Noémi had at least provided Fabian with a false alibi and perhaps been involved in the killing herself. My suspicions of her had never abated. The only reason I hadn't focused all my energy on proving her guilt was the attack that morning, which I could now explain.

It's never the obvious suspect.

Except when it is.

But if Noémi and her boyfriend were the killers, what did they hope to achieve? I suppose it would make sense for Fabian to seduce Elizabeth, but it wouldn't guarantee them an inheritance. With Noémi still in the hospital, it was Fabian I needed to talk to.

It turned out I'd missed lunch already, which is never a good thing. I was horrified to discover that, as my watch and aching legs revealed, I'd spent far longer in the detective library than I had imagined. It was now four in the afternoon.

You read a whole book and a bunch of unnecessarily long letters, then sat staring into space, ruminating on the case for about an hour. Were you hoping time would stand still?

Shut up, Brain. I'm basically Sherlock Holmes at this point.

It took me another twenty minutes just to find the Frenchman. I'd always dreamed of living in a big country house, but after that weekend, I decided I was happier with a three-bed semi-detached. As a very lazy person, I can tell you that I do not enjoy walking long distances between the lounge and the kitchen (snacks should be at arm's reach at all times).

Ed the chef-

Hang on a second. Why is Ed classed as a chef when all the female kitchen workers we've met have been plain old cooks? Sexist much?

No, not at all actually. It's got nothing to do with their gender. It's just that Ed has one of those big white hats!

My brain couldn't cope with such superior logic and had no answer to that. Anyway, where was I?

Ed the cook…

Right, Ed the chef told me that Fabian had an office beside Elizabeth's on the lower floor of the house, so I set off (using the compass on my phone's GPS to help me). It was the one area of Castleton Square Manor which I'd never visited before and was rather drab compared to the others. It had presumably once been home to countless servants but, with the reduced staff numbers, was now given over to offices and a conference room.

I found Fabian packing up his possessions into boxes. "What do you want?" I've had frostier welcomes in my life, but none sprang to mind.

"I need to talk to you."

"Well, I didn't imagine you were coming here to perform some mime." The sarcastic tone, which he had used to corral us into a photographable group the day before, was back in his voice.

It wasn't enough to scare me off. "I need to talk to you about Elizabeth."

He stopped what he was doing and studied me for a moment before replying. "It's a tragedy and I'm very sorry such a warm-hearted person was taken from us." He sounded like he was reading from a script, and it struck a remarkable contrast with the emotion that had poured out of him every other time I'd seen him.

"I know about you and Noémi." I kept my comments sufficiently vague to set him on edge.

"I don't know what you're talking about."

"She confessed that you're together. Did her mother know?"

He turned to a shelf behind the large, leather-topped desk which filled the room and pulled some folders down. "It's a free country, I see the women I want." Though his English was superlative, there was something jarring about the way he spoke. He was a very good copy rather than the genuine article.

"And what about Elizabeth herself? Were you free to see her?"

He laughed then, but I could tell he found no amusement in what he was about to say. "You British are so obsessed with who is sleeping with whom. We French learnt long ago that such things are of little importance. Yes, I was intimate with a daughter and her mother. It's no crime. I didn't kill Elizabeth. I loved her briefly before Noémi staked her claim to me."

"There was no overlapping?"

"No. Though, again, I would have no problem with such a thing."

"You didn't meet Noémi on her gap year living in Paris for example?" As I said this, there was the tiniest twitch in his left eye and it was enough for me to know I was on the right track. "She didn't get you a job here and help you write these letters?" I held up two of the papers that I'd discovered in the library.

He lugged the now loaded box down onto the floor. "All you want is a scandal. Well, I won't entertain your accusations. I've already spoken to the police and they're happy I'm innocent, I've got nothing to say to you."

I have to apologise in advance for what I said next. "Do you know who I am?"

He rolled his eyes, and I thought, *fair enough*. But going softly with him wasn't getting me anywhere, so I put on my toughest voice and leaned into the arrogance of my words. "I'm Izzy fudging Palmer! I'm not just the greatest amateur detective in Britain, I'm the only one in my lifetime that the media has bothered to cover."

He looked me up and down and, with his Gallic detachment, said, "It must be because you are tall. The media love a freak."

He didn't just call you the F-word! Are you going to take that, Izzy?

"There was another letter. It was on Elizabeth's desk when she died, but disappeared by the time you left the room. You took it. You were closest to the desk and must have slipped it into your pocket when we were busy with Elizabeth."

That was what finally broke him. His cool dissolved before my eyes. "She made me do it." He collapsed into the wooden swivel chair and his first tears sprang forth. "I swear, Noémi masterminded the whole thing."

So much for honour among thieves.

"You kissed up to Elizabeth so that she would change her will, then placed a knife in her back when you knew there were plenty of other suspects around who could be blamed." My words came out as a torrent and his crying grew louder.

"No, not that. We didn't kill her. It was just the money, nothing else."

I leaned over the desk, my face up close to his. "Why should I believe you? Why would a jury? You had the opportunity, the motive and, clearly weren't averse to a little criminal activity. Who's a more likely suspect, the conman who tampered with evidence at the crime scene, a distinguished general, or my national treasure mother?" I decided not to include the other, less wholesome suspects on that list.

"I'm not a killer!" he screamed, and his words shook the glass in the patio window. "You have to believe me. I'll tell you everything that happened, but you have to convince the police that I had nothing to do with her death."

I pulled back, which gave him a moment to catch his breath. "I want every last detail from the day you met Noémi. And if I really think you're innocent, then of course I'll help you."

He looked up at me with his big brown eyes. Though I couldn't actually feel sorry for him, I did understand the pressure of being mistaken for a killer.

I sat down in the spare chair and, his whole body still shaking, he nodded and began. "You were right. We met a few years ago in Paris. She was taking a course at the university where I studied and she hunted me." He paused to suck back in a breath. "I don't mean that metaphorically, she saw me one day in a lecture and wouldn't leave me alone until she possessed me."

Nope, sorry. Still a metaphor.

As he continued with his tale, the hints of suave sophistication that had occasionally peeked through his emotional exterior became more apparent. "Noémi Castleton is not like any other women I have slept with – and there have been very many." *Yuck!* "She is a wild animal and I was her prey. The relationship we had in Paris was not a healthy one, but my body felt like an extension of her own. When we made love, it was as if-"

"Urmmm, okay, thank you, Fabian." I was definitely blushing. "Could we get back to how you ended up living in her family home, attempting to swindle her mother? Only, I've got a lot on today."

One side of his mouth perked up as he enjoyed my squirming. "That's another problem with you British. You want to know whose bed we are all in, but then you refuse to talk about sex. It is a natural part of life. In fact it *is* life, and the sooner-"

"I just don't think mysteries need to be any racier than they already are," I blurted rather angrily, and he finally got the message to STOP TALKING ABOUT SEX ALL THE TIME!!!

"Fine… when she left Paris, I became a ghost. I had no life left in me and mourned my absence as much as her own. I had no doubt that she would have other lovers in Britain, but I didn't care. I just wanted to be with her, no matter the cost."

"So how did you get back together?"

He full on smiled then, his eyes floating off to reminisce. "I wrote her letters, of course. It is a sadly maligned art form. E-mails and text messaging hold no candle to a well-written communiqué. I recorded my desire for her, using just a pen and a whole pad of paper and, though I doubt it made her fall in love with me, it gave her the idea which united us again."

He paused, and I examined his suddenly calm, dark-featured face as I waited for him to continue. "Noémi's mother had practically cut her off at this point. She wished to live alone in London and her mother refused. Elizabeth gave her children no regular income, which made Noémi furious. She saw the possibilities that bringing me here could present and so she came to Paris to explain her plan."

His face turned sorrowful once more. With the speed at which his emotions changed, it was hard to know if any of them were real. "I am not proud of what I have done, but it was all to be with her. Noémi convinced her mother that she needed an assistant for her charity work and fixed it so that I would be the chosen candidate. No one knew of our previous connection and, as I am originally from Lyon and had lived in London as a younger man, she had no reason to suspect my connection to Paris and her daughter."

"So then you pretended to fall in love with her?"

He flicked a dismissive hand through the air. "Please! I took my time. I did not simply jump on Elizabeth. I started with little compliments each day, but not until I'd been working with her for at least a month already. Her constantly shifting appearance told me that she was insecure, and I knew that I could exploit that to make her love me. A drunken kiss after one of her galas gave me the chance to start writing my letters to describe the deep internal turmoil I was suffering over her.

"Noémi knew her mother well and knew that she would be unable to resist the version of myself we created in prose. You were correct that Noémi helped me a little, but the sentiment was all my own. I may not have been enamoured with Elizabeth in quite the way I suggested, but, for a woman of her age, she was an exquisite lover and-"

"Okay, yes. Thank you for that, but I don't think it's going to help me find the killer." He bowed his head deferentially, and I moved on to my next question. "So what did Noémi get out of you smushing lips with her mother?"

He looked down at the desk, perhaps trying to communicate how guilty he felt. "As I said, we took things slowly. I never asked Elizabeth for anything, but she was generous to me and so, when I mentioned that my mother would have to sell her house for my father's care in Lyon, she offered to pay his medical bills."

I put my most sympathetic voice on. "That must have been a great relief for you." I dropped said voice. "And how exactly did you make it look as though your father was getting the money and not Noémi?"

I thought he would show me his confident smile again, but his face remained blank. "We used an online bank account – such things are easy these days."

As good as I'd become at reading people over the previous year, remorse is a difficult thing to assess. It's far easier to fake than other emotions. We all know what a regretful person looks like. But the crease of the brow and down-turned head can be produced on command, and I genuinely couldn't tell whether a word he was saying was true.

"So that gave you both some pocket money, but I imagine that your girlfriend wanted more." I thought he might deny it, but my words hung between us for twenty seconds before he could find an answer.

"She wanted influence. That was what her plan was all about. Ever since I met her, Noémi has been afraid that her brother was outplaying her for their mother's affection. She believes that Tedwin doesn't deserve to inherit anything. Says he's weak and pathetic. You know, I think that's what drives her most. Not the money but the chance to defeat her brother after two decades of fighting."

He kept going off on these tangents (though at least this one was family friendly!) and I had to keep wrangling him back to the main discussion.

"You talked about influence. What influence did you have over Elizabeth?"

He put his hands palm down on the table in front of him. "As I mentioned, I never asked for anything from Elizabeth. I was there for the long game. I was there to help rehabilitate Noémi in her mother's eyes. In a very subtle way, I spoke of how kind and accepting Noé had been to me. I was a stranger, a foreigner, and yet she had welcomed me as one of the family. Her mother encouraged it at first, and I think we were winning her over when, all of a sudden, she broke off the relationship between us."

I had understood this much from his letters, but it led us to one of the key pieces of information I'd yet to discover. "What caused Elizabeth's change of heart?"

He breathed in, his face a picture of uncertainty. "I never found out. One week she was looking lovingly into my eyes and discussing our future together; the next she could hardly bear to be alone with me. When I asked her why, she said that our love had run its course."

"She must have found out about you and Noémi." I was thinking out loud, but it seemed to make sense.

He considered the possibility for a moment. "That's what we thought too, but then why not throw me out? I continued working for her, and Noémi and I started arguing in front of everyone to deflect suspicion. I tried my best to get back into Elizabeth's affections, but it was no good."

"I suppose she needed you for her work by then. When I spoke to her yesterday, she said that she didn't know where she'd be without you. Perhaps she knew that you and Noémi were sleeping together but nothing more – if it was just that, then she might have kept you on."

"Wait." With this one word, all his fear returned. "There's something else you don't know." He swallowed hard and I could hear how dry his throat had become. "She changed her will. I don't know exactly how, but she changed it the week before we broke up. She told me that she was going to and, I'm not sure why, but I decided not to tell Noémi."

Now this was interesting. "Didn't you trust her?"

His eyes were glistening wet once again. "It wasn't that – though I can't honestly say that trust is ever complete with Noé. I think it was mainly to protect myself. Everything had moved so quickly with Elizabeth, despite my slow and steady approach. I thought that, if she had changed her will to benefit me, I could find myself in…" He looked around the room for the right words. "In French we have an expression 'être dans le pétrin' it means to be in the place where the baker prepares his bread. Do you know what I'm saying?"

I really didn't, but, in the context, I managed to understand. "You'd be in trouble?" He nodded. "You'd be in hot water, maybe?"

He clicked his fingers at me. "That's the one I was looking for. Hot water, I would be in."

Things were starting to make sense. "That's why you've been so distressed all weekend? Because you're worried what's going to happen when they read the will?"

His silent tears became sobs. "That's exactly it. I don't want to go to prison. I haven't done anything. I mean, I know I lied to her, but she was happy when we were together. I don't think it was really so cruel." Those dark, mournful eyes peered up at me, begging for understanding.

"You know, we have another saying in English. It goes, if you lie down with dogs, you get up with fleas." I waited for a moment to check that he'd understood. He cried a little louder so I imagine he had. "If there was any criminal wrongdoing, Noémi made sure to keep out of it. It's your word against hers that she convinced you to defraud her mother. Did you keep the letters she sent you at least?"

He shook his head and I finally felt bad for him. I probably shouldn't have bothered as it was just as likely that he'd never told Noémi about the will so that he could double cross her later on.

"What about the letter you took after Elizabeth was killed?"

He brightened a fraction before replying. "Yes, I hid it behind a radiator in the hall after we left the east tower. Presumably the police never looked there, or I'd be in a cell already."

"Good, I'll fetch it myself. But there's one more thing I need if you want me to help you."

"I'll do anything." All his charm and elegance had deserted him and he was a snotty, blubbering mess. Knowing how skilful a manipulator he'd been with Elizabeth, I wasn't totally sold on his performance. It didn't make sense that he had given in so easily and confessed everything. If it was all part of their plan, then he'd go down with Noémi. And if he was innocent, he'd be fine.

To be honest, I no longer cared either way.

Chapter Thirty

Fabian mailed me a link to the photographs from the party, so that I could go through them on my phone. I was hoping they would help me cast my mind back to the moments before we discovered Elizabeth's body.

I started with the formal photos that he'd taken outside. The tight grouping in the centre of the image contained all my suspects but him. My mother had her arms out in an appropriately flamboyant style, while my stepdad Greg looked very apologetic for even being in the shot. Tedwin wore a shy smile, Noémi was as pretty as ever, and Uncle Bradley was sneezing. It was really only the General and Elizabeth herself who were noticeably out of sorts.

Elizabeth wore that same terrified expression on her face that I'd seen when she'd spoken to me in the east tower, and it only made me more confident that she knew what was coming her way. Her father meanwhile, standing beside my admirable mother, happy to be talking about his favourite royals, was all smiles. It really wasn't indicative of his normal personality.

The rest of the photos in the online folder were candid snaps from the party. There was a picture of my grandfather putting something in my grandma's purse – silver cutlery, I have to suspect – a nice one of Elizabeth with her cousins, spoilt only by the bunny ears Bradley was making over Mum's head, and a shot of my table during lunch with Noémi at her sycophantic worst. She had her hand on my shoulder and had just finished telling me how excited she got whenever she read about my cases.

Phoney.

Axel looked appropriately glum, even when he was collecting several glasses of champagne from the bar and, during the dancing, Tedwin stood alone in a corner with a maudlin expression disfiguring his face. He looked sadder than Keanu Reeves without a sandwich.

There was no smoking gun to find. No image of Noémi running upstairs with a kitchen knife. But jumping back in time like that cemented some of my existing theories. I understood the relationships between everyone now. When I'd arrived the day before, that hadn't been the case. I hadn't known whether my cousins had grown up to be decent people, or whether the General had a heart of stone. I knew my uncle was a complete waste of space and that his son deserved better, but… actually, there's no but with Bradley. The man's about as pleasant as box full of rats.

It felt like I'd already spent a lifetime in Castleton Square Manor, and it was time I put everything I'd discovered to the police. I found P.C. Chandra standing guard at the second crime scene. It made me rather glad I was a private detective and not a public one; she'd spent half her weekend standing very still, waiting for no one to come along and mess up the investigation.

"Hiya!" She looked genuinely happy to see me. "What can I do for you today?"

"I need to get a message to D.I. Fincher."

She was reaching for her radio already when a figure ducked out from behind the police tape. "Perhaps I can be of assistance?"

I had to wonder whether D.S. Osborne had been hanging out there on the off chance that I would pop by with the name of the killer.

"No, that's alright. I'll wait for Fincher."

He nodded slowly and repeatedly, as though I'd said something very smart. "That is your pre-rogative." He pronounced the word all wrong and watched me to see whether he'd got away with it. I thought he'd try to extract some info from me, but he'd got stuck in his endless nodding and couldn't break free.

"I'll let him know you were looking for him," Chandra said, without taking her eyes off her halfwit superior. "He said he'd be heading back over here before long."

"Of course," Osborne began, as though he were jumping back into an earlier conversation. "In my opinion, killers are often very close to home." He tapped his nose twice and then spun on the spot to walk down the corridor away from me like he'd made a decisive point.

"Sarge?" the young P.C. called after him. "There's nothing that way but the stairs down to the supply cupboards. Is that really where you wanted to go?"

Osborne peered over his shoulder, tapped his nose once more and disappeared down the stairs.

I looked at Chandra, she looked at me and I could tell she was doing her best not to burst into tears of laughter. "I'm not allowed to say what I think of that bloke in case it gets back to my superiors but…"

"Don't worry," I told her. "I feel exactly the same."

Fincher didn't turn up for half an hour, so I went in search of moral support and found Dean playing cards with Axel and my folks in their favourite lounge.

"Izzy, we'll be heading home tomorrow after the reading of the will," Mum shouted over as I arrived. "We wouldn't want to miss out on all the juicy-" I think Greg must have kicked her under the table just then, though Dean and Axel may have given her a punt too. "I mean, we thought it was best that we support the family at this difficult time."

She didn't sound particularly convincing and, as there was nothing else to do, I sat down with them to wait. It was alright for some. They were having a fine old time. Martha was keeping them well provided for with regular deliveries of cocktails and snacks. On seeing me, the maid darted back to the kitchen to bring me a plate of my own. It was a smorgasbord of well… smorgasbords. A platter of small dishes containing all sorts of Scandinavian treats.

"Back to square one, I'm afraid," Fincher told me as he marched into the room with that efficient energy of his. "The brother's woken up and claims the sister attacked him. I honestly don't know who to believe."

I was ready for his arrival – well, my hands were a bit ketchupy and I probably had some crumbs on my face – but I jumped up to greet him. "Have you interviewed him?"

"That's right. Seems that he and Noémi Castleton are in a stable condition. I gave them both a bit of a grilling, but they wouldn't fess up. I hope you've got something more for me."

"Here's hoping." This was all the cheer I could muster. "You'd better come with me."

Dean was up on his feet and more than willing to accompany us on the next stage of the investigation. "Let's go."

"Are you sure you don't have to get back to work?" I felt I should at least check. The poor man had spent the weekend hanging around for nothing.

"Not at all. One of the great things about having my own company is that no one can criticise me when I feel like having a day off."

"What about your chauffeur then? Isn't he camping out in your car? He could starve to death."

Dean gave me an affectionate punch on the arm as we walked through the ballroom. "Don't worry about Giles. He knows how to phone for a pizza."

Following along behind, Fincher looked worried about where we were taking him.

"It's upstairs," I explained to calm his mind, though I chose not to say what it was that we were trekking across the house in search of.

Walking past another bored constable, who was standing guard at the top of the stairs, we entered the east wing and turned along the corridor towards the spot where we'd congregated after Elizabeth died. The stairs up to her reading room were still blocked off with police tape, and, except for the sound of Bradley snoring in one of the bedrooms, the place was dead.

I came to a stop in front of the radiator under the window where Fabian had been standing the day before.

"I spoke to Elizabeth's assistant," I began, then realised I hadn't gone back far enough in my explanation. "Or rather, I spent some time in the small library around the corner from our room and discovered a series of letters in the books which Elizabeth had been reading over the last year. They were from Fabian and they were…"

Come on, Izzy. Don't be so coy! You can say it.

"They were…" What on earth is wrong with me? I've met royals, (not that I like to go on about it) solved the most brain-tickling mysteries and seen countless dead bodies.

It's still only nine actually.

Right, yes. I've seen nine dead bodies, so why do I get all red and stuttery when I talk about kissy-time?

"Well… Fabian and Elizabeth were…" I took a deep breath and then spoke in a stage whisper for some reason. "They were playing mummies and daddies!"

Bravo! You said it. You sounded like a four-year-old but you finally managed to talk about sex in public!

I ignored the expressions on my companions' faces and pressed on with the explanation. "Fabian got the job here because he was already in love with Noémi after they met when she was living in Paris. They pretended not to know one another in order for him to win favour with his boss. He seduced Elizabeth and started an affair, which is all laid out in the letters, but there was one on her desk when she died."

The two men had been hanging on my story, and Fincher was the first to react. "So, what did it say?"

"I have no idea because Fabian smuggled it out with him and it's hidden behind this radiator."

I stepped aside, like I was about to reveal my next trick, and Dean lent over the long white heater to peer down behind it. It was dark in the corridor, with the sun gone from that side of the house, but he soon caught sight of something.

"Won't be easy to get at," he said in that defeatist tone of his, just before he normally solves the problem.

Sure enough, he reached inside the preppy, red sports jacket he was wearing and pulled out a complicated pen knife. Like a dentist choosing the right tool, he took his time over the selection and finally extended a long metal pole with a gripping hand on the end, which could be opened and closed with a button on the handle.

Dean's basically Inspector Gadget. Well, Mr Gadget.

"I'll need complete silence while I attempt to grab hold of it." Now he was the one acting like a magician. "I don't want to knock it down any further."

"I'll try pushing from the bottom," Fincher said, before lying down on the floor and peering up behind the radiator.

They were both taking the operation very seriously, as I stood around waiting for the good bit. In the end, it only took Dean about ten seconds before he'd nabbed the crumpled paper and D.I. Fincher was brushing himself off.

"It's *from* Elizabeth, not to her," I said when Dean held the letter out for us to read. "It's the same handwriting as the letter she wrote me this week."

Huddled together in our little gang, I felt like a teenage adventurer from the Enid Blyton books which I'd devoured before I started my Christie obsession.

"To my dearest man," D.I. Fincher began to read aloud. He didn't really have the voice for it and read as though it were a gas bill or a piece of mildly interesting junk mail. "Can you ever forgive me for how cold I have been to you over the last months? You know that I trust you more than anyone in this house and have loved you deeply. I will never be able to explain the suspicion that gripped me, but I am beyond it now and pray that you will see just how earnestly I write these words."

His voice faded out as it became clear that the letter would be dominated by these vague, sentimental notions. There was no great clue as to who had killed her, and I could tell that Fincher was disappointed.

"So let me get this straight," he continued. "The Frenchman was swindling her out of her money, she broke off the relationship but was writing this shortly before she died to patch things up?"

I had to get everything in order in my head before I could reply. "More or less. I don't think she knew that he was using her. He was very subtle about it and never asked for money outright. She was paying his father's fictitious medical bills, which, of course, Noémi was siphoning off."

It was Dean's turn for a question. "But is that even a crime if she agreed to it and he didn't ask?"

We both turned to Fincher, who looked just as clueless as we were. "It's a tricky one. The law is a complicated business, though I reckon in this case it'd come under fraud by false representation. So yes, if they lied in order to obtain money from her, that's a crime. Course it doesn't mean they killed her, does it?"

I wasn't expecting this, and my voice betrayed my surprise. "You can't be serious? Her own daughter was plotting against her. That has to be enough to suggest intent. Perhaps Elizabeth found out what Noémi had been up to, and that's why she was killed. This letter suggests she forgave Fabian, but it doesn't mention Noémi once. She has to be behind the murder."

Even in the dim light of the hall, I could see Fincher wasn't convinced. "Where's the hard evidence? Where's the forensics? You pointed out all those little clues – the putty outside the window, the key in the door – how do they fit in if Noémi's the killer?"

I was racing for an explanation. "Perhaps they don't have to. Perhaps they were planted to frame other people. The putty made us think it was Bradley because he's a plumber, so the killer could have taken some up with them, planted a little on Elizabeth's hand and chucked the rest out of the window. And the key…" I didn't have an answer for him. The key in the lock had tripped me up from the beginning.

He looked at me face on and softened his tone. "I'm not saying you're wrong, Miss Palmer. I'm only telling you that a jury will never convict a killer based on unrelated bad behaviour. We need clear evidence and a proven motive. There's simply not enough to go on for now."

"You're letting them get away with it!" I was surprised that Dean was just as worked up as I was. "Where's the justice in that?"

Fincher sighed. It was clear he was used to such pessimistic questions. "Listen, if it was up to me, I'd lock them both away. And I'm not giving up yet. We should be able to prove the fraud and, from what I can tell, you were right about the attack this morning. All the evidence suggests that Noémi was the one doing the stabbing, but in terms of the murder, we're just not there yet."

I felt bad for him then. He nodded in that professional manner of his and, with the letter safely stowed away in an evidence bag, headed off down the corridor.

"Thank you for listening at least," I shouted after him. I was worried that sounded insincere, so followed it up with, "I really do appreciate it."

Dean looked at me with his nose all scrunched up. "There's no need to be sarcastic, Izzy. He was only doing his job."

Chapter Thirty-One

That evening passed in a daze. The remaining members of our group had dinner together, but I was hardly even aware of the food.

Sacrilege!

I was ploughing through the evidence in my head. The inspector was right. I hadn't found a path to the killer, I'd just picked the nastiest person in the house and hoped that would be enough to convince the police that she was guilty. And perhaps that wasn't the only reason. Perhaps I'd been biased against Noémi from the beginning. Essentially the biggest piece of evidence I had against her was the fact that she'd been a brattish child.

My mother, Greg and even Dean tried to be chirpy after dinner, but it was a pretty sombre affair. It's not often Mum goes more than a couple of hours without breaking into a musical number, so it was clear that no one was in the mood. I think the reality had settled in that, at that same time the following day, we'd be back at home, Noémi and Tedwin would presumably be the new owners of Castleton Square Manor and a killer would have gone unpunished.

We retired one last time to our games lounge. More cocktails were served, which livened Mum and Greg up, but there was no hope for me.

Don't be so down, mate. You can still piece it together.

Thanks, Brain, But I don't think you can cheer me up this time. What I really need is three days in bed and a samovar filled to the brim with hot chocolate.

I made my excuses and headed back upstairs for one last night's rest in that beautiful, big four-poster bed. Diving under the covers made me feel a bit better about the world. The duvet was so puffy and the blankets on top so heavy that I could barely move under them and I was happy to lie there, prone and trapped in a happy cave of my own making.

Of course, I couldn't sleep. My thoughts were a firework display, whizzing and banging to stop me from the oblivious slumber I so desperately desired. I figured the only way I'd get through this was to make a deal with my brain.

Alright, listen up. I'll go to sleep now, you can do your hypnagogic, subconscious wizardry and, in the morning, we'll wake up with the very answer we need. Have we got a deal?

Deal! And a very good one for everyone involved, if I may say so.

I don't know how long after that it took me to nod off, but I dreamed of Danny, alone in the Peruvian jungle. Well, hopefully alone. In the dream he was dressed as Tarzan – though still with his trademark black v-neck – and was swinging through the trees to rescue me from a deranged gorilla who looked awfully like my secondary school P.E. teacher, Mr Bath.

The gorilla had me trapped in his lair and, for some reason, my clothes were all covered in milk. He kept making me do star jumps, but I was really exhausted after about four of them. Then Danny arrived just in time to punch the nasty moustachioed gorilla on the nose and give me a big wet kiss before we… Well, you don't need to know what happened after that.

When I woke up the next morning, I was alone. I had to assume that Dean and the others had made a night of it, as it didn't look as though anyone had slept beside me. The new day brought new possibilities. There was already light streaming in through the curtains, and all that negativity had been swept from within me.

So lay it on me, Brain. What did you work out?

Urmmm… There was a sound in my head then, like an old factory machine starting up. Cogs whirred, levers were pulled and gears engaged. *How about we take a look at the crime scene again?*

Seriously? Is that the best you've got for me?

Or we could have breakfast first. We hardly ate a thing yesterday, every moment we're in this house not eating Ed the cook's food is a moment wasted.

I think I liked your first idea better.

Feeling weary and blue once more, I lifted the leaden blankets off me and swung my legs out. I hadn't packed for so long away so had to throw on the same clothes that I'd worn when we'd arrived. At least they were comfy (though a tiny bit musty by now).

If I'm being honest, breakfast did sound tempting, but instead, I turned out of my room towards the east tower. I knew that, two days after the killing, with the forensics team long gone, I wouldn't be disturbing much by ducking under the tape and having a look around. As I mounted the stone spiral staircase, it felt like a new opportunity.

Going into that room alone gave me the chance to view it with fresh eyes, knowing all that I had learnt since Elizabeth had died. I could finally take my time to explore that den of hidden secrets.

I stopped at the top of the stairs and looked at the lock. The key had been removed by the police but I got to take a close look at the elaborate brass plate which surrounded the keyhole. In a Christie novel, there would have been scratches on one side to suggest tampering, or a hidden cotton thread for some reason. Sadly, I didn't notice anything like that. The lock on that immensely thick door was quite new, but then I suppose keys get lost over the centuries and locks are replaced.

So, I moved on. I stepped inside and skirted the perimeter of the room, examining every item there. One advantage I had over the police who had investigated on Saturday afternoon was that I knew that whatever remained in that room had been considered insignificant.

A small cactus on one bookshelf: insignificant.

A plate with a banana skin, a packet of crispbread biscuits and an empty jam jar on top of it: insignificant!

The three mystery novels that had fallen on the floor: infinitely significant, of course, though not according to the police.

Most of the books on the shelf were non-fiction, which I suppose made sense as the crime library was downstairs. I read off the three titles which I hadn't had time to notice before. The only Christie was 'Elephants can Remember', a later work which is far from her best. I looked at the narrow space where they'd fallen from and tried to imagine the struggle that had dislodged them. If the killer was waiting for Elizabeth behind the door, she might have smashed into the bookshelf after she was attacked. This would explain the knife in her back, though not the cuts on her hands.

So that was another dead end. Unless there were two killers working together. Perhaps one was waiting in the room, while the accomplice convinced Elizabeth to head up for a chat. One knife went in her back and the second killer had a separate weapon which Elizabeth managed to fend off.

So then where did the other knife go?

Unable to answer, I moved on. I looked at those beautiful stuffed birds trapped forever in their tableau, waiting to sing. They reminded me of Elizabeth and I glanced down at the stain on the carpet where the blood had soaked in as I'd sat holding her hand. There were specks of blood on the table too, with the clean patch where the letter had been. But this was nothing new.

In fact, I wasn't searching the room; I was reliving my last visit there. My eyes weren't looking for new evidence, but re-compiling the same elements I had already witnessed. They were finding the same things that the police already knew about. I needed to look deeper.

I went back to the bookshelf and searched for more letters, but there were none to be found. I opened the drawers on her desk and searched for secret compartments, which was a hopeful endeavour but worth a try. I ran my fingers over the top of a cupboard, in case my imaginary second killer had discarded the imaginary second blade there; I found nothing.

I threw open cabinets, pulled out papers, emptied drawers and boxes and none of it did any good. In the end, I was so desperate, I climbed inside the gigantic mahogany wardrobe and checked to see whether there were any fake panels inside it. Not only did I not find any evidence, I also failed to discover a portal to Narnia, so that was disappointing.

The room had nothing new to tell me, and so, feeling increasingly depressed, I gave up. I sat down on the windowsill and accepted the fact that the case had beaten me. The key in the door, the putty under her nails, her spy husband and rotten daughter, the books and the blood and all those letters meant nothing.

I gripped the windowsill and looked out over the grounds, feeling thoroughly disappointed with myself. Even my brain didn't have any words of wisdom to impart. But, you know what? If I hadn't felt so hard done by, I would have been beaten.

"Woe is me!" I wailed aloud. "Why is my life so difficult when everyone else's is easy?" Okay, these weren't my exact words, but they were on a similar level of self-pity.

And rightly so. Without a bit of self-pity, Great Britain would never have established the widest empire in the history of-

Oh, don't start that again. But, yes. Who says that being a bit grumpy sometimes is a bad thing? Who says that feeling down in the dumps can't push us on to better things? Well, most people actually, but in this one case at least, I proved them wrong.

As I struggled with the idea of my detective agency's one hundred per cent success rate coming to an end, my hand dangled down at my side. My fingers gripped the space just under the windowsill and I discovered a soft patch.

Chapter Thirty-Two

The solicitor was due to arrive at eleven o'clock but I called D.I. Fincher to explain what I'd discovered first. He agreed that it would be best to wait for the reading of the will before proceeding and I was relieved that he was (what I have come to refer to as) an Izzy enabler. Most police officers I've met are reluctant for me to assist them. They normally tell me that I'm not allowed to have big dramatic scenes where I get to reveal how clever I am and that the best thing would simply be to arrest the guilty party and avoid any complications.

But not D.I. Fincher.

I don't know whether it was my growing cachet in the detecting community, or he was a bit of a pushover, but he was happy with what I'd discovered and saw no reason not to go along with my plan. He even agreed to bring the two convalescents back from the hospital to hear their mother's last will and testament.

Hurrrrrrrrrraaaaaaaaaaaaaaaaaay!

Shush, you! You've been no help whatsoever this time.

Hey! It was my idea to look at the crime scene again. You'd be nowhere without me.

I didn't have anything to say to that, so, feeling like a million pounds – which, let's be honest, isn't that much anymore, what with the average price of houses in Britain being twice that and a kidney – I went downstairs to find my family.

They weren't quite as prepared for what lay ahead of us as I was. Clearly, when sourpuss Izzy had gone to bed, the party had really started. There were abandoned bottles and glasses all over the lounge. Mum and Greg had fallen asleep on top of one another on the sofa and Bradley had dozed off standing up in one corner. Yet more surprising was the fact that the General, Ed and Martha were all there too. Oh, and Dean and Axel were lying top to tail on the floor.

I felt a bit guilty waking them, but as soon as I stepped into the room, my mother jerked into life, saying, "How dare you, Izzy. I haven't touched a drop."

"What happened in here?" I know it was a stupid question, but I felt I had to ask.

Mum was up on her feet pretending to be sober. "Oh, nothing, darling. Nothing at all. We had a quiet drink in Elizabeth's honour and then got a little sleepy." The pink feather boa around her neck and the monkey face paint she had on suggested that this was not the whole story.

"Why would anyone be so noisy at a time like this?" Dean suddenly yelled from the floor, before putting one arm around Axel's legs and falling back asleep.

The General looked particularly alarmed to be discovered there and, though wide awake by now, remained entirely still in the hope that no one would notice him.

I put my hands on Mum's shoulders and tried to communicate with her. "Now, listen, Mother. I'm going to need you all to sober up. The solicitor will be coming here soon to read the will and the police too."

Her face brightened. "Oh, that's wonderful, darling. Does that mean you've solved the case?"

I think I probably blushed. "It's a long story."

"It wasn't your cousin Axel, was it?" Her eyes narrowed as she laid out this new theory. "He has an unhealthy obsession with computer games that boy. He's almost as bad as Dean. Actually, now that I come to think of it, Dean's a really good suspect. I mean, talk about antisocial. Back when we first met, he could barely make eye contact! Why didn't anyone consider him?"

I spoke very clearly to make sure she understood. "Because he was sitting right next to me when the murder took place."

She wasn't convinced. "Ha, classic false alibi! The oldest trick in the book, really."

I steered her back to an armchair as she was clearly still worse for wear. "Mother, why don't we get you a nice cup of coffee?"

She threw her hands out in front of her expressively. "That's a wonderful idea, darling. Now where's that maid when we need her?" She peered around the room, unable to spot Martha who was sitting a few feet away.

"I tell you what, Mum. How about I fetch you some?"

She didn't reply directly. She closed her eyes and put her hand to her head as the first wave of headache kicked in. "I'm not going to lie, Izzy. Mummy isn't in tip-top shape this morning."

So instead of getting all the evidence clear in my head to explain the events that had brought about Elizabeth's death, I spent the next hour in the kitchen making refreshments for my beleaguered family and friends.

"That's a damn good chip sandwich, Izzy," Ed the chef said once we were all sitting down at the breakfast table. "All this food I make is a bit fancy if you ask me. Give me a nice chip butty, any day of the week."

Chip sandwiches are just about the high point of my culinary range, so he was lucky he enjoyed them. I have to admit, they were pretty darn delicious. I'd found some big fat potatoes left over from the night before and fried them up in a pan, mixed some ketchup and brown sauce together (because, why choose?) slung all that into some proper crusty white bread, which I'd pre-lathered with butter, then melted half a packet of mature cheddar cheese on top. And they say British food isn't a sophisticated form of cuisine!

That poor skinny chap Dean couldn't hold his booze the way big Ed could and was looking less sunny.

I was quietly impressed by the fact that my stepfather Greg was his usual polite self, even when dealing with a hangover.

"Nice tea too, Izzy. You can make it more when we go home," he told me, and I pretended I hadn't heard.

As we sat together eating, I felt pretty positive. I had a steaming hot chocolate, I'd solved the case, and everything was right with the world. Well, it was until Noémi showed up, looking as well and wicked as ever. Except for the bruise on her forehead, there was hardly a mark on her.

"I'm starving," she said, plonking herself down at the head of the table. "If I'd known how bad hospital food was, I'd never have got knocked out."

Martha gave me a pleading look which said, "Please, Izzy. Please deal with the little monster who I've spent my life putting up with. Just for one morning, let me have a break."

I smiled at her and went back to the kitchen to fetch our callous, mother-swindling suspect some breakfast. But I'll say this; I buttered her toast most half-heartedly. I barely reached the corners!

When the police arrived with poor Tedwin, I thought we might finally get a second victim.

His sister leaped up to launch her words at him. "You pig! Why aren't you in handcuffs after what you did to me?"

He didn't respond, but kept his eyes straight in front of him and pretended he hadn't heard. Osborne proudly escorted him over to the table, while D.I. Fincher stood guard by the door. With almost everyone there, a sense of tension filled the room. I wasn't sure whether it was the fear of what was about to be revealed or each person's hope that they would inherit the Castleton family fortune. Either way, the atmosphere was soon cut through by my buzzing phone.

"Can't talk right now, Ramesh," I murmured into my hand.

"Ahh, sorry to hear that, Iz. More dead bodies?" He didn't wait for my reply. "Anyway, bit of an emergency again. Can you ask your mother if she has a helmet with wings on?"

Mum had leaned over from her seat next to mine and was already listening in. "You know, I think I just might." I handed the phone to her and left them to their conversation.

No one had given Noémi any attention for at least sixty seconds, and so she made her presence felt again. "Why are the servants in here? And why do you all smell so… boozy?"

"I can't answer your second question." Mr Jaggard had arrived. He was a rotund, jolly chap, dressed in a solicitor's uniform (aka an unremarkable grey suit). He set a folder filled with papers on the table and then his briefcase on a chair. "But I can tell you that Mrs Martha Costello and Mr Edward Rose are here because I asked D.I. Fincher to ensure that all the beneficiaries of Elizabeth Castleton's will were assembled."

I think it took a moment for Noémi to realise that he was talking about the two employees who had waited on her for years.

"In fact, I believe we're still missing one person?" he turned to the officers for assistance but, just at that moment, P.C. Chandra walked in, marching Fabian in front of her.

"I caught this one trying to do a runner." She shoved him towards the table and he gave a nervous smile as he pulled an extra chair over.

"Jolly good, I was worried you wouldn't make it, monsieur." The solicitor was clearly familiar with the different members of the household.

He stood at the end of the long table and paused with great portent. Glancing around the faces of the group, he assessed his audience. I could already see that he had a quick mind, and it was rather nice to have someone else standing up to address the suspects for once.

"We have a lot to work through this morning and I think it's best to get down to business." He waited to check there were no objections and then, with a characteristic smile, began in earnest. "I should start by telling you all how sorry I was to hear of Mrs Castleton's death. I have served the family for half my life, but also considered Elizabeth a friend, which I believe is why she named me as the executor of her will."

He licked one finger and selected the relevant document. "As her solicitor, I was already aware of the contents after she changed it a short while ago. As her executor, I was within my rights to open it without any of the beneficiaries present, and I did so this morning in my office. Along with the will, Elizabeth included several envelopes which she asked to be passed on in the event of her death. The first of these was addressed to me and laid out the instructions for what she hoped would happen with the formal reading of the will – I should also point out that, while such events are no longer common in the twenty-first century, I was happy to indulge her love of the theatrical."

He gave me a wink, which I was rather surprised by. The weighty legalese he spoke in was undercut by the lightness of his tone and his cheerful demeanour. Having held up the document in its manila folder, he placed it carefully on the table in front of him and started to read.

"I, Elizabeth Louise Castleton, presently of Castleton Square Manor, Castleton, Derbyshire, hereby revoke all former testamentary dispositions made by me and declare this to be my last will and…" No one made a sound as his deep, sombre voice shook the table, before lightening once more. "Well, it goes on like that for quite some time and wills are rather dull things. Elizabeth's is relatively simple, but I'll summarise it for you a little nonetheless. First, she leaves the manor and the majority of its contents to her only son Tedwin."

Yelling with glee, Tedwin jumped from his chair. He immediately regretted it and had to sit back down to clutch his scars. His sister meanwhile couldn't believe what she was hearing.

"How could Mummy do this to me?"

Tedwin couldn't resist the chance to have a dig at her. "Perhaps you should have been nicer once in a while. I mean actually nice, Sis, not just pretending in order to get your own way."

Noémi's eyes flared and she reached for something to throw at him. Luckily for Tedwin, all she found was Mum's half-eaten croissant.

"I'll stab you again if you're not careful."

"Well, well, well," Osborne stepped around the table to mutter. "It sounds like we've solved the case of the stabbed-up brother and sister." No one looked impressed by his deduction, and Jaggard continued.

"If you'll wait one moment, Miss Castleton. Though your brother gets the house, you will receive your mother's liquid wealth. All funds and investments will now be transferred to your name."

"Oh, thank goodness for that." The young beauty's face turned saintly and calm. "I was terrified she would leave all her money to some damn charity."

"To her assistant Fabian Montreux, she left her collection of Montblanc pens. To her cousin Rosemarie Palmer, the contents of her many wardrobes, to her cousin Bradley Gibbs…" My uncle looked down the table expectantly, but Jaggard paused and I realised what an exceptional tease he was. "…she leaves her eternal thanks for such generous companionship over recent months. And to his son, Axel Gibbs, she transfers any remaining portion of the fifty-thousand-pound debt Bradley owes her."

The smile that had been present on Bradley's face migrated over to my cousin's. My uncle looked like he'd just seen a-

Big scary monster?

Yeah, that'll do.

"To her father, General Francis Castleton, she has set aside a generous annuity and the option to continue living in his apartment in the manor for as long as it remains within the family."

The General glanced down at his hands, but showed some relief at the announcement. His face was etched with emotion and I had to conclude that he was just as happy that his daughter had cared enough for him to make such a provision as he was about the endowment itself.

"To her faithful employee Mrs Martha Costello, she leaves the deeds to her cottage and an annuity for life." This made Martha smile and tear up in equal measure. Ed the chef was about to comfort her when his name was mentioned. "Mr Edward Rose inherits the collection of antique skillets and a lump sum which must be used for the establishment of the restaurant he has long hoped to open."

I could see that our chef/cook was taken aback by this. His eyes shot halfway up his forehead and he didn't say another word for the rest of the morning. I assumed that the bequests were now complete, but there was still one to be made.

"And finally, to her first cousin once removed, Isobel Palmer, Elizabeth leaves the contents of the crime fiction library, which is housed within the east wing of the property."

"Oh, that's so kind of her." I remained cool and nonchalant, but, inside I was jumping about and yelling even louder than Tedwin had.

Boooooooooooooooooooooooooooooooooooooks!

Jaggard closed the folder and straightened his back to look at us. When he spoke again, that cheerful tone was entirely absent. "As I believe this document shows, Elizabeth was a kind woman with a good heart. And I would be remiss in my duties if I failed to mention that, should one of you be identified as her killer, your inheritance would be forfeit."

With this important detail delivered, the mood changed once more. Tedwin met Noémi's gaze for the first time, and she sneered at him with great disdain.

Mr Jaggard graciously gestured for me to take his place as the next speaker. "Now that my job is done, I will hand over to Miss Palmer. She has my full support in this matter and I am certain that Elizabeth would have approved of her speaking to you today." Smiling anew, he moved a chair aside for me to have more space.

"Thank you, Mr Jaggard."

With all those eyes on me, I felt strangely nervous. I'd done this sort of thing countl… several times before, but this was different. My family have a special way of getting under my skin, and my previous success no longer seemed to matter when faced with such warm, supportive faces staring back at me.

Chapter Thirty-Three

I took a deep breath, told my brain not to interrupt, and began my tale. "I've only met Elizabeth a few times in my life. She and her kids stopped attending family functions after her husband Matthew died, and we only came to visit once after that. I was eleven years old and my cousins treated me worse than dirt."

"Oh, you poor thing," Noémi was quick to snipe, but it didn't break my concentration.

"I realised this weekend that, though the memory is still fresh in my mind, I have moved beyond it. But there's one person who never managed to forgive Tedwin and Noémi's years of bad behaviour, and that was their mother."

There was no interruption this time. I looked around that elegant room, with its priceless landscapes hung in each alcove and the elegant regency furniture, and it no longer impressed me as it once had.

"Elizabeth brought up her children to believe they were perfect. She idolised and idealised them, but, by the time Noémi was a teenager, she was so wild that her mother could no longer handle her. The realisation that her children weren't angels deeply affected Elizabeth and, by throwing the party this weekend, I think she wanted to make it up to those who'd been wronged."

I had a story to tell, but it was hard to know how to approach it without upsetting people too deeply or missing out important details. I carefully poured out a glass of orange juice to give myself a moment to think.

"This wasn't her only reason though. She wanted everyone to witness the person she'd become. You see, over the last couple of years, Elizabeth had transformed herself. Not just in her appearance, which underwent a dramatic change thanks to the good doctors of Harley Street, but her role in the world. She became a philanthropist – donating large sums to charities and volunteering for local projects – and I believe that she considered this to be her penitence."

"Oh, please…" Noémi was at it again. "If she suffered so much, why didn't she say anything?"

"She did, to me this weekend." I paused to let my words sink in. "I was surprised by her change of attitude since the last time we'd met. She'd already apologised in her letter for what you did to me when we were children, and she said it again when I arrived. I told her that you both seemed to have learnt from your mistakes, and she scoffed at the idea."

Funnily enough, Noémi had nothing to say to that.

"Unlike the rest of us, Elizabeth saw through her daughter's enlightened act and, even after her attempts to make amends, could not forgive Noémi."

Tedwin smiled at this, and I didn't like to point out that their mother's view of him was not a great deal rosier.

"Elizabeth's changes brought tension to the house. Her father, General Francis Castleton, had given up his claim to the estate in order for Elizabeth and her husband to run the place. But, recently, he'd become worried about her spending and did not agree with the lavish party she had planned. Remember that this was on top of the hundreds of thousands of pounds she'd already spent on plastic surgery, the small fortune she'd invested in her art collection and the improvements she'd made to the manor itself over the years."

I turned to the General. "Uncle Francis, can you tell me how she reacted to your complaints?"

He looked flustered to be called upon. "She… Well, she didn't really respond. I found it quite unnerving, actually. No matter how loud I shouted, I couldn't get through to her. All she would say was that I needn't worry; that she knew what she was doing."

"And that made you angry?" I kept all emotion from my voice, just as Elizabeth would have.

"Yes, it very well did!" It showed right then, and he made no attempt to hide it. "Or rather, I was upset that she wouldn't listen to me, but not angry with Elizabeth herself. She was my daughter, and I had the utmost respect for her." This being the Castleton family, he would not use the word *love* in public.

I gave him a warm nod and continued. "Elizabeth might have been indulging in a little retail therapy, but the Castleton estate is a wealthy one; which is a fact some people came to prey on."

Ha, Bradley's turn!

"Uncle Bradley, you asked to borrow money from your cousin,

isn't that right?"

He scratched his head like he was looking at a boiler he couldn't fix. "Something like that, yeah."

"As we heard in the will, it was fifty thousand pounds. Can you tell me why you needed to borrow so much money?"

He let out a whistle through his teeth as though this were far too sensitive topic to address. "Well, my business hasn't been doing so well the last few years and-"

"So you invested the money in your business?" I sounded quite innocent then.

"No, not the business. It helped pay for…" His words faded to a mumble.

Luckily Axel was on hand to help him out. "Dad blew it planning the wedding to his bimbo girlfriend."

All Bradley's arrogance had seeped away. He didn't even answer back to his own son for once.

I was quick with my next question. "How much have you paid back?"

"It's not so simple as all that." He kept his eyes on the table as he spoke.

"So, let's call it fifty thousand still, shall we?" I turned to address my cousin. "It might be worth you noting that down somewhere, Axel. You should probably work out a repayment plan with your dad. Elizabeth clearly wanted to make sure you were compensated for Bradley's overindulgence."

Smiling perhaps a little too broadly, I once more addressed the group. "So there's Bradley, with his business in ruins, facing a fifty-thousand-pound debt and about to marry a woman with expensive tastes. It can't have been nice for him, can it? And it must have been like acid on a wound when Elizabeth got so angry that she banished him from the house. What a terrible state of affairs he was in, but he still had his invitation to the party this weekend. A loophole to once more win favour with his dear, wealthy cousin."

Ha! Still Bradley's turn! Sock it to him, Iz!

"What did you talk about when you were together in the east tower just an hour before she died?"

He was really squirming by now, pulling at the cuffs of his paint-splattered sweater as though it was too small for him. "It's not like that. You've got me all wrong." He looked at Mum in the hope she would help him out. "I… I went there to apologise."

"Not to ask for more money?"

No one had any sympathy for Bradley right then, and he knew it. "No… Well, I suppose it might have been nice if she'd offered, like. But she didn't want to hear it."

"I bet you didn't like that."

My uncle is a stupid man; he always has been. Though he wasn't quite dim enough to incriminate himself any further.

"Ohhhh." He actually smiled at me then and his reply had a hint of venom in it. "Nice try, Ian. You want me to say how angry I was with her. So angry that I'd go back up there with a knife later on? Well, you won't get me like that."

I gazed back sweetly, just his niece asking a few questions. "No, of course not. I merely wanted to point out that, if you are the killer, going up to her reading room to scout out the scene of the crime was a good idea."

"I didn't kill her!" He got all whiny then, before Mum replied in the exact same high-pitch tone to mock him.

"Nobody said that you killed her, Brad." It might have been the first time I'd heard her speak down to her brother. "Just be quiet and listen to what Izzy – not Ian – Izzy has to say."

I mouthed a thank you to my wonderful mother and got back on with my explanation. "When I saw Elizabeth again for the first time in two decades, there was something very vulnerable about her. The strong, imposing woman I'd been terrified of as a child had been replaced by a nervous, fragile creature – and the vultures were circling."

Walking to the far end of the table, I swung my gaze around the gallery of faces. Among the spectators, Ed the chef, Mr Jaggard the solicitor and Greg the stepdad were greatly enjoying the spectacle. Noémi, meanwhile, looked like she wanted to stick a knife in my back.

"Bradley wasn't the only person who wormed money out of Elizabeth, though some people did it in a far subtler manner. As her philanthropic interests grew, her devoted daughter suggested that she should hire an assistant to help her with the day-to-day administration of her various projects. Fabian Montrose-"

"It's Montreux!" he said haughtily, which I thought was a bit arrogant considering that he knew what I was about to tell everyone.

"Fabian Montreux was an excellent administrator, and Elizabeth became dependent upon him in more ways than one. He found himself in a privileged position in the Castleton household, but also in his employer's affections as the pair soon struck up a romantic relationship."

His moment of resilience had passed and he was back to looking like he'd just sat through a particularly scary horror film about flesh-eating zombie babies.

Izzy, only you can have that effect on people.

Ahhh, thanks!

The Frenchman's head had slumped, and I almost felt sorry for him. Though not sorry enough to stop from revealing that he was a conman.

"What Elizabeth didn't know was that his appointment was no twist of fate. Fabian and Noémi had met on her gap year in Paris. This disloyal daughter had engineered her boyfriend's presence here in order to soften up Elizabeth and extract money and influence from her."

"You pair of absolute swines." I was happy to see Tedwin get some payback, but the story wasn't over.

"Don't be too hard on Fabian. He was besotted with your sister and would have done anything to be with her. Even sleeping with and swindling your mother wasn't too much for him. Fabian would die for Noémi and perhaps he would kill for her too."

"We didn't do anything illegal," Noémi was quick to announce.

"You claimed that Fabian's father was dying so that your mother would pay his hospital fees, then kept the money for yourselves. I'm pretty sure that's fraud."

"Yep," Osborne backed me up. "Sounds like fraud to me."

Noémi cast her penetrating green eyes upon him. "Fine, then prove I was involved?"

Funnily enough, the sergeant didn't have anything more to contribute.

"How about the letters which you and your lover wrote to Elizabeth? I imagine there are a fair few lies in there we could expose. Luckily, she kept them as bookmarks in the detective novels she read over the last year. The detective novels, in fact, which I just inherited."

I was standing across from Noémi and directed my vitriol towards her. "You systematically set about defrauding your mother. For what? A bit more pocket money? That flat in London you were after? What did you think would happen when she found out?"

She no longer had that bright, confident tone to her voice. There was a crack running through it as she attempted to defend herself. "She never did."

"But she knew about you and Fabian. Why else would she have called the relationship off so abruptly? And I think that the knowledge was enough for her to work out that you'd been conning her." I couldn't be sure of this, but it made sense. "You knew exactly where her old will was kept, and you knew the combination to the safe. So, tell me, do you remember who was originally set to inherit the manor?"

Her voice shrunk away and she could make nothing but a dry croak. "Tedwin and I would have shared it."

"Thank you." I stood up straight so that I towered over everyone. Sometimes being tall has its advantages. "But then, a short time ago, she changed the distribution of her legacy so that Tedwin gets everything of value."

As scared as Noémi already looked, this is what really shook her. "What do you mean? I'm set to get the cash, the investments. He only gets this musty old place."

I admit that I wanted to scream the truth in her face just then. I thought about poor eleven-year-old Izzy, crying in the detective library, and wished that I could travel back in time to tell her, *one day, everything will be alright with the world. Noémi will have her comeuppance.*

I let my wretched cousin stew in her uncertainty and turned to the solicitor. "Mr Jaggard, as the executor of the estate, I imagine you've examined the financial situation that the Castletons are in. Would you like to explain exactly what Noémi will inherit?"

He cleared his throat and stood up like a witness at a trial, but it was the General who answered for him. "I was going to tell you in private, my dear, but I'm afraid to say there isn't a lot left for you. Your mother had liquidated our investments and put all her money into this house, her charities and the art collection. Tedwin will get the lot."

Chapter Thirty-Four

I wasn't the only one who wore a smug grin just then. Tedwin, Dean and Mum looked like they were about to start a Conga line. Noémi and Fabian? Not so much. The former assistant had slumped low in his chair, and his girlfriend had transformed into a garden ornament. I tried to keep my face serious as my brain sang our favourite happy tune.

Woah! I'm going to Barbados! Diddle diddle dee dee!

"Sometimes, there is justice in the world. Elizabeth found out that her own daughter had been scamming her like a Russian troll factory. She was going to cut her off entirely, but, instead, she planned to reveal what she had discovered at just the right moment. She allowed Fabian to keep working here, but broke off their romantic relationship. He tried his best to win her over, but nothing worked.

"How did that make you feel, Noémi?" I was beginning to sound like a therapist. "To know that your mother had outplayed you?"

She was furious already, and it didn't take much needling to get her to pour forth her deeply channelled wrath. "How do you think it made me feel? You're only telling one side of this story. You've conveniently left out the fact that my millionaire mother made me live like a pauper. She paid for my time in university, but forced me into student accommodation when she could just as easily have bought me a cosy little penthouse in the city."

She had a funny idea of what it meant to be a pauper. I could have listened to her spitting like that all day and not got tired of the self-indulgent look on her pretty face.

"So you bided your time, just like her. You waited for the opportunity to get even. But what exactly happened when you went up into the tower with her?"

"You're talking nonsense." She managed to control her voice but couldn't look at me. "Tell her, Fabian."

Everyone in the room turned to look at the Frenchman, but he couldn't speak any longer. His face was running with tears, just as it had been when we'd found the body.

Noémi wouldn't give up. "Tell them what happened!"

I thought I'd make it clear to her. "Fabian can't speak right now because, despite providing you with an alibi, he saw you go upstairs with your mother and, the next thing he knew of her, she was dead."

She looked around the table in disbelief. "I didn't kill her. I swear. I'm not like that."

I sat down in a free chair. I didn't need to push my advantage or make her confess. She'd already incriminated herself in front of several police officers. I could sit back and it would still have the same outcome.

"Thank you for confirming that you went upstairs with her at least. I have to admit that I wasn't sure about that part, though I knew that Fabian was keeping something from us. After I found out about his relationship with your mother, it still didn't make sense that he would be the only one in the family in tears. You see, he isn't crying for Elizabeth. He's crying for the woman he loves. He's crying for you, because even he thinks you're a murderer."

When her response came, it was a banshee's wail. "Well, men are weak. They're all the same and, if he hadn't been such a soft-headed fool from the beginning, Mummy would have never worked out what was going on and none of this would have happened."

"You mean she wouldn't have had to die?"

"No… You've got it wrong. I didn't kill her."

This was proper rabbit-in-the-headlights stuff. Noémi Castleton, a bullying, brattish bad egg, who had spent her life sadistically manipulating everyone around her, was finally getting her just desserts. But I don't enjoy seeing people suffer, no matter how much they deserve it, so I put her out of her misery.

"No, you didn't." I placed my hand on the table in front of her and, to my surprise, she took it. "You're not the murderer, but that doesn't let you off for your other crimes."

"Wait." Fabian finally jabbered out a word. "Are you saying she didn't kill Elizabeth? I mean, I saw her-"

Noémi turned to glare at her accomplice, and he got the message to shut up.

I kept going regardless. "It's never the obvious suspect who turns out to be the killer in murder mysteries." I paused for effect. "Except when it is, and I was convinced she'd done it. I sat in the east tower this morning, putting it all together. There was a plate from Elizabeth's breakfast with a banana skin and crackers, but no knife. There was the missing letter which Fabian took when we were attending to the dying woman, and the fact that Noémi had already lied about her alibi. It was almost enough to convince me she'd done it, but there were a few things that didn't fit."

I needed to take a moment to breathe after all that fevered excitement. I stood up again and looked at the line of impressive paintings that were hung between each window. I could feel fourteen pairs of eyes on me as I slowly worked my way around the room, but I was in no hurry.

I slipped a latex glove on and took a brass key from my pocket. I held it up for all to see and smiled at D.I. Fincher who had maintained his professional demeanour throughout.

"There was the key in the door, for one thing. I couldn't land on a really good theory for why the killer had locked up after themselves when, with so many potential witnesses milling about downstairs, they would have had very little time to make a getaway. It's haunted me all weekend, in fact, but that wasn't all. There was the white, sticky powder on Elizabeth's fingers, the books on the floor which had fallen from a bookshelf as she struggled with the killer, and the wounds on her front and back that simply didn't add up."

There was silence now. Everyone in that room, even my doltish uncle, knew that we were approaching the end. "I considered all sorts of clever solutions. A particular favourite was that, just as Fabian and Noémi had faked their animosity, the two Castleton children had done the same. No one would have suspected they were working together after they'd spent the last twenty years at one another's throats. But of course, their hospitalisation yesterday put paid to that theory, right?"

I was hoping that someone would point out the flaw in this argument, and Dean was typically obliging. "Except that they're both sitting here now and their injuries were largely superficial. We know they attacked one another. Perhaps they were careful with the knife and made sure not to do too much damage."

I gave him a wink for his trouble. He'd been a faithful and reliable assistant throughout – despite banging on about spies the whole time.

"Exactly. If they were the killers, the attack threw me off the scent, especially as I couldn't tie any of the physical evidence in the reading room to Tedwin and Noémi. So, I moved on. I wondered whether

Bradley, in his infinite wisdom, had planted putty on Elizabeth's fingers to make us think it was far too obvious that he could be the killer. I considered that the General's anger at his daughter might have overflown, causing some violent instinct to kick in. But it was only this morning that the truth finally came to me."

I held that key up high between my two gloved fingers. "Why did the killer lock the door after attacking Elizabeth?" One last dramatic pause. "They didn't. On my trip up to the east tower after lunch on Saturday, I noticed that Elizabeth kept the room locked and the key in her clutch handbag when she wasn't there. This made sense to me. That room was her haven away from the rest of the house. If I lived here, I would have done the same thing and created a space just for me, for reading and thinking. A room of one's own.

"I went up there with Elizabeth and she apologised for how her children had treated me nineteen years ago. This was the second time she'd said it since I arrived, and I struggled to understand why. She was so nervous she was shaking, like there was something she was afraid of she couldn't put into words. After she was killed, I could only conclude that Elizabeth knew who her killer was but hadn't found the courage to tell me."

There was a lot to get out, a lot of evidence to connect up for them, so I kept going. "She'd followed my career as detective, she knew what I was capable of and so it was easy to believe that she called me to Castleton to save her. It's quite possible that the whole party, with all our scrounging relatives back here for a free lunch, was put on to get me here. But Elizabeth wasn't scared; that's just what she wanted me to think. No, she took me up to her room so that I could see the place. She wanted me to notice the key in the lock, the tidy state it was in and the letter on the desk. She knew that I would consider all those things and make a careful note of each of them, as that's my job.

"You see, the killer didn't lock the door, because there was no killer. In fact, this isn't the key which we found after Elizabeth died." I turned it around between my fingers so that it sparkled in the morning light that cut in through the half-drawn curtains. "She went upstairs when Bradley got so drunk that he almost maimed me. She knew that her kids would follow to continue their sycophantic competition. Her father was worried about her so he did the same, and having Fabian there – the man who had facilitated her betrayal – was surely a bonus. Everything had fallen neatly into place."

"How does any of this make sense?" Mum sounded like she was several rooms away. "You're saying Elizabeth faked her own murder, but how is that's possible?"

I took a deep breath and answered her question as succinctly as I could. "When Noémi left, her mother put one key on the outside of the thick door, and locked it on the inside with a spare. If I hadn't gone back up there this morning, we might never have found it. But sure enough, there it was, hidden in a crevice under the windowsill which she'd covered over with putty."

Tedwin's eyes were the size of lunar craters. "That makes no sense; she was covered in cuts."

"That's right. She had clear defensive wounds, which any crime fiction fan like your mother would know are sure signs of a struggle. The books on the floor and the upturned chair only added to that impression. One of the most important facts, which I should have paid more attention to, was that your mother loved murder mysteries. She'd read thousands of them – even more than I have – and she knew exactly how to fake a murder."

The General was clearly already saddened by this news and, in the same fragile voice he'd used when talking to me of his father, he asked, "But why?"

I took my time to answer him and tried to keep my tone free from judgement. "For a thousand reasons, I suppose. For all the things I've already laid out; her husband's death, Fabian's duplicity, her own failures, Bradley's greed and, most of all, her daughter's treachery."

The prodigal daughter let out a loud grunt of disapproval but had no right to argue.

I turned to Martha who, with all the deference and discretion of her position, had remained silent throughout. "Martha, you suggested I go up to the family museum where we discovered Matthew's work as a spy, but that wasn't what you wanted me to see, was it?"

Looking like she might finally cry, the long-serving maid shook her head.

"You wanted me to see how much Elizabeth loved him and how sad she'd been since he died." A nod this time and I attempted a smile back to her. "She was not a happy person. She blamed herself for her children's faults and had been missing her husband for twenty years. When she finally attempted to do something about it, first through her charity work and then her piece-by-piece dismantling of her image, a new man came along and she fell in love.

"None of us can say how deeply the discovery that Fabian was in a relationship with her daughter affected Elizabeth. Instead of confiding in one of you, she plotted her revenge. In some ways, my presence here was the biggest clue of all. Dean likes to say that murders happen wherever I go-"

"They do!" He sounded rather put out that I didn't believe him.

"Well, not this time, mate." I shot him a glum look. "This time, the killer planned the whole thing based on the fact that I would be here. She waited to invite me until the last moment, presumably afraid that I would change my mind and not come, but a phone call to my very persuasive mother made sure that wasn't the case."

Mum looked the tiniest bit guilty for once as she listened.

"You see, Elizabeth wanted me to investigate her death. She took me up to the east tower to see the room, planted Fabian's letters in the detective library for me to find and wrote a letter back to him which she left on her desk. Fabian stole the unsent letter, and, when I eventually read it, it made no sense in the timeline of their relationship. She sounded as though she still loved him, when all she really wanted was for me to find the letter and discover what Fabian and Noémi had done to her."

Tedwin raised his finger to interrupt. "I apologise for harping on about this, but you still haven't explained how my mother planted a knife in her own back."

"Sorry, you're right. I noticed early on that the wound was high up – Elizabeth was a tall woman and the knife was right between her shoulder blades. But, after I'd found the spare key that she'd hidden, the books scattered on the floor finally made sense. She'd wedged the knife in a tight gap on the bookshelf with the blade facing outwards, then thrown herself back against it. By pulling her weight down, she dislodged the knife, causing the books to fall from the shelf. If she'd managed to puncture her heart, she'd have died instantly. It was impossible to be so accurate, but she fulfilled her goal and removed any suspicion of suicide. The upturned chair and defensive wounds were added touches to throw me off the scent."

Noémi had fallen sombre and silent as the truth set in. "It was me, wasn't it? She wanted you to tell the police that I'd done it." She was stunned by the realisation. "Everything you accused me of before, they would have used all that against me if you hadn't worked it out. Mum locked the door and hid the spare key to make it look like she'd been murdered, and it was all so that she could get me sent to prison."

It gave me no joy anymore to say, "Yeah, that's pretty much it. Bradley would have made a good scapegoat and your brother had no alibi whatsoever, but you were the prime suspect all along."

Don't feel too bad about it, Iz. She did defraud her mother and assault Tedwin. She's no Mother Teresa.

Still subdued, Tedwin had something to add. "I didn't lie, you know. I really did look for a quiet spot to call someone, though I might have exaggerated about her being my girlfriend." He got all moony then, his gaze floating up to the ceiling. "At the very moment that mother locked herself in the east tower, I was sitting downstairs debating whether to call a girl I'd met out on the town on Friday night. You see, I'd just discovered that she had a fiancé, and it broke my heart a little. But she's the most extraordinary woman. I've never fallen for anyone so fast or intensely before. I decided when I was in the hospital this morning that I had to call her."

I didn't see that this was particularly relevant, but he needed to get it off his chest. Personally, I was relieved he hadn't turned out to be a complete villain like his sister. It showed that some people really could change for the better.

Everyone was still processing the hoard of revelations we'd just worked through, so I finally had another sip of orange juice and a bit of cold toast. It was odd to see so many people sitting so quietly doing nothing. Even D.I. Fincher and P.C. Chandra looked reflective, as though they were still searching for a hole in my explanation.

In the end, it was Osborne who broke the silence.

"Right, I couldn't follow much of that. Who am I supposed to arrest?"

Chapter Thirty-Five

Of everyone there, Fabian seemed the most relieved. Not only was he now free to profess his hopeless love in front of his girlfriend's family, he found another silver lining to focus on.

"This is wonderful, Noémi." He was the only person in the room smiling. "You didn't kill your mother. You won't have to go to prison."

"Yes… wonderful." I can't say she looked overly thrilled at the possibility of spending more time with him.

"I wouldn't get too excited just yet," Fincher stepped forward to inform them. "Fraud by false representation has a maximum sentence of ten years imprisonment. You'll have to attend an interview at the police station so we can get to the bottom of exactly what you've both been up to. And there's the little matter to address of Miss Castleton stabbing her brother."

Noémi looked just as miserable as when she'd found out how little she'd inherited. "Why don't you shut your stupid, cheesy mouth, Fabian?"

He clearly didn't care what she said to him and put his loving arms around the despicable creature. I wished them all the luck in the world.

Tedwin was apparently in a forgiving mood as he raised his hand to the inspector and said, "If it's up to me, I won't be pressing charges. She didn't really do me any harm. The doctors think I fainted from the sight of all the blood more than anything. She's still my sister and she's done far worse in the past."

Fincher clearly didn't to know how to take this and went to discuss the details with a colleague. Mr Jaggard had finished talking to the General about what would happen next, and there was something I needed to ask him. "I'm sorry to bother you, but I have a question."

His face had reverted to its usual smiley shape. "Of course, how may I be of assistance?"

"I assume that, in the letter she wrote you, Elizabeth left various different instructions depending on what I discovered today."

"That's right."

"So what did she want you to do if I'd come to the wrong conclusion?"

He perched on the side of the breakfast table and his head wobbled happily as he replied. “I believe you worked that out. If you’d identified Noémi as the killer, I wasn’t to tell anyone what had really happened.”

I was taken aback to hear him admit this so freely. “So, would you have gone through with Elizabeth’s wishes and let her daughter go to prison unfairly?”

Raising one hand to brush through the bristles on his chin, he considered my question. “You know, I’m not quite sure. I’ve been representing the Castletons for over forty years and have been a loyal servant all that time. Let’s just say I’m glad you got to the truth, and I didn’t have to find out how far my loyalty would stretch.”

“At least you’re honest.”

I thought that would be the end of the conversation, but he had something more to say. “Speaking of fulfilling wishes, in the letter from Elizabeth which I opened this morning, she told me to give you this.” He reached into his briefcase and pulled out a book I’d only ever dreamed of getting my hands on. “Agatha Christie, I believe you’re familiar with her work?”

I was holding the signed, first edition of Christie’s debut novel that Elizabeth had told me about. A tan leather book with a black gate design on the front and gilt lettering on the spine with the year, 1921, marked at the bottom. I opened the cover and there was Christie’s famous scribbled signature.

I would quite happily have left everyone behind right then and gone off somewhere quiet to obsess over my new favourite possession, but I had something else to do first. Poked into the middle of the book, was a white envelope with my name on. I didn’t need to ask who it was from. As I weighed it in my hand, it felt uncanny to be receiving a message from the dead.

Dear Isobel,

If I was alive right now, I would be impressed. You see, I wrote two different letters and Mr Jaggard had instructions to only give you this one if you worked out what really happened. The other didn't mention me getting murdered of course, as that would have given the game away. It simply explained the very much deserved gift I had bequeathed and encouraged you to continue in your career.

The fact that you're reading this shows that you saw through my bluff. I knew that inviting you to the party meant that you might undermine my well-laid plans, but it was a challenge I was happy to set you. I'm extremely glad you succeeded. This was also why I included the back up clause in the will to ensure that – murderer or not – Noémi would not benefit from my death. I've had a fine old time spending her inheritance over the last few months, all the more so as she hadn't the faintest idea.

If my daughter is not on the way to jail already, then so be it. I'm quite certain that a life lived without the family coffers is far more of a punishment to her than a prison sentence could be. And perhaps you think me terribly cruel to treat my own child in such a way, but, if so, then you haven't got to know my family to the extent that I had hoped.

I was born into guilt. As the inheritor of an estate that was built on the back of murder and cruelty, I have lived a conflicted existence. My behaviour in life did not meet up to my own expectations and I have tried to make amends, but the one thing I could never correct was her. Tedwin is vain and apathetic, but Noémi, as you witnessed as a child, has savagery deep within her. She has spent her adult life bullying, berating and bending us to her will. I am so glad I finally saw through her schemes.

So there you go, that's all I have to say on the matter. And my parting words to you are these; live your life without

regrets, Isobel. Do what you will, but not at the expense of those around you. Be happy and find love, for that is the most we can hope for in this world and something I never truly achieved.

With respect and admiration,

Elizabeth Louise Castleton

The scene was quiet once more. As I read the letter, the solicitor had packed up his papers and departed. The police had taken Noémi and Fabian away for a quiet chat, Martha and Ed gave a friendly wave as they left the room and, except for Bradley, who was begging his son for flexibility with the loan repayments, the others sat in quiet reflection. Tedwin had taken his grandfather's hand and the two men sat side by side, with their upper lips well stiffened.

Leaving Dean and my stepfather to their thoughts, Mum came over to congratulate and commiserate. "I can't quite believe it, Izzy. You were wonderful." Her face was wracked with sadness in that moment, and I could see how much the morning had taken out of her.

"No, I was lucky," I replied. "If I hadn't found that key, I'd never have worked out what happened."

"We make our own luck, darling. I thought you would have known that by now." She smiled her winning smile. "Elizabeth was too beholden to what others expected of her. She only lived half a life, but not you. Not my wonderful daughter, and that makes me extremely proud."

I would have either turned scarlet or burst into tears right then, so I quickly changed the subject. "Mum, why are you the only person in the room wearing face paint?"

She really laughed then. "Oh, Axel taught us a drinking game last night and I lost. Have you never played 'Monkey Monkey Drinky Drinky'? It's an awful lot of fun."

As my mother explained the rules of the game, a woman arrived wearing a very short skirt, a very low top and enough makeup to repaint the Sistine Chapel. Bradley, who until that moment had looked like he would be the next to top himself, jumped up to welcome her.

"Deidre! My beautiful Deidre. You came!"

He ran over to her, but she wasn't happy to see him. "Sorry, Brad, but

I'm not here for you." Her eyes scanned the remaining members of our party and she found who she was looking for. "Teddy, are you okay?"

Tedwin launched himself at the voluptuous new arrival. "I am now. I'm so happy to see you. If one good thing came out of this weekend, it's the two of us meeting. Now that I've found you, Deidre, I will never let you go."

Uncle Bradley looked shell-shocked as the young lovers kissed in front of him.

Ahhh, poor guy!

You can't seriously feel sorry for him? The man who referred to me at his last birthday party as "the Billie Jean King of the family" even though I can't play tennis and I'm not American (or gay).

But he looks so sad.

"Pull yourself together, Bradley," I was surprised to hear my mother tell him. "What did you expect, dating someone not even half your age?"

Bradley whimpered out a sad reply. "But… She's just so pretty."

My monkey/mother pulled on his arm so that her brother was facing her. "It's time you grew up. No more debts, no more pretending you're something you're not, and definitely no more young girlfriends. You're going to focus on saving your business and start treating your son with the respect he deserves."

His head bowed, he squeaked out, "Yes, Rosie." And my mother spent the next half an hour providing the kick up the bum that someone should have dealt him many years earlier.

Chapter Thirty-Six

I had lunch with my favourite people in the whole of Castleton Square Manor; Martha the maid, Ed the chef and Barrington the butler – who seemed like a great bloke and someone I should have spent more time getting to know – or at least considered as a suspect.

"A tragedy," Ed declared in his typically dramatic tone as we sat around the kitchen table and Barrington served drinks.

"It's just so sad that she would take her own life," Martha added, but I wasn't convinced.

"I'm not sure that's the word I'd use. Yes, Elizabeth had a tragic existence, but she brought a lot of it on herself." I slurped my hot chocolate. "She blamed her children for her own failings. If anyone made them monsters, it was her."

"I hate to agree with my fake fiancée," Dean added. "But the fact that Elizabeth could concoct this plan in the first place means she's as bad as Noémi in my book."

We fell silent then and even Ed didn't have anything more to say.

"I still think it's sad," Martha eventually said, in a tiny voice, and I had to give her a hug at last.

After a long goodbye, we packed our bags and Dean called his driver to take us home.

"So was a *Private I Detective Agency* investigation everything you'd hoped it would be?" I asked my friend as we waited on the drive for my mother to lug her luggage down to us and Greg to take photos of the house.

"And more!" Dean was resolutely chipper. "I have to say, I think I enjoyed it a bit too much when Noémi realised that she wasn't inheriting a fortune. I didn't like to say it, as she's your cousin, but that girl is a nasty piece of work. I saw it the moment we met her."

I eyed him side on, trying to work out if he was telling the truth or just hoping to sound clever. "Oh, yeah? But you were also convinced that the dead father's career as a spy would be significant, and it was barely a red herring."

He sniffed noisily. "Fine, I'm no Izzy Palmer."

He'd cheered me up after a difficult weekend, and I couldn't help smiling. "No, but you're a pretty good Ramesh. So thanks for being here."

"Watch out," he said, pointing back up the stairs. "The new lord of the manor and his lovely girlfriend are coming. Do you want me to tell them any more lies about what a wonderful person you are? I could claim that you're a sweeter singer than your mother and a finer painter than your stepdad."

"I think I'd rather just be myself for the moment, thanks." As I finished speaking, an ecstatic-looking Tedwin and Deidre arrived.

"Thank you, Izzy," he told me, and he sounded quite sincere. "I didn't have a chance to say it before, but I don't know what would have happened if you hadn't been here."

"Oh… urmmm, anytime." I always know just the wrong thing to say. "Do you think you're going to stay on in the manor?"

He looked at his new love before speaking. "We've been talking about it and, once we've generated a little cash by selling Mother's art collection, we plan to open this place up to the public to provide a regular income." He looked back up at the building. "I'm told it was quite the architectural marvel, in its day. I've always thought it was selfish to keep it to ourselves."

"I'm sure you'll make a real go of it," my business expert companion predicted.

Her arm entwined in my cousin's, Deidre looked shy as she said, "We know we're probably going a bit fast but, if things work out between us, Tedwin just told me that we could get married in Bermuda next year."

He suddenly had a giddy air to him that I hadn't witnessed before. His face was seventy per cent smile. "When you feel the way I do right now, there's no way it could go wrong."

"And I've always wanted to get married in the Bahamas!" Deidre sang.

"No, darling, the Bahamas are in the Caribbean." Tedwin began as he pulled his beloved off for a walk around the property and an impromptu geography lesson. "Bermuda is in…"

Mum finally turned up, with Axel and the General carrying her bags. Once I'd given them a hug goodbye, and reminded my cousin not to let my uncle push him around anymore, we got in the car and Giles pulled away. I looked through the back window to see Bradley standing in front of the house, waving sadly. Perhaps I felt a tiniest little smidgen of sympathy for him, but I'm sure that the next time he called me Ian it would be forgotten.

On the journey home, I had no excuse not to look at my phone and so I opened up Danny's messages from that week. There were plenty of them and I could see he'd been freaking out just like me. The very last one seemed promising though.

I'm sorry, Iz, we've both been a bit crazy this week. We're obviously not brilliant on the phone and I think we need to get used to it. If you don't want to call anymore or only want to talk when there's something really important to say, that's okay with me. Just as long as we can message as often as before. Long-distance relationships are not much fun, but you're my best friend and I'm convinced we can make this work.

Thinking about the final letter that Elizabeth had written me, I knew what I had to do.

To my lovely Danny. Thank you so much for being patient with me as I acted like a coward and ignored your messages. I'd stupidly got it into my head you were going to break up with me and that we'd never talk again. I wholeheartedly approve of your suggestion and have one of my own: How about we watch a movie tonight?

As soon as I hit enter, Danny appeared online and started typing. I only had to wait a few seconds as the little dots rippled on my screen for his message to appear.

Amazing idea. What should we watch?

Urmmm… Anything but Star Wars?

Our journey home passed in two shakes of a greyhound's tail, mainly thanks to the fact that I spent the whole time chatting to my favourite Danny. Outside of the unnatural confines of a video call, conversation came easily to us and, within a few hours of discussing our favourite films, we'd settled on what we wanted to watch – and, yes, it was an Agatha Christie adaptation, but only because he'd never seen the Marlene Dietrich version of 'Witness for the Prosecution'.

When we pulled into my road, we were greeted by an unexpected sight.

"Give me one minute, Izzy." Ramesh told me as I got out of the car. "We're practically finished."

I should probably have prepared myself for such an event, but couldn't help wondering why he was dressed as a Roman gladiator, complete with sculpted breast plate, a lion's head shield and an authentic-looking sword.

Come on, Izzy. That's a surprisingly muted outfit by Ramesh's standards. And the leather sandals really show off his calf muscles.

My father had a welder's apron and helmet on and was kneeling down beside his old motorbike and sidecar which had been transformed into a chariot.

"What on earth are you doing?" Dean asked, so that I didn't have to.

"What does it look like?" Ramesh was as transparent as ever.

I turned to my dad, who can normally be relied on to give a sensible answer.

"Ramesh and I have been working on this all weekend for-"

"For the big proposal I have planned!" Ramesh interrupted as he boarded his chariot.

"To Patricia?"

"Yes, Izzy. It's customary to ask the person you're in a relationship with to marry you rather than a complete stranger." He stood on the converted sidecar and gripped the wooden frame that my father had added.

"Isn't it wonderful?" Dad pulled off his apron to reveal his centurion costume before placing the winged helmet on his head and mounting his bike. "We're on our way to see her now."

I was still a little confused. "Wait, didn't you already ask her to marry you?"

"Yes, but she was very busy and took a few weeks to get back to me. Then, when she did, she thought it was a joke anyway." Judging by his tone, Ramesh couldn't see the need to explain such petty details. "She said there was no way I'd do anything so half-heartedly." I guess this explained his pre-engagement at least.

"So why the chariot?"

"Her favourite film is Ben Hurrrrrrrrrrr," he shouted from halfway down the road, as Dad had already revved off.

"Lord Edgington Investigates..."

Have you discovered my new 1920s mystery series?
It's available now at **amazon**.

A little music, a little dancing, a little murder at the spring ball.

Find out how Izzy's adventure began…

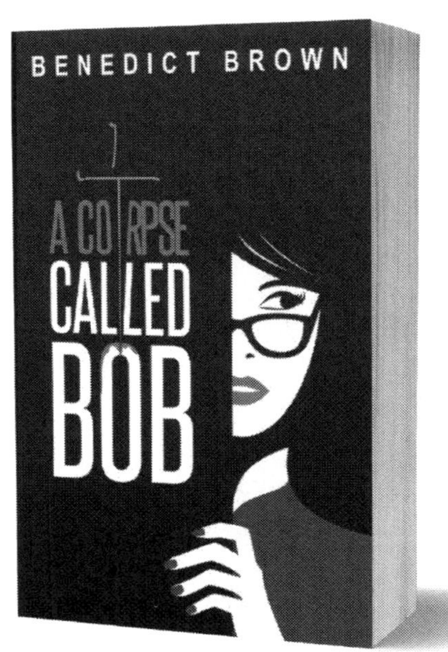

"A CORPSE CALLED BOB" (BOOK ONE)

Izzy just found her horrible boss murdered in his office and all her dreams are about to come true! Miss Marple meets Bridget Jones in a fast and funny new detective series with a hilarious cast of characters and a wicked resolution you'll never see coming. Read now to discover why one Amazon reviewer called it, "***Sheer murder mystery bliss.***"

About this Book

I always knew Izzy and Rosie's wider family were going to be weird and I hope her quirky personality makes more sense now. If you read back through the books, you'll find references to some of them, Bradley and Axel got a mention in **"A Corpse in London"** and this whole plot came out of the backstory to **"A Corpse in the Country"** when we heard about Izzy's first visit to Castleton Square Manor.

That book is a clear companion piece to this one. Another country house mystery for Izzy to solve, another mad, rich, warring family to pick a culprit from and I got to return to one of my favourite themes – the way that our family histories impact upon the present. The only family I grew up with was my Mum's kind-hearted bunch of weirdos, so this preoccupation must come from my Dad's side. Dad was an only child with very few relatives and a stern, distant father whose parents left him to be raised by his grandparents. Dad broke this cycle by being a truly loving man and the opposite of his ancestors – much like Rosie Palmer. His family were incredibly poor, but he did have a rich aunt who was swindled out of her grand house and savings on her deathbed. So all those stories I grew up with no doubt helped me craft the darker characters in these books.

There is another co-text I have to mention, which is the first in my new series **"Murder at the Spring Ball"**. I wrote the two books back to back over the winter and wanted them to be linked in small ways. I decided not to feature the butler too prominently in this one though as I think Gladwell and Fellowes have done a pretty good job already.

The house this time wasn't based on one particular place and is flashier than those in the other books. I chose Derbyshire simply because, as a child, whenever we visited, my history teacher mother would insist on a trip to a stately home. One of the most beautiful buildings in the world, Chatsworth House, is there too.

Izzy will be back in **"A Corpse in a Quaint English Village"** in the summer, and I think there's the matter of a **"Corpse at a Wedding"** to get to before long! For this year at least, I'm going to be alternating between Izzy and Lord Edgington so I hope you like both series!

The next **Izzy Palmer Mystery**
will be available in **summer 2021** at amazon

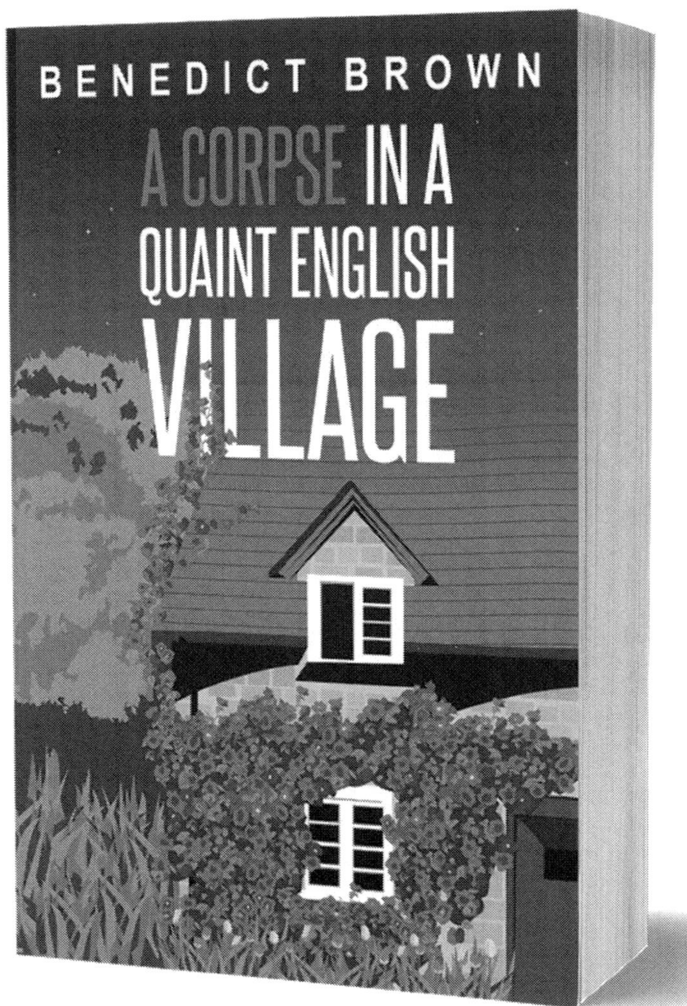

**A weekend away in the countryside,
what could possibly go wrong?**

Acknowledgements

I'm sorry for D.S. Osborne. I've tried to portray the police positively throughout this series and I hope D.I. Fincher balances him out. Osborne was originally an inspector, but he was demoted in the final draft to take into account just how bad he is at his job. Sorry again to Keanu Reeves; I'm sure you're a very happy person, with or without a sandwich. Sorry to geography teachers (like my mother) for Deidre's lack of knowledge. Sorry to French people, and especially my in-laws, if I in anyway suggested that you are the slightest bit impolite. (SPOILER ALERT…) I'm sorry if anyone feels the conclusion of the mystery is too tricky. I try to be fair in my books, and still feel there's plenty of evidence for you to spot, but admit this one is out of leftfield. However, people really have done such things. There's a fascinating story in the New York Times about a man who used a shotgun attached to a weather balloon to achieve his goal!

Thank you, as always, to my wife and daughter for being my absolute favourite people, to my family for reading my books and my crack team of experts – Paul Bickley (**policing**), Karen Baugh Menuhin (**marketing**) and Mar Pérez (**dead people**) for knowing lots of stuff when I don't. Thanks to all the writers who have helped too, especially Pete, Suzanne, Rose and, as ever, Lucy Middlemass. I also have to thank my wonderful readers. I love hearing from you, so feel free to get in touch if the urge takes you. And please keep leaving positive **reviews on** Amazon. They really help!

Last, but most of all, I must thank my team of super early readers, the Martins, the Hoggs, Lori Willis and Esther Lamin, I'm greatly indebted to each of you. And the wider team have offered such great advice too, so thank you to Rebecca Brooks, Ferne Miller, Craig Jones, Mindy Denkin, Melinda Kimlinger, Emma James, Namoi Lamont, Katharine Reibig, Linsey Neale, Sarah Brown, Karen Davis, Taylor Rain, Brenda, Christine Folks McGraw, Terri Roller, Margaret Liddle, Tracy Humphries, Anja Peerdeman, Barbara Hackel, Kathryn Davenport, Vanessa Rivington, Sandra Hoff, Helena George and Marion Davis. And if there's anyone I've missed off please get in touch and let me know!

Get your **Free** Izzy Palmer Novellas...

If you'd like to hear about forthcoming releases and download my free novellas, sign up to the Izzy Palmer readers' club via my website. I'll never spam you or inundate you with stuff you're not interested in, but I'd love to keep in contact.

www.benedictbrown.net

About Me

Writing has always been my passion. It was my favourite half-an-hour a week at primary school, and I started on my first, truly abysmal book as a teenager. So it wasn't a difficult decision to study literature at university which led to a masters in Creative Writing.

I'm a Welsh-Irish-Englishman originally from **South London** but now living with my French/Spanish wife and presumably quite confused infant daughter in **Burgos**, a beautiful medieval city in the north of Spain. I write overlooking the Castilian countryside, trying not to be distracted by the vultures, hawks and red kites that fly past my window each day.

I previously spent years focussing on kids' books and wrote everything from fairy tales to environmental dystopian fantasies right through to issue-based teen fiction. My book **"The Princess and The Peach"** was long-listed for the Chicken House prize in The Times and an American producer even talked about adapting it into a film. I'll be slowly publishing those books over the next year on Amazon.

"A Corpse in a Locked Room" is the sixth Izzy Palmer novel and number seven **"A Corpse in a Quaint English Village"** will be coming in the late summer. If you feel like telling me what you think about Izzy, my writing or the world at large, I'd love to hear from you, so feel free to get in touch via...

www.benedictbrown.net

Made in United States
Orlando, FL
18 March 2024